"[An] engrossing series . . . The author takes great care to detail the everyday life of the time, but weaves these details through the narrative in a very natural way. The social structure, the class differences, and daily life in a keep are very much a part of the mystery, and readers will feel that they've made a trip back through time to witness these events."
—*CA Reviews*

The Alehouse Murders

"An excellent mystery, very suspenseful and clever, with a sympathetic sleuth sure to captivate readers."
—Sharon Kay Penman,
New York Times bestselling author

"I loved *The Alehouse Murders*. Combining marvelous period detail with characters whose emotions and personalities would ring true in any era, Maureen Ash has launched a terrific new historical mystery series. I'll be standing in line for the next Templar Knight Mystery."
—Jayne Ann Krentz,
New York Times bestselling author of *Sizzle and Burn*

"A deft re-creation of a time and place, with characters you'll want to meet again."
—Margaret Frazer, national bestselling
author of *A Play of Lords*

"A delightful addition to the medieval mystery list. It is well researched and, even better, well written, with distinct, interesting characters and plot twists that I didn't expect . . . I look forward to more books in the series."
—Sharan Newman, author of *The Shanghai Tunnel*

continued . . .

Berkley Prime Crime titles by Maureen Ash

THE ALEHOUSE MURDERS
DEATH OF A SQUIRE
A PLAGUE OF POISON
MURDER FOR CHRIST'S MASS

Murder for Christ's Mass

A Templar Knight Mystery

MAUREEN ASH

BERKLEY PRIME CRIME, NEW YORK

THE BERKLEY PUBLISHING GROUP
Published by the Penguin Group
Penguin Group (USA) Inc.
375 Hudson Street, New York, New York 10014, USA
Penguin Group (Canada), 90 Eglinton Avenue East, Suite 700, Toronto, Ontario M4P 2Y3, Canada
(a division of Pearson Penguin Canada Inc.)
Penguin Books Ltd., 80 Strand, London WC2R 0RL, England
Penguin Group Ireland, 25 St. Stephen's Green, Dublin 2, Ireland (a division of Penguin Books Ltd.)
Penguin Group (Australia), 250 Camberwell Road, Camberwell, Victoria 3124, Australia
(a division of Pearson Australia Group Pty. Ltd.)
Penguin Books India Pvt. Ltd., 11 Community Centre, Panchsheel Park, New Delhi—110 017, India
Penguin Group (NZ), 67 Apollo Drive, Rosedale, North Shore 0632, New Zealand
(a division of Pearson New Zealand Ltd.)
Penguin Books (South Africa) (Pty.) Ltd., 24 Sturdee Avenue, Rosebank, Johannesburg 2196,
South Africa

Penguin Books Ltd., Registered Offices: 80 Strand, London WC2R 0RL, England

This is a work of fiction. Names, characters, places, and incidents either are the product of the author's
imagination or are used fictitiously, and any resemblance to actual persons, living or dead, business
establishments, events, or locales is entirely coincidental. The publisher does not have any control over
and does not assume any responsibility for author or third-party websites or their content.

MURDER FOR CHRIST'S MASS

A Berkley Prime Crime Book / published by arrangement with the author

PRINTING HISTORY
Berkley Prime Crime mass-market edition / December 2009

Copyright © 2009 by Maureen Ash.
Cover illustration by Griesback & Martucci.
Cover design by Judith Lagerman.
Interior text design by Kristin del Rosario.

ISBN: 978-0-425-23157-9

BERKLEY® PRIME CRIME
Berkley Prime Crime Books are published by The Berkley Publishing Group,
a division of Penguin Group (USA) Inc.,
375 Hudson Street, New York, New York 10014.
BERKLEY® PRIME CRIME and the PRIME CRIME logo are trademarks of Penguin Group (USA) Inc.

PRINTED IN THE UNITED STATES OF AMERICA

10 9 8 7 6 5 4 3 2 1

I would like to add here a word of appreciation for Emily Beth Rapoport, my editor at Berkley Prime Crime. Her supportive attitude and insightful guidance have been invaluable while I have been writing the Templar Knight Mysteries. Thank you, Emily.

List Of Characters

PRINCIPAL CHARACTERS

Bascot de Marins—A Templar knight

Gianni—A mute Italian boy, servant to Bascot

Nicolaa de la Haye—Hereditary castellan of Lincoln castle

Gerard Camville—Nicolaa's husband and sheriff of Lincoln

Richard Camville—Gerard and Nicolaa's son

Roget—Captain of Gerard Camville's town guard

Ernulf—Serjeant of Lincoln garrison

John Blund—Secretary to Nicolaa de la Haye

Lambert—Clerical assistant to John Blund

Everard d'Arderon—Preceptor of the Templar enclave in Lincoln

Miles de Laxton—A knight in Gerard Camville's retinue

VISITING NOBILITY

Gilbert Bassett—Lord of Drayton in Oxfordshire

Egelina Bassett—Gilbert's wife

Eustachia Bassett—Elder daughter of Gilbert and Egelina

Lucia Bassett—Younger daughter of Gilbert and Egelina

Ralph of Turville—Egelina Bassett's cousin

Maud of Turville—Ralph's wife

Stephen of Turville—Ralph and Maud's son

TOWNSFOLK

Walter Legerton—Exchanger in the Lincoln mint

Silvana Legerton—Walter's sister

Helias de Stow—Moneyer in the Lincoln mint

Blanche de Stow—Helias's wife

Peter Brand—Clerk to Helias de Stow

Simon Partager—Assayer in the employ of Walter Legerton

Iseult Partager—Simon's wife

Cerlo—A Lincoln stonemason

Warner Tasser—A Lincoln silversmith

Roger Fardein—Apprentice to Warner Tasser

One

✦⚬✦

THE STONE QUARRY LAY STILL AND SILENT UNDER THE maelstrom of wind and raging clouds scudding in the skies above. The early darkness of a winter evening had already fallen and the deep pit was shrouded in gloom. At intermittent moments, the racing clouds parted for an instant and allowed the beams of a full moon to dance a chiaroscuro of flickering shadows across the steep walls of stone. The night air was cold, its intensity heightened by a bitter wind blowing from the northeast. To the man who stood at the top of the cliff face overlooking the quarry, it was an eerie scene and made him apprehensive. In the daytime, when quarrymen were at work cutting and hauling blocks of stone, the huge pit would be full of activity, but now, in the darkness, it was a lonely place. Although he was only a few hundred yards from the walls of Lincoln town, it seemed as though he were stranded in a desolate spot far from the comforting presence of civilization. He started suddenly as the distant cry of a wolf was borne to him on the gusting wind. Wrapping his cloak closer about him, he damned the person he expected to meet for being late. It must be nearly an hour past the time agreed for their appointment.

A short distance from where he stood was a small shack. It was only large enough to contain a few small tools and some coils of rope but, nonetheless, the door was fastened with a stout lock. A few flakes of wind-driven snow blew onto the man's cheeks, stinging his exposed flesh like needles. If he was going to wait any longer, he needed to find shelter, and the shack was the only place available. Even if he could not break the lock to gain entry, there might be some relief from the wind on the leeward side of the walls.

Deciding he would wait just a few more minutes, he turned to make his way towards the shed when he thought he saw a movement on the narrow track leading from the main road to the cliff top. The shifting shadows caused by the passage of the clouds made it difficult to be sure, and he stopped and stared in that direction, shielding his eyes from the wind by cupping his hands on either side of his face. After a few moments, he decided he was mistaken. Patting the leather sack tied to his belt to make sure it was still securely in place, he resumed his steps towards the shed.

He had almost reached the small building when he was hit from behind, a heavy clout that took his breath away and brought him to his knees. Instinctively he tried to roll away but was too slow, and again a crushing blow descended on his skull, this time on the side of his head. As he struggled to regain his reeling senses, a booted foot pushed him onto his back and there was the brief glimmer of a knife arcing towards his chest. The blade took him directly in the heart. He was dead within seconds.

The attacker knelt beside his victim, feeling within the folds of the dead man's clothing for the pouch he carried. The murderer had difficulty removing it and used his knife to cut it free, not noticing that his efforts had loosened the neck of the sack slightly, and one of the coins it contained spilled out onto the ground. Once the pouch was safely stowed inside his tunic, he dragged the corpse to the edge of the cliff and shoved it over. The body fell with silent quickness and landed with a barely perceptible thud beside an enormous limestone block. As the killer crept back behind the shack, the wind increased in strength. Soon it would bring more snow, the flakes driving almost sideways in the vanguard of the incoming storm. By the time the midnight hour arrived, a mantle of white would cover the floor of the quarry and render the body of the dead man indistinguishable from the other snow-covered mounds of stone.

Two

✦✦✦

Lincoln
December 25, 1201

THE SNOWSTORM LASTED ONE NIGHT AND A DAY. WHEN the last errant flake fluttered down from a leaden-coloured sky, it left the high knoll on which the castle and cathedral stood and the streets of the town on the hillside below covered in a deep blanket of snow. On the heels of the storm the temperature rose sharply and within a few hours rain began to fall, gently at first, then in a torrential downpour that turned the snow into a mire of slush. As the hours passed, the slush began to melt and rivulets of water gushed down the hill towards the banks of the Witham River. It was not until late in the afternoon on the eve of Christ's Mass that the sky finally ceased its outpouring of moisture.

At midnight, the townspeople flocked to the cathedral for the first Mass of this auspicious day, the Angel's Mass, and a few hours later, at dawn, to the second service, the Shepherd's Mass, determinedly slogging their way through huge puddles of water as they trekked up the hill to the grounds of the Minster. By the time the dawn service was over, an uncertain winter sun had appeared and everyone hoped it would continue to shine for the third and last Mass of the day, the Divine Word. Whatever the weather held in store, all were resolved it would not spoil their enjoyment of the holy day or anticipation of the festive evening meal.

Among the crowd of people leaving the cathedral after the Shepherd's Mass was Bascot de Marins, a Templar knight temporarily staying in Lincoln. Over the socket of his missing right eye he wore a black leather patch, and there were premature strands of grey in his dark hair and beard. By his side trotted his mute servant, Gianni, a boy about thirteen years of age. Both of them were imbued with a sense of well-being after hearing the hymns of praise honouring the Christ child and, as they walked across the grounds of the Minster in the direction of the castle, Bascot reached in the scrip at his belt and took out a couple of *candi*, boiled lumps of sugar made from sweet canes in the Holy Land and imported into England by the Templar Order. Tossing one to Gianni, he suppressed a chuckle at the boy's expression of delight as he caught the sweet and popped it in his mouth. In the two years they had known each other, the Templar had become as fond of the lad as if he were his own true son. Soon, in the spring, Bascot would be leaving Lincoln to rejoin the ranks of the Order, and it saddened him to think it might be years, if ever, before he saw Gianni again. He was determined to spend as much time as possible with the boy over the holy days of Christ's Mass. The pair munched contentedly on the *candi* as they left the Minster grounds and, crossing the broad highway of Ermine Street, entered the bail of Lincoln castle.

Ahead of them, a large complement of household servants were hurrying from attendance at the dawn service towards the steps that led up to the keep, all intent on taking up the various duties involved in the preparation of the sumptuous evening feast. An extra effort was to be made this year, for Nicolaa de la Haye, the castellan of the castle, and her husband, Gerard Camville, the sheriff of Lincoln, were entertaining guests who had arrived just before the onset of the snowstorm. Gilbert Bassett, lord of Drayton in Oxfordshire, had brought his wife and family to Lincoln to share the holy days and, on the feast of Epiphany, to attend the betrothal of his eldest daughter, Eustachia, to Gerard and Nicolaa's only son and heir, Richard. The match was considered to be most suitable by all the parties involved, for not only was Eustachia possessed of a considerable dower; her father was an old and trusted friend of the sheriff. Lady Nicolaa intended to ensure the Bassetts' stay in Lincoln castle was both comfortable and entertaining.

Eustachia's younger sister, Lucia, was also in the party of the visiting baron, along with Ralph of Turville, an amiable knight who was a cousin of Gilbert's wife Egelina. With Turville were his wife, Maud, and their twelve-year-old son, Stephen, a lad born with a badly cleft upper lip and separated palate. Conscious that others often found his appearance unsightly, Stephen had adopted the habit of wrapping a silken scarf around the lower part of his face. Since the deformities made it difficult for him to speak clearly, he was extremely shy and rarely attempted to communicate with anyone other than his parents.

When Bascot and Gianni entered the hall, a massive

log was burning in the cavernous fireplace. It brought a welcome glow of warmth and light to the huge, high-ceilinged room. The sheriff, his wife, and most of their guests were nowhere to be seen, the ladies having repaired to Nicolaa de la Haye's solar to engage in some comfortable gossip, while the sheriff had invited his old friend Gilbert Bassett to share a flagon of wine in his private chamber. Of those of high station, only Richard Camville and Ralph of Turville were in the hall, waiting for two menservants to set up a pair of tables painted with chequered squares so they could play a game of Quek. Near them was Turville's young son, Stephen, standing close to the wall, his muffler in place, watching in an unobtrusive manner as the servants went about their task.

When the game commenced, Bascot walked over to the table and stood watching the play. It was a relatively simple game that involved tossing a pair of dice onto the chequered board and betting whether they would land on light or dark squares. As gambling for money on a holy day was frowned upon, the stakes were in hazelnuts instead of silver pennies, and a stack of these were piled at the elbows of each of the players. The competitors seemed evenly matched, with Richard winning one or two throws in succession and then Turville gaining the advantage. Both men were in good spirits and laughing all the while; it was not long before some of the household knights gathered to watch the game, and young Stephen was softly clapping his hands together with approval each time his father won a toss.

The better part of an hour had passed when Bascot, lost in enjoyment of the good-natured rivalry of the game, heard his name whispered. He turned to find Eudo, Nicolaa de la Haye's steward, standing respectfully behind him.

"Sir Bascot, one of the stonemasons from the cathedral has come to report the finding of a dead body in the church quarry. He also said he thinks the man was murdered. I am reluctant to disturb Sir Gerard while he is entertaining his guest. Would you be prepared to take the responsibility of judging whether the matter is of sufficient importance to interrupt him?"

Bascot knew why Eudo had chosen to bring his concern to him instead of one of the other household knights. During the two years the Templar had been staying in Lincoln, he had been involved, on several separate occasions, in uncovering the perpetrators of secret murder. Suspicious deaths were an occurrence with which Bascot had, unfortunately, more than a passing familiarity.

Bascot nodded his assent to the steward, and he and Gianni followed Eudo across the hall to where the mason, a man with a weather-beaten face and appearing to be of an age somewhere in his middle forties, was waiting. The mason was nervously twisting a rough leather cap between his fingers. He held his head at an odd angle as the Templar approached, turning his face first towards Bascot and then Eudo as he peered at each of them in turn.

"This is Cerlo, Sir Bascot," Eudo said. "He is employed by the cathedral and is, at present, in charge of the quarry." The steward instructed the mason to tell the Templar about the body he had found.

The mason glanced nervously at Bascot, and then dropped his head. Cerlo had heard tell of the Templar knight and how he had been a captive of the Saracens in the Holy Land for eight long years before making a daring escape from a Muslim pirate ship. It was said he had undergone terrible torture, including having his right eye put out with a hot poker, and that he had survived only because of his true devotion to Our Lord Jesus Christ. Tales about the Templar and his courage abounded and most of the townsfolk held the knight in awe because of his uncanny ability to track down murderers. The majority of Lincoln's citizens believed God had chosen the Templar as an avenging angel, but there were others who were unnerved by his quiet and aloof manner and claimed his success was due to heathen powers he had learned from his captors in the Holy Land. Whatever the truth was, the pale blue glitter of the Templar's remaining eye unnerved Cerlo as he struggled to comply with the steward's direction.

"'Tis a terrible matter, lord," he finally said self-consciously, "and I thought as how the sheriff should know of it straight away, even though 'tis Christ's Mass day."

"If necessary, I will ensure he is informed," Bascot responded quietly. "Tell me how you came to discover the body."

Cerlo nodded and his voice dropped to a thready whisper. "I went along to the pit at daybreak with one of the quarrymen to see if water from the rain and melted snow was draining from the site," he explained. "I was worried the struts on the heavy sledges might have become waterlogged. We noticed the body almost as soon as we arrived. It was wedged between a block of stone and the bottom of the cliff face."

The mason twisted his cap so hard it seemed it

would be rent in pieces as he added, "It looks as though he's been there for some days, perhaps from before the snow fell, but I . . . but I think he's been murdered, lord. There's a fearful stab wound in his chest."

"Did you recognise him?" Bascot asked.

Cerlo nodded uncomfortably. "Aye. His name is Peter Brand. He's clerk to Helias de Stow, the moneyer in charge of the Lincoln mint."

Three

✠

BASCOT WENT OVER TO RICHARD CAMVILLE AND ASKED if he could speak to him for a moment. The sheriff's son motioned for one of the household knights who had been watching the game of Quek to take his place and he and Bascot went a little apart from the group. Richard listened with undivided attention as the Templar told him the news the mason had brought.

In appearance and temperament, Richard Camville was a composite of his parents and their antecedents, favouring neither one side nor the other. His tall, well-muscled body and flaming red hair had been inherited from his n.aternal grandfather, but he had about him a good portion of his father's aggressiveness and restless manner, which had fortunately been tempered by a shrewdness passed down from his mother. His response was quick and decisive.

"I do not know the man the mason has found but I am, of course, acquainted with de Stow and will see that my father is apprised of what has passed," he said.

"Since Coroner Pinchbeck is away from Lincoln at the moment, someone in authority needs to view the body and note any pertinent details as to the cause of death." Richard gave a grimace. "Even if Pinchbeck were here, I doubt he would be willing to turn out on a holy day to inspect a corpse, since he usually proves reluctant to do so any other time." He gave Bascot a direct look. "In the past you have been involved, at my mother's behest, in cases of secret murder. Are you willing to be so again, as my father's representative?"

Bascot smiled inwardly. Richard was just as diplomatic as his mother who, on every previous occasion of a suspicious death, had asked for his help and not demanded it even though, as he was temporarily in her service, he was duty bound to comply with any orders she gave. Although he, too, had no wish to spend the day of Christ's Mass viewing a corpse, what Richard said about the coroner was true. Alan of Pinchbeck was an indolent man, content to leave the duties of his office to others if at all possible. The royal post of coroner was an unpaid one and while Pinchbeck enjoyed the prestige that holding the office bestowed on him, he was more than willing to have Gerard Camville, in his capacity as sheriff, investigate the circumstances of any sudden death.

Bascot nodded his agreement to undertake the task. "Do you wish me to make arrangements for the safekeeping of the body?"

"I think it would be best to have it removed to the Priory of All Saints for the nonce," Richard replied. "Until arrangements have been made for the relatives of the dead man to be notified, the infirmarian at the priory will care for the corpse in the proper manner and see it readied for burial."

After assuring the sheriff's son he would report what he found as soon as he returned from the quarry, Bascot called to Gianni and told the boy to go to the scriptorium and fetch his portable wax tablet and stylus. Gianni spent two or three hours a day studying the art of scribing under the direction of Lady Nicolaa's secretarius, John Blund, and kept his writing implements in the chamber where the clerks carried out their duties. A few minutes later, the boy returned and together he and the Templar followed Cerlo out of the hall.

"The road to the quarry is a mucky mess, Sir Bascot," the mason said as they descended the steps that led down from the keep. "You might want to ride there, instead of walk, even though 'tis not a far distance."

While Bascot waited for a groom to saddle a horse, the mason set off to wait for the Templar at the quarry, which was located a little way from the cathedral outside the eastern boundary of the city wall. When the mount was ready, Bascot, with Gianni riding pillion behind, guided his mount through the crowds still thronging the precincts of the Minster to the gate in the city wall. Once they were through the portal, they found that the track leading to the quarry, as Cerlo had claimed, was badly mired from the recent rain.

The mason was waiting for them a little distance from the gate, along a footpath leading off the main road to the top of the cliff face. Despite the mud, he had made good speed on foot. There was a shed near the spot where Cerlo was standing, and Bascot guided his mount towards it and, after he and Gianni had dismounted, tethered the horse to an iron ring in the door, and walked up to the mason.

"That's where he is, lord," the mason said as they

approached, pointing down over the lip of the precipice. "Down there. I told the quarryman to wait with him 'til I come back."

Bascot looked in the direction Cerlo was pointing. The floor of the quarry was perhaps fifty or sixty feet beneath the top of the rock face and littered with stone blocks of varying sizes. There were still a few small clumps of snow on the ground and atop the pieces of stone. In the middle of the pit was a huge sledge that had been partially loaded with cut blocks, and a giant winch, its arm extending skywards. Large covers of cowhides sewn together were draped over the sledge and the mechanism of the winch, but the edges did not quite reach to the ground and rivulets of water streamed alongside the metal-rimmed wood on the bases of both pieces of equipment. Almost at the foot of the cliff, and perhaps a space of about four feet from it, was a large stone block. Beside it stood the quarryman, the hood of his cloak drawn up over his head. At his feet lay the body of Peter Brand, partially shielded from view by an old piece of sacking.

"I don't know how long he's been lying there, lord," the mason said with some agitation. "That there block beside him has been waiting to be cut into smaller pieces for some time, but we haven't been able to work 'cause of the bad weather, so none of us have been down in the pit since before the snowstorm started. I covered him up as best I could for decency's sake," Cerlo added. "We'd just come to have a look at the sledge when we saw his feet sticking out." The mason shook his head. "'Twasn't a sight to cheer a man on such a holy day."

"I'll need to go down and examine him," Bascot

said and pointed to a broad opening on the far side of the quarry where the walls of the pit were much lower. "Is that the quickest way to go?"

"'Tis the only way, lord," Cerlo replied. "You'll have to go down Masons Row to the far end and along by the stables where we keeps the mules to reach it."

Bascot nodded and he and Gianni remounted the grey gelding and followed Cerlo as he trudged back towards the gate and then turned down onto the main track he called Masons Row. It was a long thruway, about a mile in length, with a number of buildings at the far end, just before it turned back on itself and descended onto lower ground and led to the opening Bascot had seen.

"There's drainage holes bored alongside of this track," Cerlo said as they went down the stone flags of the pathway, "and sometimes they get blocked with stone dust. That's what I come to check this morning, but it seems they've stayed clear."

After traversing the breadth of the quarry, Bascot and Gianni once again dismounted and walked up to where the body lay. The quarryman gave the Templar a respectful nod and removed the sacking laid over the corpse.

The dead man was lying almost flat on his back, his left shoulder resting against the stone block. His head was tilted at an awkward angle and one leg folded beneath the other. Kneeling beside him, Bascot could see the right side of his head was crushed, but not so badly that it distorted his features. Peter Brand looked to be a young man of about twenty-five years of age, with soft contours to his cheek and brow that were almost feminine in their delicacy. A sparse beard covered his narrow chin and both it and his hair were a pale blond colour. His tunic and hose were of serviceable wool, as was his cloak, and the fabric was sodden with moisture. Tiny remnants of slush trapped in the folds of his clothing fell out and started to melt as Bascot pushed the material aside to examine the body. On the clerk's chest, the remains of a bloodstain could be seen around a jagged slash in his tunic. Probing with his fingers, Bascot found that the wound, narrow and very deep, had been a forceful one. It angled straight into the heart, the blade slightly nicking a rib before entering the vital organ, and was most likely administered by a long, thin dagger. The man had indeed, as the mason said, been murdered.

The Templar felt a surge of outrage rise in his throat. Murder was surely the most evil of all the sins committed by mankind. It mocked the justice of God. As he thought of the terror that must have gripped Brand in the moments before the murderer struck, he could almost hear the devil laughing. It was with great difficulty that he swallowed his anger and forced himself to instruct Gianni, who was standing beside him, to write down the conclusion he had reached about the type of weapon used in the killing.

The boy complied quickly, perching himself on a nearby lump of stone before removing the wax tablet and stylus from the pouch on his belt and carefully lifting the wooden cover of the tablet to expose the surface of the wax. He then began to write his master's description of the deathblow with a sure and steady hand. His notes would be transcribed onto parchment and the surface of the wax smoothed clean for reuse. Watching the boy's competent movements, the Templar felt his anger slowly abate and pride in Gianni's proficiency burgeon in its place.

It had been a little more than two years since Bascot, on his way home to England after escaping from the Saracens, had found the boy on a wharf in Palermo on the island of Sicily. Gianni had been feebly struggling with a couple of mangy dogs for possession of a dead pigeon that was no more than a mangled lump of blood and feathers. The boy had been in the last stages of starvation, his slender frame stick thin and his liquid brown eyes two dark pools of despair. It had taken all of Bascot's patience to win the boy's trust and persuade him to become his servant. Now Gianni was not only healthy, but had before him a promising future as a clerk.

Confident the details of the body's condition would be recorded efficiently, Bascot returned his attention to the corpse. A cursory examination of the clerk's head on the side that had not been crushed revealed another, slighter depression. It could have been caused by the fall, but it was also feasible the victim had been dealt a blow to his head that had rendered him unconscious before he was stabbed. Running his fingers over the dead man's limbs, the Templar found the bones on the left side were sound, but those on the right were broken in several places and the shoulder dislocated. He looked closely at the skin of Brand's face. It was a mottled white in colour, as were the backs of his hands and fingers, and the nails had a bluish tinge. From this and the fact that the death rigor had already come and gone, it would appear that Brand had been dead for at least two days and, as there were no traces of snow underneath the corpse, probably since before the snowstorm began four days earlier.

As Gianni noted these facts, the Templar asked Cerlo how he had been able to identify the dead man. "Was he known to you? Has he ever had occasion to visit the quarry?"

The mason shook his head. "'Tis only because Master de Stow is the moneyer, lord, and well-known about the town, as are those who work for him. As far as I know, his clerk has never been to the quarry at all." Cerlo cocked his head in the peculiar manner Bascot had noted before and looked toward the quarryman for confirmation.

"Aye, lord, that's so," the quarryman agreed. "Every one of us is interested in the men who makes the coins we're paid with. Must be a little like working in heaven to be surrounded by so much richness every day." He looked around him at the stones littering the quarry floor, and added, "On days when 'tis high summer, workin' down here can seem just the opposite, like slaving in the pit of hell."

"And you are certain neither of you saw him in the quarry in the days before the snow fell?"

When both men shook their heads, Bascot said he would need to question the other men who worked in the pit to find out if any of them had noted the clerk's presence on the work site, but Cerlo forestalled him.

"If Brand was killed during the two days before the storm began," he told Bascot, "there were none of the other men here. The pit was shut down because the winch broke and we had to stop work while new parts was made for it. Then the storm came before the parts was ready, so the quarry's been closed for all that time. 'Twas only us two stayed here." Cerlo nodded to the quarryman. "He looks after the mules, so he sleeps in the stables. And I lives in one of the houses on Masons Row."

"And neither of you came down into the quarry while the winch was inoperative?" Bascot asked.

The quarryman shook his head. "I stayed in the warm with the mules. Wasn't no need to go down t'pit."

"And you, Cerlo?"

"I kept indoors to do a few little jobs around the house, sharpening my tools and the like."

"It must have been while the quarry was idle that he was killed, lord," the quarryman observed. "He would have been seen for certain whiles any of us was workin' here, 'cause he's layin' right out in plain sight."

Bascot concurred and again examined the injuries on Brand's body. After a few moments, he motioned to the top of the cliff and said, "It seems probable that this man was first stabbed, and then fell—or was pushed—from up there after the knife wound was inflicted. If he had fallen first, there would have been no need to stab him; he would have already been dead."

"I thought that's the way it must have happened," the mason agreed, "for only the intervention of God could save a man's life after such a tumble."

Bascot searched Brand's clothing and found nothing except a short piece of leather thong, of the type used to secure a scrip to a belt, caught up in the folds of the dead man's cloak.

"I think this man had a purse on his belt and it has been cut off," Bascot said. "It may be that robbery was the reason for this crime. My servant and I will search above to see if there are any signs of a struggle."

Cerlo nodded. "Will you be wanting me or the quarryman any further, lord?"

"Only to transport the corpse to the Priory of All Saints," Bascot replied. "Ask for the infirmarian, Brother Jehan, and tell him I sent you with a request that he take care of the body of this unfortunate soul until arrangements can be made for burial."

The mason assured Bascot they would do as he asked and told the quarryman to fetch a large wheelbarrow and some more lengths of sacking to wrap the body securely.

Leaving them to their task, Bascot and Gianni rode back to the cliff top. The thin layer of earth that covered the area was almost afloat with water and, when they dismounted to search the ground, it squelched beneath the soles of their boots. The pair walked slowly for about twenty yards along the lip of the steep drop and all around the shack, and then began to search farther back in case the body had been dragged for a distance before being pushed into the quarry. There was nothing to indicate a struggle, but the heavy fall of rain had pounded the earth so severely that the few blades of grass attempting to grow had been flattened into the ground. Any evidence of footsteps or scuff marks had been obliterated by the downpour. Just as Bascot was about to concede defeat, Gianni clapped his hands together loudly and the Templar looked up to see the boy wearing a smile on his face. Bascot went over to see what he had found and Gianni held out his hand, palm upwards. On it lay a silver penny. Although slightly tarnished, its brightness shone through the layer of mud on the surface.

Bascot took the coin and rubbed it on the front of his tunic so he could examine it more closely. "It's an old coin," he said to Gianni, "and appears to be from the reign of King Stephen. If I am right, it is at least fifty years old, maybe more, and is surprisingly unworn in view of its age."

He held it out for the boy to see. There, inscribed on the surface, was a portrait of the king, depicted with a diadem on his head and, in his right hand, a sceptre. Around the edge was the inscription *STEFNE REX*. On the reverse side was a cross of the type with broadened and split ends called moline and a design of fleur-de-lis.

Gianni peered at it, and then, with a questioning look, took the coin from his master and hefted it in his palm. Moving his hand up and down slightly, he looked at the Templar in puzzlement.

"Yes, it may be short weighted," Bascot answered to the boy's unspoken question. "I believe many coins made during that period did not have a full complement of silver. That was a sad time in England's history, Gianni, for the king battled for many years with his cousin, Matilda, for possession of the throne, and coinage was issued not only by the king, but by many barons and bishops as well. I remember my grandsire telling me that most of the minters in Stephen's reign did not observe the criterion established in earlier times regarding the silver-weight of a penny. This fault was not corrected until King Henry came to the throne."

He smiled as he recalled the time when his grandfather had, cursing, told Bascot and his brothers of those days, and how the silver the old man had so carefully hoarded was not worth as much as he thought so he had been unable to raise enough funds to buy a young stallion to replace his aging destrier. His grandsire had spat on the ground in disgust at the memory and told his grandsons to always be wary of accepting coin of the realm at face value.

Bascot took the coin back from Gianni and looked down at the scarred earth beneath his feet, pondering how long the penny could have lain there. "This must have been dropped recently; otherwise it would be more badly stained. But it is strange that a coin of such age has not been exchanged for one of new issue."

Thoughtfully, he placed the coin in his scrip along with the piece of leather thong. "It may have been dropped by someone who had no connection with the murder—one of the stone workers, perhaps—but I shall show it to the sheriff nonetheless. It would appear the clerk was robbed and since Brand worked in a place that is closely involved with exchanging old coins for new, it is a coincidence that must not be overlooked."

He and Gianni made another careful search of the ground, but found nothing more. Remounting the grey, they rode back to Lincoln castle.

Four

✦✝✦

WHEN BASCOT AND GIANNI RETURNED TO THE HALL, Richard Camville was leaning against the wall watching Ralph of Turville and one of the household knights play Quek. The sheriff's son was in a disgruntled mood. After he had informed his father of the stonemason's discovery, he had not been able to settle back into his enjoyment of the game. He had looked forward to this visit from Eustachia and was taking pleasure in her company; the possibility of a murder intruding upon the festivities—and their betrothal ceremony—had destroyed his good humour. As Bascot and his servant walked across the hall towards him, threading their way through servants bustling about preparing the evening meal, Richard felt his glumness lighten a little. The Templar had proved himself extremely competent in solving the mysteries that surrounded crimes of murder, and perhaps he would be so again in this latest instance. Then all of the company would be able to enjoy the celebrations without distraction.

As Bascot approached, Richard wondered what it was in the Templar's nature that made him so insightful of the motives that drove a man, or woman, to commit heinous crimes. He thought back to the day of Bascot's arrival in Lincoln two years before. De Marins had only recently returned from the Holy Land at that time and had seemed a broken man, both in body and in spirit. He had been sent to Lincoln castle by the Order with a request to Richard's mother, Nicolaa de la Haye, that she give the Templar shelter while he recovered from injuries sustained during his incarceration by the Saracens, and also in the hope that a period spent in the familiar surroundings of a castle would help him recover his waning faith. De Marins's recuperation had been slow but, as the months passed, Nicolaa had begun to recognise the intrinsic worth of the man consigned to her care. If the knight had not decided to rejoin his brothers in the Templar Order, she would gladly have given him a place in her retinue.

Richard's impression of the Templar was of a reticent man who was sometimes difficult to understand, but these minor failings were more than compensated for by his rigid code of honour and tenacious sense of duty. He also possessed, in contrast to most men of knightly status, a deep empathy for anyone unfortunate enough to find themselves in desperate circumstances, such as the mute boy he had taken as his servant. Was it these characteristics that gave him a heightened sensitivity to the baseness in others, or had his long imprisonment fostered an insight that comes only to those who have endured great suffering? Richard did not know the answer to these questions, but of one thing he

was certain—de Marins could be tireless in his quest
for truth. If there was any mystery surrounding this
latest death, the sheriff's son had every confidence the
Templar would not rest until he unravelled it.

As Bascot came up to him, Richard asked if he had
found confirmation that the clerk had, as the mason
said, been murdered.

"Yes," Bascot replied. "There can be no doubt the
man's life was purposely taken."

Richard sighed resignedly. "My father said if that
was the case, he would like to hear the details directly
upon your return."

Bascot nodded and, after giving Gianni instructions
to go to the scriptorium and transcribe the notes he had
taken, followed Richard to the sheriff's chamber. It
was a large room, littered with items of personal use
such as spare leather jerkins, boots and tack for horses.
On one side of the room were two large ironbound
chests with heavy triple locks in which the sheriff kept
the fees he collected on behalf of the crown. When
Richard and Bascot entered the room, the sheriff was
seated with his guest, Gilbert Bassett, in front of a
roaring fire, drinking wine. Gerard Camville bade them
help themselves to a cup of wine and then asked the
Templar what he had found at the quarry.

"The clerk was killed by a stab wound to the heart,
lord," Bascot replied. "Death would have been immediate, and although the mason found his body lying on
the quarry floor, I do not think Brand died there. It
seems likely he was fatally stabbed atop the cliff face
on the western side of the quarry and his body pushed
over the edge into the pit. From the condition of his
corpse, I would say Brand has been dead at least four

days. It is likely he was killed on the day the snow-storm began, or the one before."

Camville nodded and got up from his seat. He was a man of large proportions, with thick muscles swelling at neck and thighs, and black hair cut high on the nape of his neck in the old Norman fashion. When he rose, he emanated an aura of physical power so strong it made the chamber seem too small to contain his presence. Usually belligerent by nature, Camville had been in a mellower mood since the arrival of his old friend Gilbert Bassett. But even the congenial company of a fellow baron did not stop the sheriff from indulging in his habit of pacing, and that was what he did now, striding up and down the room with a catlike tread as he mused on what he had been told.

"The quarry is a strange place for a clerk to have been in such weather," he said reflectively. "Did you find any hint as to why he was there?"

"No, lord, I did not," Bascot replied. "The men who found the body told me the quarry was shut down for two days before the storm began, and so the pit was deserted, most of the men having gone into Lincoln, and the two who remained stayed inside their lodgings. Whatever his purpose, there was nothing on the clerk's person to give any indication of what it might have been. His purse was missing, and the only evidence I could find that he had been wearing one was this, which was caught in the folds of his cloak." Bascot laid the piece of leather thong on the table.

Camville picked it up. "Looks as though it might be part of a fastener for a scrip," he said. "Robbery must have been the reason for his death. Someone lured him there and murdered him for whatever his purse contained. A common enough crime."

"There was also this coin, lord, at the top of the cliff face, but it may not have been part of whatever money Brand had on him. It looks to be from a very old minting." Bascot placed the coin on the table beside the piece of leather thong Camville had inspected.

The sheriff's interest, which had been dismissive at first, now became more alert. He picked up the coin and examined it. "Have you cleaned this, de Marins?"

Bascot shook his head. "I rubbed off some of the surface dirt, that is all."

Bassett rose from his seat and came to where Camville stood, approaching the sheriff with an easy familiarity that spoke of the close nature of their mutual regard. He was a smaller man than the sheriff, but his compact body was solid with muscle and his face, with its prominent nose and hazel eyes, had a hawkish look. Camville handed the coin to his friend and the baron examined it carefully.

"This is from Stephen's time on the throne," Bassett remarked, "and must have been kept securely stored since it was made. It is so pristine it could have been struck from a die only yesterday."

"Did you say this coin was found near the spot where you believe the clerk to have been killed?" Camville asked Bascot.

When the Templar nodded, the sheriff glanced at Bassett with a look that held some significance.

"What is it, Father?" Richard asked. "Why is the coin of so much interest to both of you?"

"It is the state of its preservation," Camville said slowly. "Random coins of this age do turn up from time to time, but they are usually in halves or quarters or else very worn, with clipped edges." He held the coin up to the light of the candle on the table. "But this one is in excellent condition. I am wondering if it could have been part of a trove. There were many people in Lincoln town who felt it prudent during Stephen's reign to secrete any valuables they possessed."

All of them were aware that in 1141, during the years when King Stephen had a less than tenacious hold on the throne, he engaged in a significant battle at Lincoln with the supporters of his rival, Matilda, daughter of the recently deceased King Henry I. Quite a few of the more affluent townspeople, fearing for the security of their wealth, hid their money to keep it safe until the danger was past.

"But that was over sixty years ago, Father," Richard protested. "Surely any troves from that time would have been discovered by now."

Bassett was quick to refute Richard's supposition. "That may not be so, Richard. During my father's lifetime, and while he was sheriff of Oxford, there were perhaps a half dozen caches unearthed in the district. Two of them contained coins of Saxon minting and dated from before King William's conquest of England in 1066. They had lain undiscovered for more than a hundred years."

Camville carefully laid the coin back on the table. "I do not like the appearance of this coin near the place where the clerk was murdered. If we assume it was on his person, then why was he carrying it about with him? Brand worked in the mint, which is adjacent to the office of the exchanger. It would have been a simple task for him to turn it in."

The office of exchanger was a relatively new institution, formed by order of the late King Henry II in 1180. The effect of the new office had been to separate the minting of coins from their distribution and so lessen the opportunities for corruption. The exchanger's office was also the place where old or foreign coins could be exchanged for new. If a treasure trove had been found, or even a single coin from one, it should have been taken to the exchanger with an explanation of how it had come into the possession of the person who surrendered it. Not to follow this directive was an offence against the crown, for if the heirs of the original owner of the coins could not be found, or there were none living, the proceeds of such a find became the property of the king. Concealment was considered treasonable and the penalties were dire.

"It could be that the provenance of the coin is genuine, lord," Bascot said. "If someone found it recently—in a crack between the stones of a wall or in the bottom of an old chest, for instance—and gave it to Brand with a request he exchange it for one of current issue, the clerk may not have had time to carry out the transaction before he was killed."

Camville considered the Templar's suggestion. "Yes, you could be right," he admitted. "But still, I would like to be sure. Brand was murdered and, considering the place he worked, this coin may be connected to his death. If this penny was part of an unreported trove and Brand was privy to its discovery, the safekeeping of such a secret could have been the motive for his killing."

"You will need to be very careful, Father, in how

you handle any questions you pose about the coin. The exchanger, Walter Legerton, is not a man to be trifled with. If he realises you suspect the existence of a trove, he will surely report the matter to the Exchequer in London. And if the king hears of it . . ."

"I know what you are warning me of, Richard," Camville growled. "I am well aware that King John holds me in scant regard—as I do him—and, whether there is a trove or not, he will be quick to accuse me of conspiring to keep its contents from his grasping fingers."

He spoke to Bascot. "Are any others beside yourself and your servant aware you found this coin?"

"No, lord," the Templar replied. "The mason and quarryman were not with us when we searched the top of the cliff."

"Good," Camville exclaimed. "Then, for now, we will keep it between ourselves."

The sheriff resumed his pacing for a few moments before he spoke again. "De Marins, as a Templar, your probity is beyond question. If you are my representative in this matter, it will allay any suspicions about the intent of the investigation. Now that you know what is involved, are you willing to make an enquiry into the clerk's murder on my behalf?"

Although Gerard Camville was nominal lord over the estates Nicolaa de la Haye held through her inheritance from her father, including the castellanship of the castle, it suited the sheriff's indolent nature to leave the management of the vast demesne in his wife's hands. Camville's attitude to the responsibilities of the shrievality, however, was completely different. The office of sheriff was a lucrative one and Gerard guarded his rights jealously; an accusation of wrongdoing, even if not proved, might indeed bring reprisals from the king and could result in Camville's removal from office. The sheriff and the king had no liking for each other, although they had once joined forces in rebellion against King Richard during a time when John, then a prince, had attempted to wrest the throne of England from his elder brother's grasp. Now that John was king, he was suspicious of the nobles who had supported him, fearing they would once again show a willingness to change their allegiance and conspire against him. He was therefore wary of Camville, deeming him factious. Only the king's longstanding friendship with Nicolaa de la Haye and his confidence in her loyalty kept John from depriving her husband of the sheriff's post, but Camville was well aware that John would not hesitate to do so if he felt he had just cause.

When Bascot and Gianni had first arrived in Lincoln, Gerard Camville and his wife had willingly given the weary pair shelter and treated them with courtesy. For that kindness alone, the Templar owed them both a debt of gratitude. But he also had a genuine liking for Lady Nicolaa and a great deal of respect for her husband. He was more than willing to make every effort he could to keep the sheriff's reputation free of odium.

The Templar gave his reply without hesitation. "I will be pleased to assist you in whatever way I can, lord."

The sheriff gave a grunt of satisfaction and Bascot asked if he knew whether anyone had reported Brand's absence over the days the clerk had been missing.

"No," Camville replied, "the town bailiff always tells me immediately of such cases and there has been no recent report of any missing persons. The last one was some months ago when a draper came to the bailiff claiming his daughter had been abducted. And even that was a false alarm, for the girl had run off with her lover. It is not often people disappear in Lincoln without someone being aware of their whereabouts."

"Do you know if the clerk had any family, Father?" Richard asked. "If he did, I would have thought one of them would have been distressed by his disappearance."

The sheriff thought for a moment. "As far as I recall, Brand came to Lincoln with Helias de Stow and his family when the moneyer took up his post a little over a year ago. Both of them lived in Grantham before that. But even if the clerk did not have any kin in town, I would have thought de Stow would have wondered why his clerk was not at his place of work. It is curious he did not mention it to someone in authority."

He paused, and then said decisively, "That is the best place to start your investigation, de Marins, with the moneyer. There is not much that can be done today while the celebrations for Christ's Mass are being held. Most of the town will be either at the cathedral or feasting with family and friends, the moneyer amongst them. But tomorrow morning de Stow is likely to be at home; his house is the one that stands next to the mint on the other side to the exchange. Go there and ask him if Brand was due to be at work over the days the clerk has been missing and, if he was, why de Stow did not mention his absence to the bailiff. Even if his answer satisfies you, try also to determine, in a discreet fashion, if the clerk had a legitimate reason for carrying such an old coin on his person."

"It might also be profitable to ask Cerlo if he or any

of the quarrymen have been atop the cliff face in the last week or two," Bascot suggested. "It could be that one of them, or a visitor to the quarry, dropped the coin. If so, their possession of it may prove legitimate. It could be a keepsake handed down by a relative or simply a token kept for good luck. If it was, it will have no connection with a trove."

"Let us hope that is what happened," Camville said curtly. "I would much prefer to find that Brand's killing is a simple case of murder committed during the course of a robbery than because of some conspiracy involving hidden treasure. But all the same, de Marins, make no mention of finding the coin to anyone you question. As I said, I want its existence kept privily for the nonce."

"And if Coroner Pinchbeck should return to Lincoln before you are satisfied about the provenance of the penny, Father, will you tell him about it?" Richard asked dubiously. "The investigation of a trove is as much within his writ as yours and it would greatly enhance his standing with the king if he can claim the credit for finding one. He will be very irate if you do not tell him."

Camville scowled in disgust. "No, I will say nothing to him until I know whether my suspicions are valid or not. The man is a lazy bastard and takes advantage of my help whenever he has the opportunity to do so. Let him remain in ignorance until I am ready to enlighten him."

Five

✦✦✦

Later that afternoon, after the Mass of the Divine Word, the task of decorating the hall had been completed, and, as the company assembled, they looked about them appreciatively. On the walls hung circlets of holly depicting the crown of thorns that Jesus wore, the bright red berries nestling amongst the dark green leaves symbolising drops of His precious blood. Ropes of ivy and sprigs of bay festooned the tables and the room flared with light from a multitude of torches and beeswax candles. In the hearth, the trunk of an oak tree burned and the heady scent of cloves wafted from mounds of spiced winter apples heaped in bowls on the tables. The ambience was warm and welcoming.

As the cathedral bells rang out the hour of Vespers, flagons of wine and ale were brought in and cups filled. At the high table on the dais, Gerard Camville sat with his wife and guests. On his left were Gilbert Bassett and his wife, Egelina; their daughter Eustachia was keeping company with Richard farther down the board. The young couple made a handsome pair, Richard's bright red hair and fair complexion a startling contrast to the dark tresses and deep brown eyes of the woman he would soon pledge to make his wife.

On the sheriff's right hand, beside Lady Nicolaa, sat Ralph of Turville and his wife, Maud, with Eustachia's younger sister, Lucia, watching protectively over Turville's young son, Stephen. Gesticulating with her hands towards the musicians that had begun to play quietly at the back of the hall, Lucia talked volubly to Stephen while the boy, silent behind his silken muffler, nodded in response.

Just below the dais, where the household knights sat, Bascot took his customary seat above the ornately worked silver saltcellar that marked the dividing line between those of high rank and low. He gave a friendly nod to John Blund, secretarius to Nicolaa de la Haye, who was seated on his left in the space reserved for those who were foremost among the upper servants of the household.

Blund was an elderly man, a sparse figure with eyes of faded blue and thinning hair. His demeanour was gentle, but his face had an intelligent cast and there was a hint of fastidiousness in his erect bearing. Across the board from Blund was Lambert, the secretary's assistant, a man of about thirty years of age and unprepossessing appearance, his lantern-jawed visage wearing its habitual introspective expression. His aspect lightened, however, when he saw Gianni and he gave the boy a companionable smile. It was Lambert's responsibility, under Blund's direction, to instruct the Templar's servant in the rules of grammar and logic, and he seemed to have formed a comradely liking for the lad, even taking the time to learn the hand signals Gianni used to communicate with his master in the hope it would facilitate the lessons he gave the boy. When Lambert nodded respectfully in the Templar's direction, Bascot returned the greeting with warmth.

Once everyone was seated, the steward, Eudo, gave a signal to the musicians and they struck up a lively air, the strings of rebec and citole providing a harmonious background to the sweet piping of flutes. As the opening strains commenced, a procession of servants came through the door that led to the kitchen, the foremost carrying wide-mouthed bowls of wassail—a costly brew of mulled ale, ginger, nutmeg and cinnamon topped with sops, or slices, of toasted stale bread. One of these bowls was laid on every table, even those at the back of the hall where the servants of lowest rank were seated, and as each of them were set down, everyone shouted the old Saxon cry of *waes hael,* to wish one another "good health." Following the bowls of wassail was a huge board carried by a half dozen servants, on which was laid a whole roasted pig, including the head, its mouth stuffed with an apple. This was placed on a small table near the dais so Eudo could carve it before it was served to those seated at the high table. In the wake of the roast pig came trays laid with slices of venison and goose— for the delectation of the knights and upper household servants—and, at the end of the train, umble pies— minced offal baked in coffins of pastry filled with thick gravy. These were for those of menial rank. There were also platters of boiled turnip, parsnip, onions and carrots, and loaves of bread piled high in wicker baskets.

After all these delicacies had been devoured, bowls of frumenty, a thick porridge made of boiled wheat, eggs and dried fruit, would be served along with creamy slices of cheese and a plenitude of winter apples and plum conserve. It was a time of rare feasting and one that everyone—those of high station as well as low—looked forward to all the year long.

As Gianni heaped Bascot's trencher with chunks of venison, the Templar gave the boy permission, once he finished his task, to take a seat alongside Lambert. Normally Gianni would wait until Bascot had eaten his meal before he was allowed to get his own food, but the day of Christ's Mass was one of leniency and goodwill, and the Templar felt that the boy, whose eyes were shining with expectation as he dished up his master's food, could be allowed the laxity. The rest of the household knights seated alongside Bascot were allowing their servants the same liberty and, on the dais, Nicolaa de la Haye gave the pages serving the high table leave to join in the feast. Even the cook and kitchen scullions sat down at a table near the door and helped themselves to the food they had spent so many hours preparing.

The air of merriment increased as tumblers entered the hall and began to cavort among the throng, playing silly tricks as they did so. Some snatched apples from the very mouths of those who were eating them and made them disappear, while others surprised the serving maids by pretending to pull bright ribbons from the necks of their gowns. As the acrobats amused the company, the musicians strolled around the perimeter of the room, playing merry tunes.

As Bascot looked across at Gianni, who was hungrily tucking into the leg of a goose, the Templar once

again felt a pang of sadness that he would be leaving
Lincoln in a few months' time. It had not been so very
long since he had decided it would be necessary for
him to leave the Templar Order to ensure the safety of
Gianni's welfare. It had only been through the intervention of Amery St. Maur, master of the Templar Order in England, that Bascot's sacrifice had not been
necessary. St. Maur had given Bascot sanction to remain in Lincoln until next Eastertide while Gianni
completed his training as a clerk and, at the end of that
time, if the boy showed competence, Nicolaa de la
Haye had promised Gianni a post in her retinue. Since
then, Gianni had applied himself to his studies with an
industry that gave no doubt he would win the castellan's approval and realise his dream of becoming a
clerk. Pride in the boy's accomplishments warred with
regret in Bascot's heart. He longed to rejoin his Templar brothers in their battle against the infidel but, at
the same time, he knew he would sorely miss the
young lad.

John Blund saw the emotion that clouded the Templar's face and spoke in a whisper too soft for Gianni
to hear. "Do not be concerned for the boy, Sir Bascot.
Once you are gone from Lincoln, I assure you I will
personally oversee his welfare and, if the infirmities of
old age or my death should make me incapable of ful-
filling that duty, Lady Nicolaa has promised to take my
place."

"I know that, Master Blund, and am grateful for it,"
Bascot replied earnestly. "But I shall miss his company
all the same."

"And he yours," Blund rejoined. "But even though
both of your lives will change after you are gone from

Lincoln, your affection for one another will not. Many a father would wish such closeness with his son as you have with Gianni. It is a true blessing and should be cherished, even if it must be done in absence."

Bascot accepted the wisdom in the secretary's words and both men resumed their enjoyment of the viands on their trenchers. Some moments later, Blund spoke again, inclining his head in the direction of the high table. "It would seem young Master Stephen is most interested in the way Gianni is conversing with Lambert."

Bascot glanced up and saw that Turville's son was watching intently as Gianni moved his hands quickly in Lambert's direction, conveying how much he was enjoying the food on his plate by pointing to his trencher, his mouth and his stomach in rapid succession, then giving a light clap of his hands. Lambert nodded in response and then remarked that he wished they could eat such fare at every meal, and Gianni made another quick movement of his fingers in a signal of hearty agreement. At the high table, Stephen Turville placed his hand on Lucia's arm to get her attention and pointed in Gianni's direction.

"Because of his impediment, Turville's boy speaks little," Blund said. "And even when he does, there are few that can understand him, his speech is so distorted. I think he is admiring the way in which Gianni, despite his muteness, communicates with others." The secretary became reflective. "While he was learning the gestures, Lambert wrote down a description of them as an aid to memory and I read through the notes he made. Some are obvious, but others are not, not until you are told what they signify. I wonder if it would be worthwhile to make a permanent record of them. Such a manual might be of interest to tutors who have the task of teaching others afflicted with similar difficulties to your servant and Master Stephen, or to those who have been born deaf and never heard the spoken word. I am sure Lambert would be only too pleased to make a copy for any local scholar who shows interest in such a guide. And I would be more than willing to dedicate my own labour to such a charitable task."

Bascot agreed that such a record might be useful, but, as he did so, both his and the secretary's attention were caught by the antics of one of the tumblers. The acrobat had been tossing coloured balls in the air, spinning about as he did so, and was now importuning one of the knights to give him a silver penny to include in his display of dexterity. Amid shouts of encouragement from his companions, the knight reluctantly parted with the coin, whereupon the tumbler began to toss the balls again, deftly twisting the coin between his fingers as he did so. The exhibition ended with the acrobat throwing the coin into the air along with the balls and catching the penny on the point of his chin as the balls fell neatly into the palm of his hand. As his audience gave voice to their admiration, the performer suddenly flipped over backwards in a somersault, and when he landed upright, the coin had disappeared. The knight who had contributed the silver penny let out a roar of disapproval and made a lunge for the acrobat but the tumbler danced nimbly out of the way and darted towards a heap of discarded apple cores lying on the table. Reaching into the pile, the tumbler extracted the coin and presented it to the knight with an exaggerated bow.

As the companions of the disgruntled knight broke

up in laughter, Bascot was reminded of the silver penny Gianni had found and of the investigation Gerard Camville had asked him to make into the murder of Peter Brand. By now the mason would have told others of the clerk's death and the news would have spread to Brand's friends and acquaintances in Lincoln, perhaps even to any relatives the clerk had in Grantham. For them, the day of Christ's Mass would forever be overshadowed by the murder of one they held dear. He sent up a silent prayer that God would, once again, assist him in his quest to discover the identity of a person who had committed the grisly crime of murder.

Six

❖━❖

WITHIN THE LARGE BAIL OF LINCOLN CASTLE THERE are two keeps; an impressive fortress used as the primary residence of Gerard Camville and Nicolaa de la Haye and an older, much smaller, stone tower housing the armoury at ground level and a few sleeping chambers above. Bascot and Gianni shared a room at the top of the older keep and the next morning, as the cathedral bells rang out the hour of Prime, the Templar awoke and decided to make an early start on his investigation into Peter Brand's murder. Gianni was still fast asleep, curled up in a ball on his straw pallet on the floor, and Bascot pushed his black leather eye patch into place before gently shaking the boy by the shoulder to waken him. After kneeling for a few moments in morning prayer, the pair put on their boots and cloaks and took coverings for their heads—Gianni a fur-lined bonnet he had been given by Ernulf, serjeant of the castle garrison, and Bascot the black quilted arming cap he wore under his helm. The pair then went down into the bail and across to the hall.

Few of the castle household were astir. The feast of Christ's Mass had lasted late into the evening and everyone was suffering from tiredness and overindulgence in food and drink. The only sign of activity was in the hall where a few sleepy servants were gathering up all the scraps of food remaining from the festive meal. These leftovers would be placed in wicker panniers and taken to the nearby church where they would be given as alms to the poor in honour of St. Stephen, the martyr whose holy day was celebrated after that of Christ's birth.

Since it was unlikely the morning meal would be served until all the food remnants had been bundled up, Bascot sent Gianni outside to the building that housed the kitchen to fetch some bread and cheese to break their fast while he went to the stables and ordered a horse to be saddled. As Gianni was excused from his duties in the scriptorium for the holy day, the Templar hoisted the boy up onto the pillion seat behind him and then guided his mount out of the bail. Before he went to the mint to speak to Brand's employer, Bascot wanted to find Cerlo and ask the mason if anyone had been atop the cliff face in the days before the clerk had been murdered. If there had not been, it would have to be assumed that Brand or his killer had dropped the silver penny and Gerard Camville's suspicion that a treasure trove might be involved in the slaying must be pursued.

The morning air was crisp, but the temperature had risen slightly and their cloaks provided enough warmth to feel no discomfort as they rode across Ermine Street and entered the grounds of the Minster. Only a small number of townspeople were on their way to attend early Mass at the cathedral and Bascot was able to trot quickly past them, through Priory Gate and out onto the road leading to the quarry. As they neared the stone pit, they could hear the sounds of men at work; the creak of the huge wheel affixed to the winch, the thud of stone blocks settling on the sledges and the shouts of men urging mules to their task of pulling the heavy conveyances. Although today was a holy day, not everyone was allowed to spend it at leisure, and it appeared that work was being carried out in the quarry as usual, perhaps to make up for the time lost while the pit had been shut down.

Passing the little track that led to the top of the cliff face, Bascot rode down Masons Row, heading for the buildings at the far end. He remembered passing them the day before when he had gone down into the quarry to view the clerk's body—a small row of one-storey houses, a workshop and stables—and hoped he would be able to find someone in one of the buildings that could tell him Cerlo's whereabouts.

Just as they were nearing the first of the houses, a man clad in a cloak of coarse wool came trudging up the road from the direction of the workshop. His head was covered with a peaked cap that had a square piece of leather attached to the back to protect his neck. All his clothes, as well as his face, were covered in a fine layer of stone dust. Slung over his shoulder was a bag of tools, an assortment of chisels and hammers, some of which were protruding from the top of the sack.

The Templar hailed the man as he drew near and asked for the mason. "I'm not sure where he is, lord," was the reply. "I don't work in the quarry; I just come to measure some pieces of stone in the workshop. But he might be at home." The stone worker turned and pointed to the small row of dwellings. "All t'other lodgings are empty 'til the summer, but Cerlo lives all year round in the last one along."

Bascot guided his mount to the dwelling that had been indicated, dismounted and, leaving Gianni to hold the reins of the horse, went up to the door of Cerlo's house. Although it was small, the building was substantial in construction, with walls of stone and a roof of slate tiles. When Bascot knocked at the door, it was opened by a woman of mature years, with greying hair pulled tidily back under a linen coif and garbed in a dark blue gown. One of her hands was heavily bandaged and she held her arm awkwardly, resting it gingerly against her waist. Seeing the Templar badge on the shoulder of Bascot's tunic, she quickly gave a curtsey of deference and, when he enquired after Cerlo, told him she was the mason's wife and, if he would come inside, she would take him to her husband.

Cerlo was sitting at the back of the only room the dwelling possessed, a bowl of boiled wheat and a loaf of coarse rye bread on a small table in front of him. He jumped to his feet when Bascot entered and made haste to offer the Templar a stool and a cup of ale.

Bascot accepted the ale, but not the seat, and said, "I have come to ask if you know whether any of the quarrymen have been working atop the cliff face in the last two weeks or so, or if there have been any visitors to the site during that time who walked along there."

Cerlo's face registered surprise at the question and he pondered it for a moment before he replied. "There are a few masons from the town that come to buy stone, but I don't recollect any having been here since afore Michaelmas. As to the quarrymen, 'tis only when

there's need to make a fresh breach in the west face
they have cause to go up there, and we haven't done
any cutting on that side since summer. We do keep a
few tools in the shack there, but it's just a little way
from the main road. They wouldn't need to walk along
the cliff top to get to it."

Bascot nodded. The answer had been what he expected, but it dashed any hope the coin might have been
dropped accidentally. The Templar could see Cerlo was
wondering why the question had been asked, but Bascot
did not enlighten him, merely thanked the mason for his
time and the ale, and left the house.

Hoping information would be more forthcoming at
Brand's place of employment, Bascot and Gianni re-
traced their earlier passage through the Minster to Ermine Street and turned south towards the town. Once
through Bailgate, the huge portal that separated the
castle and cathedral from the rest of Lincoln, the Templar was careful to guide his mount slowly along the
slippery incline on the other side of the massive arch—
aptly named Steep Hill—and onto the main street of
Mikelgate. Gerard Camville had said the moneyer,
Helias de Stow, lived in a house next to the mint,
which was situated in the lower reaches of town near
the church of St. Mary Crackpole.

The streets were sparsely populated; most of the
wooden shutters that protected the fronts of the shops
were fastened shut and the fowl and flesh markets
closed. It did not take Bascot long to ride down the
main thoroughfare and reach the turn he needed.

As the Templar guided his horse towards de Stow's
house, he had to thread his way through a group of
people queuing for alms outside St. Mary Crackpole

church. It was an odd name for a house of God but the latter part of the name was derived from a corruption of the Old Norse words *kraka* for a water-crake and *pol* for a pool, because of the birds that had inhabited a large pond originally on the site. Most of the people outside the little church were women with young children, but there were a few men amongst them, all clad in clothes that were threadbare and did not afford much protection against the stiff breeze that had suddenly arisen. Some of the younger children were grizzling and many of the women had expressions of stoic fortitude on their careworn faces.

Just beyond the church gate and on the opposite side of the street was the mint, a strongly fortified building adjoining the exchange where Walter Legerton carried out his work. De Stow's house was a sturdy stone-walled building of three storeys on the other side, and separated from the mint by a narrow passageway.

Bascot tied the reins of his horse to a hitching rail in front of the moneyer's house, went up to the door and rapped on it. A young maidservant with a solemn expression answered his knock. When asked to inform her master of Bascot's presence, she sniffed loudly, then nodded and led the Templar inside and to an inner door just off the entryway. Opening it, she announced the visitor's name, and motioned for Bascot to go in.

Leaving Gianni in the vestibule, the Templar entered the room. It was large and comfortably, but not lavishly, appointed. On the surface of a table in the middle of the chamber were sheets of parchment, a quill and inkpot. The deep reds and greens in the tapestries that hung on the walls gleamed in the radiance of logs burning in the fireplace. Helias de Stow came forward before Bascot had gone more than two paces into the room. A short, round-faced man with an almost bald pate, the little hair that the moneyer possessed was dark in colour and grew in a long fringe from just above his ears down to his shoulders. His eyes were dark, and set deeply under sparse brows, giving him a sharp interrogative look, but his mouth was kindly set and generous in its curve.

"Have you come about the death of my poor clerk?" de Stow asked. When Bascot confirmed he had, the moneyer offered his visitor a cup of wine, which the Templar accepted. Once both men were seated and had full cups in front of them, de Stow explained how, the day before, Cerlo had approached him after the afternoon Mass at the cathedral and told of Brand's death.

"Cerlo said that he believed Peter to have been murdered. Is that true, Sir Bascot?"

"It is," the Templar replied. "The sheriff has sent me to gather as much information as possible about your clerk in the hope it will aid his search for the murderer. Cerlo will have told you that Brand's body was found in the quarry. From the condition of his corpse, it would appear your clerk was killed four or five days ago. Do you know of any reason why he would have gone to the pit?"

De Stow shook his head sadly. "Not that I can think of. It is indeed puzzling. I gave Peter permission to visit his mother in Grantham over the holy days and thought he had left to go there." The moneyer shook his head and flashed a contrite glance at Bascot. "It is to my regret that the last words I spoke to him were said in anger. He asked to leave early on his last day of work and I was annoyed by his request because there was still a lot of work to be done. Although I gave him permission, I also gave him the rough edge of my tongue."

"And which day was that?"

"The fourth one before Christ's Mass, the day the snowstorm started."

"The road to Grantham would have been impassable by morning. Did you not wonder why he had not turned back and returned to Lincoln?"

"He was going to travel by boat, not road. He made arrangements with the owner of a vessel taking supplies to Grantham to give him passage. The boat was due to leave very early the next morning and Peter was going to sleep on board overnight rather than stay in his room and have to rise well before dawn to be at the riverside in time for the boat's departure. After he left, I didn't expect to see him again until after the holy days were over. I did wonder how he had fared on the river in such terrible weather, but there was no reason to doubt he had gone."

The moneyer took a sip of his wine and gestured towards the parchment that was lying on the table. "Now I find it is my sad duty to tell his mother that her only child is dead. I am trying to compose a letter to send her, but the words do not come easily."

"I was told that both you and your clerk came to Lincoln from Grantham about a year ago. Is that correct?"

De Stow nodded. "Yes. The previous moneyer here in Lincoln died after a sudden illness and Master Legerton sent a letter to the Exchequer in London recommending me for the post." He looked up at the

Templar with a smile that contained a touch of pride. "As you will probably know, Sir Bascot, all moneyers are under contract to the crown and must be deemed trustworthy as well as proficient. When the office of the Lincoln moneyer became vacant, Master Legerton came to Grantham and asked if I would be interested in the post. We had been acquainted from the time when his father was alive; his sire was a silversmith and he and I belonged to the same guild. When Legerton came to tell me about the moneyer's post, he said he would rather work with a man he knew than some stranger sent by the Exchequer. I gladly agreed to the terms he suggested and, along with my wife and children, asked Peter to come with me. He was an excellent clerk and I valued his services."

Bascot, mindful that he must try to extract information about the coin Gianni had found without making de Stow aware he was doing so, asked the moneyer about the responsibilities of Brand's post and if the delivery of coins was involved.

"We found no scrip on Brand's body, Master de Stow, and so it may be that the reason for his death was robbery and he lost his life in a struggle with the thief. Did he, in the course of his duties, ever carry sums of money on his person?"

De Stow shook his head. "All the pennies we produce are given into the care of the exchanger. The mint is not involved in the transfer of coins."

"Was Brand paid well? Is it likely he would have been carrying enough money to make it worthwhile to rob him?"

"I doubt it, Sir Bascot," de Stow replied with a wry smile. "Peter was paid only a clerk's wage of one and a half pence a day plus an additional halfpenny that I offered him as an inducement to accompany me here. I allowed him to take his meals with my family and gave him lodging in a room over the stables in my yard for a minimal sum, but he left the rest of his salary in my keeping. Every two months or so, he would withdraw what he had saved and take the money to Grantham for his mother. She is a widow and Peter's father, who was a tanner, did not leave any provision for her after he died. Because of his mother's reliance on him, Peter was forced to be parsimonious; he rarely even visited an alehouse because he was reluctant to part with the cost of a pint of ale. His leisure time was usually spent in his room or in the company of myself, and my family. It is hardly likely he would have been carrying enough money to tempt a thief."

De Stow's dark eyes grew moist. "He was a good lad. We shall all miss him."

With a widowed mother to support, it was possible Brand had been driven to find desperate measures to provide for her, Bascot thought. Had the clerk been involved in a theft from the mint, and had that theft involved, as Camville suspected, the contents of an unreported trove?

"Do you know if Brand had any close friends in Lincoln, one of the men who work in the mint perhaps, someone he knew well enough to confide his reason for going to the quarry?" Bascot asked.

De Stow leaned forward and refilled their wine cups. "Not that I am aware of. As I said, he rarely went out and, although Peter was amiable enough, I do not think he formed a particular fellowship with any of my other employees, which is not particularly surprising.

The three hammermen are all older than he, and married with children. They would not have much in common with an unattached young man. And the converse applies to my two apprentices. They are both some years younger than Peter; one is sixteen and the other nineteen. They would be more comfortable consorting with lads their own age."

"What about those on Legerton's staff?"

"Master Legerton has only one employee, an assayer named Simon Partager, who also fulfills the duties of clerk. Partager was recently married and, outside of the three days in the week that the exchange is open, spends the rest of his time at Legerton's house in Canwick, where he and his new wife lodge. A man in the hazy throes of newlywed bliss does not seek out the company of an unmarried clerk.

"Apart from those I have mentioned, the only other people that Peter would have met in the course of his duties are the guards that keep the mint secure," de Stow went on, "but all of them are, by the nature of their calling, men of rough disposition, former men-at-arms and the like. There are six altogether, four in my hire and two in Legerton's. I doubt whether Peter would have formed more than a nodding acquaintance with any of them."

"What about women?" Bascot asked. "Did Brand have a liaison with any?"

"Not in Lincoln, no," de Stow replied, "but there is a young woman who lives in Grantham that he hoped to make his wife. They were not betrothed, but I know Peter was anxious to secure her promise to wed. But he had not seen her since his last visit home and that was over six weeks ago. Unless his visit to the quarry was something he had planned well in advance, it is unlikely he would have mentioned it to her."

Bascot nodded. On the surface, it seemed de Stow did not have any information that might be helpful, but the Templar had one last question. "You said Brand was a competent clerk and a dutiful son, but what about his faults? All men possess one or two; it is not likely he was an exception. It may be that a facet of his personality—a tendency to be argumentative, perhaps—was offensive to someone and gave cause to wish his death."

De Stow was shaking his head even as Bascot spoke. "He was a mild-mannered lad and would not have had the temerity to exchange angry words with anyone, even in strong disagreement. He could be a little irritating at times over his obsession with the maid in Grantham. There was another suitor for her hand, apparently, and he was worried she would accept the other lad. Peter thought she might run out of patience while he saved up the money they needed to wed, which was difficult for him to do since nearly all of his salary went to support his mother. He often spoke about her, even during a working day and to any of my other employees who would listen, extolling the girl's virtues and her comeliness, saying his heart would be broken if he lost her. As you can imagine, they all thought his fixation with the maid was amusing, and I had to reprimand him more than once for distracting them from their work. Apart from that, there was little to discommend him. His work was exemplary; he kept the room he rented from me in good order and was courteous to my wife and two young daughters. I would not have offered him a post as my clerk had he been otherwise."

Deciding no further information was likely to be forthcoming, Bascot told de Stow he would like to speak to the men who had worked with Brand. Despite what the moneyer had said about the clerk not being on familiar terms with any of them, it was still possible he might have mentioned his reason for going to the quarry, if only in casual conversation.

De Stow rose from his seat. "Of course. You may do so today, if you wish, for all my men are at work. I usually give them leave to be absent on St. Stephen's day, but we have a large order to fill for the exchanger and I promised them a small bonus if they reported for duty."

"Then, Master de Stow, perhaps you would be good enough to take me to the mint."

Seven

❖

THE MONEYER LED BASCOT, WITH GIANNI KEEPING
pace behind, out of his home and to the door of the
mint. A guard was on duty outside, a burly individual
with watchful eyes and a short sword slung from his
belt. He nodded to de Stow as the moneyer, the Templar and Gianni went inside and into a small square
entrance hall where another guard was stationed. This
sentry was, in appearance, similar to the guard that had
been on the outside door; a little taller and rangier in
build perhaps, but also armed and clad in a leather
gambeson. He, too, gave a nod of respect as de Stow,
using a key on a chain attached to his belt, unlocked
yet another door and led his visitors through the portal,
turning the key behind them. The security on the premises was vigilant.

On the other side of the inner door was a huge chamber,
the far wall of which was fitted with a forge surrounded by
a double layer of stone. The atmosphere was filled with
heat generated by the furnace and the acrid tang of metal. It

was also noisy, the roar of the fire and the clang of tools making a clamorous din. In front of the furnace, two men were operating a bellows and another overseeing the contents of a crucible that sat in the depths of the red-hot embers. On the floor beside them was a large tray filled with sand containing moulds of hardened clay in the shape of long, thin cylinders. Into these, the man in charge of the crucible was carefully pouring a stream of molten silver from a scoop attached to the end of a long pole. De Stow explained to Bascot that not only was refined silver ore used to produce coins, but worn pennies brought in to be exchanged for new were also melted down for the same purpose.

"That is what they are doing now," the moneyer said. "Legerton had a large amount of silver paid in by a merchant who trades abroad and there were quite a number of foreign coins included. The coins are, of course, melted down separately from the ore, and must be assayed to test for impurities. Once they, or the ore, have been melted down, the molten metal is poured into those cylinders. When the cylinders are cool, they are sliced into thin rounds that are the approximate weight of a silver penny."

Gianni's eyes grew large at the sight of so much wealth and he listened intently as de Stow went on to name his employees and describe the various tasks in which they were engaged. There were a number of sturdy rough-hewn tables placed in rows in the middle of the room, and at two of them workers were using small hammers and tiny anvils to beat the newly annealed discs into a desired thickness and recheck the weight on a set of scales. The discs were then passed to another table where hammermen worked alongside one another, striking the blank rounds of silver between two dies provided by the Exchequer in London. The moneyer explained that the bottom die, mounted in a small block of solid iron, bore the imprint of the king and his name, while the upper die, a long, thin rod of the same metal, had one end fashioned in the design of a short cross in a circle. As they watched, one of the hammermen fixed a blank disc onto the surface of the bottom die and, grasping the upper die firmly in his hand, positioned the imprinted end over it. Once he was satisfied the disc and dies were correctly aligned, he brought his hammer down sharply on top of the upper die to produce a coin that was imprinted with both the obverse and reverse images at the same time. The newly minted penny was then given to a worker at an adjoining table to polish with a buffing rag. The whole procedure was slow and tedious, requiring studied concentration.

Casements fitted with protective iron grills were set in the walls on either side of the forge and, despite the cold winter temperature outside, the shutters had been thrown open in an attempt to lessen the stifling heat. In one corner, a bell with a pull rope hung from the ceiling. Lined up on the floor nearby were a half dozen stout wooden chests banded with iron and fitted with triple locks. Standing beside them was another guard who, like the men on duty at the doors, was clad in a leather tunic studded with iron rings and had a short sword in a scabbard depending from his belt.

De Stow motioned to a door near where the guard stood. "That leads through to the exchanger's office," he said. He then gestured towards a shelf where a set of scales and a pile of empty leather sacks were laid. "And that is where his assayer keeps his equipment. Usually it is stored in Legerton's office but when they are both away, Partager brings it in here for safekeeping."

The Templar looked around the room. "You said you had four guards in your hire. I see only three; is the other off duty?"

"He is," de Stow said. "All the guards live in quarters in the yard at the back. I also keep two mastiffs there and the dogs patrol the grounds at night. The guards rotate their shifts, so that after working hours there is one on duty in here and one asleep in their quarters, while the other two are at liberty to spend some time in the town if they choose. If anything untoward should occur after the mint is closed, the inside guard would ring the bell to sound the alarm and bring the other man, and the dogs, to his assistance."

"You keep a secure mint, moneyer," the Templar said. "Your precautions are admirable."

De Stow gave a smile of pleasure; it was obvious he was gratified by the compliment.

Bascot nodded at the iron chests. "The coins you produce—are they kept in those chests?"

"Yes, as are those brought in for changing. Two of them contain blocks of refined silver from the mine. As I said, the assayer tests all the old coins before they are melted down. He usually uses only a touchstone and his scales, but there are some occasions when he feels it necessary to assay the silver by melting it with lead in a crucible. When he wishes to do that, he uses my forge."

Bascot nodded. If any coins from the reign of King Stephen had been brought in to be exchanged, Peter Brand would have had access to the place where they were kept, but so would all the rest of de Stow and

Legerton's employees, including the guards. "I assume only you and the exchanger are in possession of keys to the coffers?" he asked de Stow.

The moneyer nodded, patting the pouch he wore on his belt. "Each of them has three separate locks and a different key is required to open each one. I hold the master keys to all of them and Legerton has duplicates. We keep them on our persons at all times. Even when I lie down for my night's rest, I place the keys in a strongbox beside my bed and keep the key to the box on a chain about my neck. I imagine Master Legerton takes the same precautions. I also check the contents of each chest every morning before work is begun and again at the end of every working day, to ensure that no discrepancy has occurred in the interim."

The security here would be difficult to infiltrate, Bascot thought, but if either de Stow or Legerton allowed himself a moment of carelessness with his keys, it would not be impossible for anyone with enough daring to steal them and gain access to the contents of the chests.

"What about the silver ore you use—how is the security of that controlled?"

De Stow gave Bascot a searching look accompanied by a cynical smile. His shrewd dark eyes took on a hard alertness as he said, "I assume you are asking these questions because you believe my clerk may have stolen coins or silver blocks from here and had them on his person when he was killed. Is that not so, Sir Bascot?"

"It would provide a motive, moneyer, especially if the person who murdered him was aware they were in his possession."

De Stow shook his head. "My clerk was an honest man, Sir Bascot, but even if he had not been, he would not have had the opportunity to steal from the mint. Besides, Peter has been gone some days and I have been doing his job since he left. If there was a shortage, I would have discovered it by now, and there is not."

After pausing for a moment, he continued. "But, to answer your question. The blocks of solid silver from the royal mine are delivered to these premises by armed guards. I then weigh them to ensure they tally with the figures I have been given by the overseer of the mine and make separate checks all through the stages of production until they are turned into coinage. That is why I have need of a clerk, for there are many figures to be recorded, but I can assure you that I double-check all of them. There is no margin for error— or pilfering."

"I will take you at your word, Master de Stow," Bascot replied. "Now I would like to speak to your employees. From what you tell me, Brand must have gone to the quarry late in the afternoon of the day he was killed. I want to ask if any of your workers know the reason he did so."

The moneyer called each of the men up in turn, the hammermen first, then the apprentices, and Bascot explained to each of them that he was conducting an investigation into Brand's death on Gerard Camville's behalf and wanted to know if the clerk had told any of them about his intention of going to the pit. The Templar also told Gianni, who was standing beside him, to take out his wax tablet and write down the names of each of those he interviewed and make a brief note of their responses. Most of de Stow's employees looked apprehensive while this was being done, which was what the Templar intended. They were far less likely to lie if they knew their names were included in a report for the sheriff. Each of them denied having seen Brand after he left the mint on the day of his death or any knowledge of why he would have gone to the quarry. The three guards on duty were subjected to the same questions and gave the same answers, as did the one that was sleeping in the guardroom in the yard behind the mint when de Stow sent one of his employees to rouse him.

Once Bascot had finished his questioning, he told de Stow he would also like to speak to Master Legerton and his assayer and asked if they were on the exchange premises.

"Not today," the moneyer replied. "The exchange was closed on the eve of Christ's Mass and Legerton went to his manor in Canwick for the holy days. Partager will have gone with him, I expect. The men hired to guard the exchange would not remain here during that time, for they are only needed when Legerton is in his office. All of them should return tomorrow, when the exchange is due to open for custom."

Bascot told de Stow he would come back in the morning to speak to Legerton and his staff. The Templar then casually asked, as though in passing, about the condition of the coins brought in for exchange. "I suppose most of them are fourthings or halfpennies that need to be made into whole coin, are they not?"

"Yes," de Stow replied. "And there are always a few that have edges badly worn from usage. Sometimes there are a few coins from other countries included, but not often. The large number of foreign coins we are melting down today is an exception, rather than otherwise."

"When I was in my childhood," Bascot added in an offhand manner, "I remember my grandsire complaining about coins from King Stephen's reign being clipped, but I suppose the new design of a short cross brought in by King Henry twenty years ago stopped that illegal practice."

"It did, Sir Bascot. And when King Henry gave an order that all old coins, especially those from King Stephen's reign, should be exchanged for ones of new issue, everyone was only too pleased to submit to his decree, for some of the parings were so deftly done it was difficult to tell whether a coin was short weighted or not. I do not believe there are many left from before King Henry's time now, except for the odd single coin or two. I have hardly seen any these last ten years."

Reluctant to press the subject of coins from Stephen's reign any further lest de Stow become suspicious of the reason for his interest, Bascot asked the moneyer to show him the room where Peter Brand had lodged. De Stow led him outside the mint and back into his own house, then through a door into the yard.

"His room is up there, over the horse stall," the moneyer said, pointing to a wooden building of two storeys with double doors at the bottom. A staircase wound up the outside wall. The top of the building was completely enclosed except for a small casement window and a narrow door at the top of the stairway.

Bascot followed de Stow up the stairs and into the room where Peter Brand had lodged. It was neat and tidy, with a palliasse covered by a pair of thick blankets. There were few of the clerk's possessions in the room; some blank pieces of parchment and some scribing tools lay on a small table, and a spare pair of hose and a lightweight summer cloak hung from a peg behind the door. On the floor near the bed was a smallish bag of heavy linen that Bascot told Gianni to open and search. When the boy did so, he extracted a tunic of good wool, another pair of hose and a small package carefully wrapped in a piece of soft cloth. Looking to his master for permission, he unrolled the parcel and found a tiny ring of silver gilt inside, which he handed to the Templar.

Bascot glanced at the clothing and then examined the ring. "It would appear your clerk intended to return for this bag before he left on his journey to Grantham," he said. "Not only would he have needed the change of clothing, I doubt whether he would have left without taking this." He held up the ring so the moneyer could see it more clearly. It was fashioned in a design of clasping hands popular for betrothal rings. "A hopeful gift for your clerk's sweetheart, I would think."

De Stow nodded sadly. "You are right, Sir Bascot. Its presence here also indicates that Peter lied to me."

"How so?" Bascot asked.

The moneyer gave a regretful sigh. "When Peter asked to leave early on his last day of work, he told me he needed to do so because he had to pick up his good tunic from a fuller who was cleansing it. The fuller's premises are on the way to the river where the boat Peter was to take lay at anchor. It would not make sense for him to go and collect his tunic and then come all the way back here just to get his extra hose and the

ring. He would have taken the bag with him and collected his tunic on the way to the quay."

"Then he must have picked up his tunic on a previous day, for it is here and looks newly cleansed." At de
Stow's disappointed nod of confirmation, Bascot
added, "And the reason he asked to leave early must
have been so he could go to the quarry for some purpose he did not wish to reveal to you."

"I suppose it must," de Stow remarked glumly.

A SHORT TIME LATER, BASCOT AND GIANNI LEFT DE
Stow's house and retrieved the Templar's horse. As
they rode past St. Mary Crackpole church towards
Mikelgate, Bascot looked up at the sky. The pale blue
above them was unmarred except for a few grey clouds
and even though there was a bank of darkness in the
east, he thought it unlikely that any rain or snow would
fall during the next few hours. He turned his mount
down Mikelgate towards Stonebow, the principal gate
out of the lower part of the town and, once they had
passed through it, went along Briggate towards the
bridge that crossed the Witham River. The village of
Canwick, where Walter Legerton had his manor house,
was only about two miles' distance from the river.

While de Stow had seemed genuinely disturbed by the
death of Peter Brand, and anxious for the sorrow it would
cause his mother, Bascot had learned from his dealing
with those involved in previous cases of secret murder
that a perpetrator was often skilled at concealing his true
thoughts behind a mask of innocence. If de Stow had
been honest when he claimed he had only learned of
Brand's death through his chance meeting with Cerlo the

day before, then Legerton, who had been absent from Lincoln for the last two days, might not yet have heard of the clerk's murder. If that was the case, it might be profitable to witness the exchanger's reaction when he heard news of the stabbing. If he was not involved in the clerk's murder, or in the concealment of a treasure trove, his surprise would be genuine. But if he had some knowledge of the circumstances surrounding Brand's death, he might not have sufficient cunning to conceal it.

AFTER THE TEMPLAR AND HIS SERVANT HAD GONE, Helias de Stow went back to his chamber, reseated himself at his desk and stared blankly at the piece of parchment lying on its surface. Although he picked up his quill and dipped it in the inkpot, he still could not bring himself to write the words that would tell Peter's mother her son was dead.

De Stow sighed heavily, laid his pen down and rested his head in his hands, his fingers digging into the top of his bald pate as he did so. Peter's death and the subsequent visit of the Templar had unnerved him. The moneyer had always taken pride in presenting a confident image to his family and employees but now he felt as though that facade was cracking. It had been a mistake to move to Lincoln, but it was an error he could not have foreseen. When Legerton had offered to recommend him for the post of king's moneyer in Lincoln, it had seemed an attractive proposition. There were two royal mints in Grantham and the one in which de Stow worked had been the smaller of the two and of less consequence. The stipend for the Lincoln post was much higher than he had been earning in

Grantham, as was the commission he, and Legerton, received on the amount of coinage that passed through their hands.

The problems that plagued him had begun to arise during the move from one town to the other. He and Blanche had sent their furniture to Lincoln by river barge and, during the journey, the barge had capsized. All their belongings, except for some clothing and personal possessions they had taken with them on their journey by road, had been lost and required a considerable sum to replace. Then Helias had arrived at the Lincoln mint and found some minor equipment was in need of replacement—the bellows for the forge were starting to rot and two of the hammermen's tables were full of woodworm. He had also been dismayed to discover that a few stones in the outer wall were loose and in need of repair. Although the latter was not extremely urgent, it could not be delayed too long lest the security of the mint be compromised. Legerton had assured the moneyer he would be reimbursed by the crown for these necessities, but the promised payment had not arrived. When the cost of bringing the mint up to a reasonable standard was added to the sum needed to replace most of the household furniture, de Stow's savings had not been enough to cover the total outlay. He had been forced to take desperate measures to try to extricate himself from his predicament and was worried they would prove disastrous. And now there was Peter's untimely death to exacerbate the whole sorry situation.

De Stow took a sip of wine and tried to compose his thoughts. He must continue with the arrangements he had made and trust all would eventually be resolved in a satisfactory manner. Resolutely he picked up the quill and returned his attention to the composition of his letter to Peter's mother, choosing his words carefully. He must try, as much as possible, to minimise the gorier details of her son's death.

Eight

+-+-+

I N FRONT OF A BLAZING FIRE IN THE SOLAR, NICOLAA de la Haye sat with her female guests, all of whom, once Richard was wed to Eustachia, would be related to her by marriage. She was having difficulty in giving her full attention to the conversation of the other women, for her mind kept drifting to the conversation she had had with her husband the previous evening. Gerard's concern that an unreported trove could be involved in the murder of the clerk was, in her opinion, well-founded.

Tales of corruption among those who manufactured and distributed coins of the realm were not uncommon and, because it was now the season of Christ's Mass, Nicolaa recalled the story she had been told of an event that had taken place seventy-five years before at this very same time of year. The first King Henry had been on the throne then and, having discovered that a number of his moneyers were guilty of abasing the silver pennies issued in his name, had summoned them to Winchester and confronted them with their crimes.

One by one, and despite the fact that he and his court were celebrating the holy days of Christ's birth, the king had sentenced them all to be emasculated and their right hands cut off.

Nicolaa shivered, her diminutive, slightly plump frame overcome with a tremor of fear. If John believed that Gerard was part of any scheme that involved embezzling monies rightfully due to the crown, not even her friendship with the king, and the trust he had always placed in her, would deter him from subjecting her husband to the same harsh punishment.

Her attention was caught by a remark directed to her by Egelina Bassett, Eustachia's mother, who was voicing her concern that the weather would not hold fine for the day of her daughter's betrothal. Egelina and Nicolaa had been friends for many years through the acquaintanceship of their husbands, and although Egelina was not an overly intelligent woman, Nicolaa was very fond of her and admired the loving firmness with which she had raised both of her girls.

Eustachia was of a more serious mien than her younger sister, but had inherited her father's acumen and would, Nicolaa thought, make a suitable wife for Richard. Her son had spent the years of his training for knighthood in Gilbert Bassett's household and had always spoken of his admiration for the baron's elder daughter, claiming she combined good sense with womanly grace. Although her son did not realise it, Nicolaa was sure Richard's favourable impression of Eustachia was mainly due to the fact that the girl had the wit to discern that most men preferred a woman who listened rather than chattered. Eustachia was also sensible in the matter of her appearance; her colouring was dark, almost Italianate, and today she was wearing a gown of muted blue set with trimmings of dark green that contrasted subtly with her skin and gave it a rosy glow. While her features were not completely handsome—her eyes were set a little too close together and her teeth were crooked—her expression was pleasing, and she possessed an even temper. There was no doubt in Nicolaa's mind that Eustachia was very fond of Richard; the castellan had seen the tender expression that came over the girl's face whenever she looked his way. All in all, the castellan thought, the match was pleasing to both young people. Since marriages among the nobility were usually arranged for the purpose of forging a favourable alliance, it was not often the two people concerned embarked on a marriage based on love, or even mutual regard. That Richard and Eustachia would be an exception to this generality was a rarity for which Nicolaa was thankful.

The castellan's gaze went to Lucia, the younger of Egelina and Gilbert's two daughters. The sisters were a contrast in opposites. Lucia had a pretty face that was always animated, hair of rich auburn and an entrancing smile that showed off her small even teeth to advantage. Even though she was only sixteen years of age, her figure was already lush, with a swelling bosom and lissom hips. At the moment, Lucia was speaking volubly to her cousin Maud of Turville about Maud's son, Stephen, telling the boy's mother that Stephen had been most interested in the gestures the Templar's mute servant had been using to convey his thoughts to the clerk that sat beside him at the banquet last night. She was also expressing her opinion that she thought Stephen should be taught some of them.

"I think he would benefit greatly from the knowledge, Maud," Lucia said earnestly. "I know that because of Stephen's disfigurement Ralph decided to keep him at home rather than send him to another lord for training in knighthood, but that decision has made him withdrawn in the company of others. If Stephen could use gestures to convey his wishes to your servants, and to converse with you and his father, I am sure it would swell his confidence."

Maud's response to the suggestion was one of agitation. Although she doted on her son, she was a timid and indecisive woman whose self-confidence had been sorely strained by the fact that the only heir she had given her husband had been marked in such a terrible manner.

"I will have to ask Ralph about your suggestion, Lucia," Maud said, her hands fluttering ineffectually over the embroidery in her lap. "Our physician at home said I must have startled a hare while Stephen was in my womb and the malicious creature took its revenge by causing my son's disfigurement. The doctor has made up an ointment he is sure will heal the cleft and I have been applying it every morning without fail for the last ten days."

She looked around at the other women, her eyes full of hope. "The physician said it would take some weeks before any difference would be noticed, but I am sure the fissure in his lip is already beginning to close. If it does, then he will not need to learn any other means of communication, for he will be able to speak clearly."

Her companions smiled at her in an attempt at reassurance but Nicolaa saw the doubt in Egelina's face, and felt the same herself. She had heard there were

occasions when a split in a newborn child's lip could
be corrected by sewing the cleft together with catgut
and leaving the stitches in place until the flesh had
grown together, but this was only effective if the gap
was very slight and the repair done immediately after
birth. Nicolaa had seen Stephen when he was just a
few months old and the malformation had been a deep
one; it started at the base of his nose and exposed
nearly all his front teeth. And even if this rift should be
improved by the physician's ointment, the cleft in his
palate would still remain. It was very doubtful he
would be able to speak without distortion unless both
of these deformities were corrected.

"And even if the ointment doesn't heal his lip,"
Maud said to Lucia with an unusual flash of temerity,
"there would be little point in Stephen learning the
gestures, for once we return home, no one except he
would know what they meant."

"But many of the movements are simple and easily
comprehended, Maud," Lucia protested, "even by those
not familiar with the meaning of them. I have seen the
Templar's servant use them with many people—to say
'please' and 'thank you' for example, or to ask that a
particular dish be passed to him when he is serving his
master. Besides," she added defiantly, "I am willing to
learn them even if you are not. Then, when I am in
Stephen's company, he can convey his thoughts to me
and we can have speech together."

Lucia gave her cousin a disdainful glance as she
added, "I would have thought that you, as his mother,
would be anxious to do likewise."

Egelina gave her younger daughter a reproving look
for her impertinence and changed the direction of the

conversation by asking Eustachia if she had made a choice of material for her wedding gown, even though a date had not yet been set for her daughter and Richard's marriage. It was a question to which her elder daughter responded with alacrity, conscious of her mother's purpose. The awkward moment passed but it was nonetheless obvious that Lucia's disapproval, and the reason for it, had impressed Maud. She, in common with most people, even those of the nobility, was not literate and although Stephen had been taught to read and write by a private tutor, she could not communicate with him through the written word because of her inability to read. But if, like Lucia, she learned the gestures the Templar's mute servant used, she would be able to hold a conversation with the son she loved so dearly. Hesitantly, in a whispered aside, Maud promised her young cousin that she would speak to her husband about the matter.

As the women fell to suggesting materials that might be suitable for Eustachia's gown, and offering advice on trimmings, shoes and jewels, Nicolaa returned to her consideration of the motive behind the murder of the clerk. She was glad Gerard had asked Bascot de Marins to investigate the death. The Templar had a forte for uncovering the truth behind men's actions, and if the murder was connected to embezzlement in the mint, she was sure he would discover it.

If the worst happened and de Marins found that a treasure trove was also involved in the crime, the king would need to be quickly apprised of the situation. In such an explosive situation, she decided, it would be best if she took upon herself the responsibility for doing so. She had enjoyed a long friendship with the king and, unlike Gerard and many other nobles, had a fondness for John. His suspicious nature was the result of being used as a pawn by the squabbling members of his family throughout the whole of his life; in truth he was intelligent, witty and, when the occasion demanded it, a more than competent military commander. Even though the king and Gerard were not complaisant with each other, she knew that John held her own person in high esteem and would not question her honesty. For her husband's well-being, it was fortunate this was so.

THE WITHAM RIVER HAD FLOODED ITS BANKS WHEN the heavy rains had fallen on Lincoln two days before, and the water was just now beginning to recede as Bascot and Gianni crossed the bridge below Briggate. The ground on both sides of the river was marshy, and it was not until they took a lane that led eastward towards Canwick and the ground began to rise that their mount could step out freely, its hooves finally unhindered by the sucking mud. As they rode, the Templar spoke to Gianni over his shoulder and instructed the boy to keep his wax tablet tucked in his scrip while they were at the manor house.

"Sir Richard told me that Legerton is very conscious of his rights as an officer of the crown and can sometimes be supercilious because of it," Bascot said to the boy. "I do not wish to make it seem we have come to interrogate him. I shall merely say I have come to ask if he has any knowledge of the reason Peter Brand was at the quarry on the night he was killed. That does not mean, Gianni, that you are not to keep your ears stretched wide, and your eyes also. If you see anything you think might be of import, store it away in your mind and write it down when we have returned to the castle."

Bascot felt Gianni give his shoulder two gentle taps, a signal that meant he understood. Two were for yes, three for no. It was fortuitous that, because of the celebration of the feast day, Gianni had not been required to assist John Blund and Lambert in the scriptorium. The boy had a sharp intelligence that had been invaluable during the previous cases of secret murder the Templar investigated; he hoped it would prove so again.

Walter Legerton's manor house was small in size but impressive nonetheless. Encircled by a protective wall of stone, it was set in the middle of a large yard surrounded by outbuildings that comprised stables, storehouses and a blacksmith's forge. The house itself was a solid rectangle in shape, half-timbered and three storeys high, with the lower floor partially submerged below ground level to serve as a cellar for the storage of provisions or as a place of safety during times of unrest. The topmost floor, which was of wood, was set with wider windows than the second storey, and the eaves on the tiled roof were decorated with carvings at each corner. There were two chimneys of turret design, one at the end of each outside wall. It appeared to be either a recently erected structure or an old one that had been completely refurbished. Whichever it was, Bascot thought, it gave the impression that its owner was a man of some wealth.

The Templar was hailed by the guard on the gate and asked his name and the purpose of his visit. Once Bascot told him, the guard sent a servant running to the house and, after a few moments, Legerton's steward

appeared. Bowing low, the steward said he would be
pleased to take the Templar to his master and, calling
for a groom to take charge of Bascot's horse, led his
two visitors across the yard.

The main door to the house was made of thick
planks of oak, but swung easily open at the steward's
command to the doorward and, as it did so, strains of
music could be heard coming from inside. Across a
narrow entryway a door led into the hall, a large chamber with a high ceiling of crisscrossed oak beams
where, in an open space in the middle of the room,
about a dozen people were engaged in a lively dance
called an *estampie*. At the far end, on a shallow dais,
was a table at which five people—two of them young
boys—were sitting. Other, smaller, tables all laid with
food, and at which a number of people were seated,
were scattered around the perimeter of the room.

"If you will wait here, Sir Bascot, I shall tell Master
Legerton of your arrival," the steward said and
threaded his way past the dancers to the table on
the dais.

Leaning down, the steward spoke in a respectful
manner to the man seated in the central position. He
had a full head of thick dark hair and a florid, well-
fleshed face. His attire was sumptuous; an expensive
scarlet wool tunic enclosed his muscular frame and
atop his head he wore a matching soft cap adorned
with a brooch of silver filigree. As he listened to the
steward, he turned his gaze in the Templar's direction.
Finally he nodded and rose from his seat. There was a
look of irritation on his face as he came down the
length of the room, but it was smoothed over by the
time he reached Bascot.

"I am Walter Legerton," he said. "My steward tells me you wish to speak to me privily."

"That is correct," Bascot told him, "and to your assayer, Simon Partager."

"May I ask what this is about?" Legerton enquired. "As you can see, we have a number of guests—family and friends—who have come to celebrate the holy days. They will not look kindly on my deserting them."

The exchanger's tone was tinged with impatience and Bascot felt his choler rise. He tried to curtail it, however, and answered in a polite, if chilly, manner. "Master de Stow's clerk, Peter Brand, was found dead yesterday in the cathedral quarry. He was murdered. Sheriff Camville has asked me to investigate the matter. I have come to ask you, and your assayer, if you have any knowledge that may assist us in apprehending his killer."

Legerton's face paled a little, but his response contained a hint of peevishness. "I am sorry to hear of Brand's death, but he was a clerk. Apart from seeing him about the mint in de Stow's company, I have barely spoken to the man. How could I be expected to know anything that would be pertinent to his murder?"

"I have been instructed to ask for information from everyone who came into contact with Brand," Bascot replied brusquely, wondering if the exchanger was as heartless as he seemed or if his manner was a screen to hide a deeper emotion. "If you have a chamber where I may speak to you and your assayer apart from your guests, the matter should not require you to be absent from your company for more than a few minutes."

Bascot's tone left Legerton in no doubt that he found the exchanger's attitude annoying. Legerton also recalled that while de Marins had said he had come on behalf of Sheriff Camville, the knight was in the temporary service of Nicolaa de la Haye, who was reputed to be on terms of great friendship with the king. In the exchanger's position as a royal official, it would not do to jeopardize his continuance in the post by leaving himself open to complaint from anyone who had King John's ear. He gave Bascot an assurance of his cooperation and, directing his steward to ask Partager to attend him, led the Templar to a small chamber just off the entryway. Gianni unobtrusively followed his master through the door. Although there was a brazier burning in a corner, there was little else in the room aside from a small table set with two wine cups and a large chest bound with iron bands and sealed with a stout lock.

"This is where my household accounts and duplicate records of transactions at the exchange are kept," Legerton explained. "The room is not used for any other purpose, so we will not be disturbed."

As Bascot nodded in response, there was a light tap at the door and the assayer, Simon Partager, entered the room. He was a man of about Bascot's own age, mid-thirties, with a thin, sensitive face and weary eyes. His hair was light brown in colour, as was his neatly trimmed beard, and his clothing was of practical design and quality. Bascot recalled catching a glimpse of him in the exchanger's hall a few moments before. Partager had been in the company of a fair-haired woman who was pretty of face and coy in demeanour. Although seated beside the assayer, she had been engaged in animated conversation with the man across the table from her, giving him admiring glances as they spoke together.

"Sir Bascot has just told me that Helias's clerk, Peter Brand, has been murdered," Legerton said to the assayer. "His body was found in the cathedral quarry yesterday and Sir Bascot has come to ask if either of us know anything that may indicate why he was killed."

Partager's face registered an expression of shock, but it was difficult to tell if it was genuine or feigned. The muscles in his jaw tightened for a moment and then he said, "That is terrible news. He was a likeable young man. Are you . . . are you sure he was murdered?"

"Since he was stabbed through the heart," Bascot said dryly, "I think the assumption he was murdered can be taken as a true one."

The Templar paused slightly to watch both men's reaction to the gory detail and then said, "It would appear that Brand was murdered four days before Christ's Mass, the day the snowstorm began, since he was last seen at work earlier that day. I am trying to find out why Brand was in the quarry that afternoon. Do either of you know the reason?"

Legerton did not even deign to answer. He had already said he had hardly spoken to the clerk and his impatient manner indicated he had consented to the interview with the Templar only on sufferance. Partager, however, gave a reply.

"I have no knowledge of Peter's movements outside the mint, Sir Bascot, and know nothing of his personal affairs," he said in a stiff manner. "He certainly never made mention, in my hearing, that he had any intention of going to the quarry on that day or at any other time."

Bascot turned to the exchanger. "I am told you at-

tend your office on three days of the week, Master
Legerton. I presume you use the quarters above for
your night's rest at those times. Is that correct?"

The exchanger bridled a bit at the question, but answered all the same. "Yes, I do."

"And you, Master Partager, do you stay there as
well when you are at work?"

The assayer replied that he did, since there was
more than one bedchamber in the lodgings. "I often
stay there alone," he added, "on those occasions when
my duties require that I remain at the exchange after
Master Legerton has gone home." There was a hint of
bitterness in his tone.

Bascot had noted Legerton's unspoken objection to
the query and explained his reason for asking it. "I am
trying to ascertain the security of the exchange. There
is reason to believe Brand was robbed at the time of his
murder and since de Stow tells me the clerk did not
possess a great deal of money, I am wondering if he
had perhaps stolen from his place of work and was
attacked for the contents of his scrip. De Stow explained the precautions that are taken to keep all the
silver safe but, as you are probably aware, any determined and clever thief can find a way through even the
most stringent safeguards."

"Impossible," Legerton expostulated. "De Stow and
I have the only keys and there are guards on the premises at all times. Besides, if any was missing, it would
be noticed as soon as the twice-daily inventory is done
by de Stow and his clerk. . . ."

He trailed off as he realised that since the murdered
man had been in a position of trust, it was possible he
had, as Bascot suggested, taken advantage of the privi-

lege to steal. "I must return immediately to Lincoln and ensure there is no shortage in the coinage I store in the mint," he said in distraction. "Simon, find my steward and tell him to order a groom to saddle my horse. . . ."

"There is no need," Bascot said bluntly. "I spoke with de Stow before I came here and he assures me he has taken a tally of the coinage and all is correct and accounted for. I am satisfied that nothing has been stolen from the mint; it is the exchange I am concerned with. Do you keep any money there that Brand may have had access to, but which is not within the moneyer's control?"

"No, no, I do not keep any silver there," Legerton said distractedly, still half in motion to leave the room. His face full of worry, he sought further assurance. "And you are certain that de Stow found nothing missing from the coffers?"

"Brand was killed some days ago," Bascot told him, "and, since the moneyer has been carrying out the clerk's duties during that time, he would quickly have discovered any shortage."

Legerton relaxed as he heard the certainty in the Templar's response and his former impatience returned. "Are there any other questions you wish to ask?" he said abruptly.

"Not at the moment," Bascot replied, his words just as blunt. "If any should arise, you will be informed of the need to make yourself available, either by myself or Sheriff Camville."

The Templar left the manor house with a feeling of unease. As the steward shut the door behind him and Gianni, he thought over his conversation with Legerton and the assayer. There had seemed to be a trace of tension underlying the exchanger's supercilious attitude and Partager's stilted responses. Was it due to the shock of learning the brutal manner of Brand's death or had it been spawned by another, more ominous reason, such as a guilty conscience?

Nine

❖

As Bascot and Gianni were on their way back
to Lincoln, snow began to fall, not as fiercely as it had
done on the fourth day before Christ's Mass, but with a
steadiness that told of more to come. By the time they
reached the castle ward, the ground was covered in a
layer of white more than an inch thick.

After stabling their mount, they crossed the ward
and went into the keep in search of Gerard Camville.
On being told by Eudo that the sheriff had gone to the
kennels, the Templar told Gianni to wait inside and
went back out into the falling snow.

The building where the hounds were kept was a low-
ceilinged wooden structure attached to a fenced compound on the north side of the bail. As the Templar
ducked his head and went in under the shallow lintel of
the doorway, the rank odour of dog filled his nostrils,
even though fresh straw lay over the entire floor. One
side of the building, partitioned off by a screen of wood,
was filled with dogs of every description—mastiffs,

lymer and gaze hounds, harriers and the mongrels called velters. Except for a few favoured dogs that were allowed to roam freely in the hall, all the castle canines were kept within the walls of the kennel and compound except when being exercised or accompanying a hunting party. At the moment, they were being fed a meal of raw offal by two kennel servants and were relatively quiet.

On the other side of the partition were a few stalls used for whelping or to house a dog that was ailing. It was in one of these that Bascot found Camville, down on his knees beside a sick lymer hound, a bitch, that was lying on her side and panting. Her dark eyes were dull and filled with pain. With the sheriff was the kennel master, a sturdily built man with straggly dark hair and a pugnacious jaw, and he was explaining to the sheriff what had happened to the dog as Bascot approached.

"The wound in her paw turned corrupt a few days ago, lord," the kennel master said. "She sliced it open during a scuffle with a male. He kept trying to mount her when she wasn't ready and they fought. When it first swelled, I cut it open to release the poison and then washed the wound with water and wine, but to no avail. I fear she will not recover."

Camville nodded his agreement. "She is a courageous hound and has borne me many fine pups. I will be sorry to lose her."

As though the dog understood his words, she raised her head slightly and tried to lick the sheriff's hand. Camville ran a hand gently over her muzzle and stood up. "Do what is necessary," he said to the kennel master. "But make sure she does not suffer. And despatch the male that attacked her as well. He does not deserve to live when he was the cause of her death."

As the sheriff rose to his feet, he saw Bascot. Camville's compassion for the sick dog did not surprise the Templar. The sheriff was a hard taskmaster, but to those who proved steadfast in his service—human or animal—he gave a full measure of loyalty in return.

Camville joined Bascot and they left the kennels. As they walked back across the ward to the keep, the Templar related the results of his interviews with de Stow and his employees, and the reactions of Legerton and the assayer. The sheriff grunted in dissatisfaction.

"Mealy-mouthed whoresons, all of them," he exclaimed. "If any of them is involved in the clerk's murder, we'll have a hard time proving it. And if a trove is at the root of this killing, whoever it was that conspired with the clerk will have it well hidden by now."

"It may be Brand confided something pertinent to his mother or the girl he wished to marry during his visits to Grantham," Bascot suggested. "It might be worthwhile to speak to them."

Camville looked up at the louring sky, which was already as dark as evening even though it was only the middle of the afternoon. Snow was still falling, lightly, but relentlessly. "This snow does not look as though it will abate and, if it does not, all roads will be impassable by morning. It is more than twenty miles to Grantham. We will have to wait for the weather to clear before the journey can be made, much as it galls me to do so."

THE SHERIFF'S FORECAST OF MORE SNOW PROVED TRUE. Over the next two days, it drifted down in a sporadic fashion and was soon deep enough to reach a tall

man's knees. By the third day, when it finally ceased
to fall and the air was crisp and cold, it underwent another mercurial change as the temperature suddenly rose
and a downpour of rain began. Although not such a del-
uge as previously, it was still heavy enough to turn the
snow once again into a morass of dirty slush. During
this time, a roaring fire was kept going in the hall, and
the troupe of minstrels, acrobats and mummers that
Nicolaa de la Haye had hired continued to weave their
way amongst the throng in the hall, playing music on
their instruments, performing tumbling feats and acting
out plays with a religious theme in an effort to keep everyone amused. In the evenings, the trestle tables were
pushed against the walls and ring dances—commonly
called carols—were held. Each of these rings was comprised of equal ranks, with those from the high table
who wished to dance forming a circle just below the
dais, upper servants in the next and, at the back of
the hall, maidservants and varlets. While the musicians
played and sang songs of good cheer, the dancers joined
hands and twirled in a circle, joining in the words of the
song as they did so.

All the younger people were enthusiastic about par-
ticipating in the dancing, with Richard leading Eustachia out for every set, their carol completed by Lucia
and one of the household knights or squires. Although
it was a time of jollity, the enforced confinement
caused by the dismal weather slowly began to take its
toll and everyone grew restless.

The tension was broken when Camville's hunt master
came into the hall just as the midday meal was ending and
told his lord a boar had been sighted in the sheriff's chase.
"It is a large male and in its prime," the huntsman said.

"The snow that fell in the chase was not as deep as within the town and, with the rain, has melted to only a thin covering among the trees. Providing the weather holds clear tomorrow, the ground will not be too treacherous for horses. If you wish to hold a hunt, lord, the boar will prove a worthy adversary."

Gilbert Bassett, sitting next to Camville, heard the huntsman's words and a slow smile spread over his face. "I have a fancy for some wild pig, Gerard," he said. "And the pleasure of snaring one will surely increase my appetite."

Camville shared his friend's anticipation and gave orders that a hunt be arranged for the next morning. As the news spread around the hall, the spirits of the men rose perceptibly.

Nicolaa de la Haye's female guests also felt a modicum of relief. The temper of their menfolk had grown increasingly testy from the enforced inactivity, and the men's absence from the keep meant the women would be able to retire to the solar and spend the day in leisurely conversation. It was traditional for gifts to be exchanged on the first day of the New Year, and the women were eager to compare the presents they intended to bestow and to speculate about what they hoped to receive.

Only Stephen, Ralph of Turville's young son, was disconsolate. Even though a couple of older pages about the same age as the lad were to accompany the hunting party, Stephen's mother, Maud, begged her husband to deny their son permission, insisting the boy should stay in the shelter of the keep lest the coldness of the weather bring on one of the ear aches that plagued him at this time of year.

When Ralph reluctantly concurred with his wife and told the boy he must remain behind, Lucia resurrected her notion of teaching Stephen some of the gestures Gianni used to communicate, begging Maud to reconsider her earlier refusal to allow the lesson. Conscious of the pleading look in her son's eyes, Maud relented and gave her permission. Lucia did not give her cousin any time to change her mind. She immediately got up from her seat at the end of the table on the dais and made her way to where Nicolaa de la Haye sat.

CHE NEXT MORNING, THE EVE OF THE FIRST DAY OF THE New Year, Bascot stood in the bail and watched Gianni race across the ward to the keep. The Templar had readily acceded to Lucia's request, which had been put to him by Lady Nicolaa on the girl's behalf. Bascot suspected Gianni's eagerness to participate in tutelage of the young Turville heir was not completely due to the honour of having the castellan make a personal request for his services, but primarily because he had been told that Lucia Bassett intended to be present during the lesson. The boy had been giving the young noblewoman admiring glances ever since she arrived and, although Lucia was a few years older than Gianni, Bascot guessed the lad had arrived at the age when young males start to become painfully aware of the attractions of female pulchritude. Neither age nor rank had ever been a barrier to the onset of love's awakening desires, and the crimson blush that spread over Gianni's face when Bascot told him about the arrangements was a good indication the boy was smitten with the fair Lucia.

Nicolaa suggested the young people, after the midday meal, hold the instruction in the chamber she used to administer the details of her vast demesne. It was private and supplied with a good quantity of parchment and writing implements. She also asked Lambert to attend the lesson so he could act as a translator for Gianni's gestures and directed the clerk to write down a brief description of the movements so that Stephen, who was literate, could use the notes for reference.

As Gianni's eager steps took him into the keep, the hunt master came out into the bail and gave a loud blast on his horn. In response, saddled horses were led from the stables and the kennel master strode from the compound where the dogs were kept, a pack of mastiffs and boarhounds at his heels. Outside the kitchen, panniers containing flagons of wine were hastily strapped to the back of a sturdy palfrey to provide refreshment for members of the hunting party.

As the barking of the dogs sounded loud on the cold air, Gerard Camville and Gilbert Bassett left the keep and came down into the bail. Behind them were Richard, Ralph of Turville and the household knights. All were wrapped in heavy cloaks and wore close-fitting caps lined with fur.

The sheriff mounted his horse and looked about him. Satisfied all was in order, he raised his hand. The gateward on the western gate blew a signal on his horn and the heavy doors were pulled open by two men-at-

arms. As the party rode through the opening and out
into the countryside, a wide swathe of churned-up mud
and slush marked their passage.

Once the sounds of jingling harnesses and yelp-
ing dogs had faded into the distance, Bascot felt a
fleeting stab of regret that he was not accompanying
the hunters. The sport was forbidden to brothers of
the Templar Order because it was believed that such
secular pleasure would detract from the monks' devotion to their religious duties. Although Bascot
agreed with the sentiment of the rule, he still felt a
craving to indulge in the excitement of the chase.
Resolutely he pushed his longing aside. He had been
too long away from the company of his brothers, he
decided, and since it was unlikely that either Lady
Nicolaa or her husband would require his presence
until later in the day, he would go and spend the
morning at the Templar enclave and immerse himself in the familiarity of the Order's regime.

THE LINCOLN ENCLAVE OF THE TEMPLAR ORDER WAS
modest in size and located on the eastern shoulder of
the hill upon which the castle and Minster stood and
just below the area where the stone quarry lay. Although not a large commandery, Lincoln was on the
main route from southeast England to the north
coast and the preceptory often fulfilled the function
of a staging post for messengers, and a harbour for
travelling brothers in need of a night's rest. Sparsely
manned at this time of year when movement about
the countryside was limited, it still had a comple-

ment of a dozen men-at-arms, a serjeant, a priest and a draper, all under the command of the preceptor, Everard d'Arderon. There was also a small number of lay servants—a cook, a blacksmith and several grooms.

When Bascot arrived, a huge wagon was in the encampment, drawn up outside the storehouse where the goods received in fee from local Templar properties were kept. It also housed a supply of commodities that had been produced in the Holy Land and were sent to enclaves throughout the kingdom for the purposes of trade, such as rare spices and *candi*.

Bales containing some of the more staple items were being loaded on the cart as Bascot entered the preceptory. Preceptor d'Arderon was standing alongside the wagon, a piece of parchment in his hands, directing a pair of men-at-arms in placement of the goods. D'Arderon, an older knight with a bluff countenance and neatly clipped greying beard, greeted his visitor warmly and, when Bascot asked the destination of the supplies, explained they were part of a shipment being sent to Tomar in Portugal, a Templar castle that was a bastion against the ever-increasing threat of encroachment by the Moors.

"This wagonload of goods will join two others that are due to stop here on their way from the preceptory in York," d'Arderon explained. "Once they have all reached London, the goods will be loaded aboard ship and taken to Portugal. Most will go to the enclave in Tomar, but some of it is needed by brothers in nearby Almourol. Those infidel bastards in the south of Portugal give our men no time to forage for themselves."

The Templar castles at both Tomar and Almourol—twelve miles south of Tomar—had been built about thirty years before at the behest of a Portuguese Templar Master, Gualdim Pais, who had died in 1195. It was an area of much unrest as the Moors battled to retake territories that had been reclaimed from them with great difficulty and loss of life by the Christian populace of northern Portugal. If the heathens were not kept back in both Portugal and Spain, there was a danger they would overwhelm the whole of the Iberian Peninsula.

As d'Arderon had been speaking, Bascot noticed the preceptor looked very tired. Usually hale and hearty despite his sixty-odd years, there were now lines of strain etched on his face, and Bascot recalled the preceptor had recently suffered a bout of tertian fever, a recurring ailment that had been the cause of his being relieved of duty in Outremer two years before, and sent to take up the post of preceptor for the Lincoln enclave. It had been hoped that the softer climes of England would provide some relief from his ailment. And so they had, but the bouts still came upon him at times and although of far less intensity than formerly, they were nonetheless debilitating.

"I do not have any duties at the castle for the next couple of hours, Preceptor, and would be more than pleased to carry out any task you care to assign me."

D'Arderon clapped him on the shoulder. "I look forward to the day when you will be back in our ranks for good, de Marins. Until then, you are welcome for however long a time you can spend."

The preceptor looked to where two grooms were

exercising the enclave's horses, walking them around the perimeter of the training ground that lay in the centre of the commandery. Usually the mounts were taken out onto the hillside below the preceptory and given a daily run, but the fall of snow over the last few days had precluded this. On the far side of the compound was a forge where a blacksmith was fitting new horseshoes on d'Arderon's big black stallion. The animal was frisky and trying to bite the groom attempting to hold it steady. The blacksmith was having great difficulty completing his task.

"If you would finish overseeing the loading of this wagon, de Marins," the preceptor said, handing Bascot the paper he had been holding, "I will go and subdue my mount. Although he is unmatched as a destrier, he is also fractious, and needs a firm hand."

Bascot took the parchment and for the rest of the morning supervised the loading of sacks of grain, barrels of salted herring, some lengths of timber suitable for palings and a number of casks containing crossbow quarrels.

After the cart was loaded and securely covered with a protective sheet of leather hides, Bascot reluctantly bid d'Arderon farewell and left the preceptory.

As he rode back to Lincoln castle, he felt a sense of well-being, instilled by the hours he had spent in the company of men who, like himself, had dedicated their lives to the service of Christ. The desire to accompany the hunting party that had so suddenly engulfed him that morning was completely expunged. As he entered the Minster grounds and rode across it in the direction of the castle, he looked toward the Priory of All Saints where the body of Peter Brand was being kept. The memory of the clerk's broken body and the fatal wound in his chest surged into the Templar's mind. Although forbidden to hunt game, it seemed as though God had ordained he be a stalker of murderers.

Ten
✠

As Bascot was returning from the preceptory, the hunting party was also on their way back to the castle. All were in high good humour. As they rode, they recalled the high points of the chase, especially the moment when the boar was killed.

It had been shortly after they entered the sheriff's chase—the edge of which was a marshy patch of ground threaded with small streams—that the dogs had flushed the boar from its lair beneath a snow-covered mound of dead bracken. At first the pig attacked and wounded one of the dogs with its sharp yellow tusks, but then, realising there were too many adversaries to be overcome, it sped off into a wooded area. The chase was an arduous one. With the dogs snapping and snarling at it heels, the boar darted farther into the trees, zigzagging back and forth, occasionally executing one of the sudden turns its short legs could perform so well and lunging at its pursuers.

The quarry was finally brought to bay in the bed of an old dried-up stream. At the far end of the shallow depression were the decaying remains of a long-deserted beaver's lodge, now covered in a thin layer of melting snow. The boar, finding its passage blocked by the pile of debris, turned and faced its enemies. It was a mature animal, and large, standing more than a metre high at the shoulder and weighing at least two hundred pounds. The dogs, still growling and barking but wary of the gleaming tusks, managed to hold it there until the hunt party caught up.

Leaving their horses a safe distance from where the pig was trapped, the men dismounted and the hunt master sent two of his assistants up onto the banks of the streambed, one on either side. Each of the huntsmen carried a large net that could be cast over the boar if the need arose. The men of the party, Camville and Bassett in the lead, armed themselves with short cross-hafted boar spears.

The area around the streambed was heavily wooded, all the trees denuded of leaves and the branches laden with dribbles of slushy snow. The feral stench of the boar permeated the air and the menacing snarls of the boarhounds and mastiffs echoed loudly in the narrow space.

Motioning to the others to spread out behind, the two barons walked slowly forward. As they did so, one of the mastiffs, excited beyond caution, made a sudden dash at the boar. The pig was ready for him and caught the mastiff in mid-leap, ripping a gash in the dog's underbelly and then, with an insolent fling of its head, tossed its attacker over its back. The dog fell heavily and did not move, its intestines trailing streaks of blood in the sparse covering of snow. It gave one feeble whimper and died.

The boar tried to back away from the approaching men, its tiny hooves scrabbling in the slush-covered stone of the streambed until its hindquarters touched the tumble of decaying wood that had once been the beaver's lodge. There it stopped, head swinging from side to side and little red eyes glaring.

The sheriff and his friend moved forward. They had no need to speak or even look at each other as they moved into position; Camville directly in front of the boar, Bassett a few feet to the sheriff's right. They had fought alongside each other since the days of their youth, following King Henry II in his campaigns to defend his lands across the Narrow Sea and afterwards, when the king's sons defied him in attempts to wrest the crown from their father's head. In a battle, or on a hunt, the two barons moved in familiar concert, accustomed to facing danger as comrades-in-arms.

Suddenly another of the mastiffs, ignoring the hunt master's order to stay back, leapt at the boar. The pig reacted with lightning speed, propelling itself forward towards the dog, clumps of dirt, pebbles and slush whirling from beneath its hooves as it came to meet its adversary. Barely in time, the dog lurched to one side and the sharp tusks missed by inches. But even though the mastiff was no longer in its path, the boar did not lessen its speed, and the momentum of its charge carried it straight towards Bassett. Kneeling down and holding his spear at the ready, the baron braced himself for the impact, but just as the clash between man and animal was imminent, the boar veered to one side, seeking an escape route through the narrow space between Bassett and the sheriff.

Camville raised his spear, holding it with both hands as the animal attempted to run past him. With one swift movement, he plunged it deep into the pig's neck. The struggle between them was violent, the boar thrashing against the steel impaled in its flesh and the sheriff determined not to release his hold. The hunt master's assistants ran forward with their nets, but there was no need of their help. Using his great strength, Camville threw his legs astride the boar and, leaning his full weight against the spear, thrust it in farther and farther until the animal, with one final spasm and a horrendous squeal, stilled into death.

Now, riding home, the story of the kill was recounted again and again. The dead pig, gutted and tied to a stout branch carried by the hunt master's assistants, was a trophy worthy of celebration, and the men passed a flagon of wine back and forth as they rode. One of the squires began to sing a hunting song and the others joined in, their voices ringing out in a paean of victory over the stillness of the winter countryside.

It was not until they were nearing the castle that anything occurred to disturb their good humour. The path leading to the western gate ran parallel to the city walls and traversed the incline at the top of the hill on which the castle and Minster stood. As the hunt party rode along the path, the hounds, which had been fed on the boar's entrails and were trotting along docilely, suddenly became attracted to a drift of snow at the wayside. One of the mastiffs snuffled at the pile and, despite the hunt master's shouted order to rejoin the pack, the dog began to dig. Almost at once, two of the other hounds joined the first and added their labour to his, their powerful chest muscles driving their paws deep into the snow, unheeding of the repeated order to stop. Cursing, the hunt master got down from his horse and pulled out the short whip he carried at his belt. Wading into the group of recalcitrant hounds, he yelled at them to fall back, swinging the whip above their heads as he did so. The dogs retreated, but only for a moment, then circled back to the same spot.

Frustrated, the hunt master now swung his whip in earnest but as the dogs, this time, obeyed his order, he stopped short and stared down at the hole they had made. Relaxing his grip on the whip, he lifted his head and walked back to the path.

"What is it, man?" Gerard Camville asked roughly. "What ails the dogs?"

"They have found a body, lord, buried under the snow," was the reply.

The sheriff shrugged. "It is most likely a beggar who died of exposure. I will have some men come and remove—"

The hunt master interrupted him with a shake of his head. "I do not believe it is a beggar, lord, and even if it is, he did not die from the foulness of the weather. There is a stab wound in his chest. He has been murdered."

WHEN BASCOT GUIDED HIS HORSE THROUGH THE eastern gate into the bail, the hunting party had already returned. He was just in time to see Gerard Camville issue a terse order to Ernulf, the serjeant of the castle garrison, before disappearing up the wooden staircase that led to the door of the keep. As he did so, the Templar noticed that a party of four men-at-arms, moving at a quick pace, were leaving the ward by the western gate.

As Ernulf turned away from the staircase and started to walk across the ward in the direction of the barracks, he noticed Bascot and called to him, an expression of relief on his face.

"De Marins, I was just about to send one of my men to find you. Sir Gerard requests you attend him immediately."

"What's amiss, Ernulf?" the Templar asked. "I saw your men leaving. Is there some trouble in the sheriff's chase?"

The grizzled serjeant shook his head. "Not in the forest, no, but right here in Lincoln. As the hunt party was returning, the dogs found a body buried under the snow just outside the city wall. My men have gone to fetch the corpse into the ward."

Ernulf gave Bascot a sorrowful look as he continued. "Not only is the man dead, but he's been murdered. Stabbed through the heart, just like the clerk. I reckon the reason the sheriff wants to speak to you is that he figures there's a connection between this corpse and the one found in the quarry."

Bascot felt a chill settle over him that was not caused by the coldness of the winter air. "Who is the dead man, then? Is it someone who knew Brand?"

Ernulf rubbed the greying stubble on his unshaven chin. "Don't rightly know about that, but they both worked with silver in one form or another. The dead man's name is Roger Fardein and he was apprentice to a silversmith in the town."

When Bascot went into the keep and up to the sheriff's chamber, Camville confirmed the name and occupation of the man buried under the snow.

"Fardein was apprentice to a man named Warner Tasser," the sheriff explained as he walked up and down the chamber, a cup of wine in his hand and his voice filled with fury. The good humour instilled in him by the success of the hunt was gone. The faces of Gilbert Bassett and Richard Camville, also in the chamber, mirrored the sheriff's anger.

"Tasser is a man of ill repute," Gerard went on. "He has been fined by his guild twice for debasing the silver content in pieces his workshop produces. And, a few years ago, he was implicated in having disposed of items that had been stolen—accused of melting them down in his forge and fashioning them into new ones. Nothing could be proven against him at that time, but I am certain he was guilty of the charge."

Camville stopped in his pacing and banged his wine cup down on the table. "And now his apprentice is dead, killed in just the same way as the clerk. Both dead men were employed in a place where silver is kept. There is a link between the two murders; I am sure. And I would wager Tasser is involved."

"You cannot be sure of that, Father," Richard protested. "It may only be happenstance."

Camville snorted. "Two men murdered in the same way, by a blow to the head and stabbed, and both left in a place where they would not be found quickly— what is there not to be sure about?"

"I did not mean they were not killed by the same person, only that it may not have been Tasser," Richard replied. "He has not, as far as I am aware, any connection with the mint. His workshop produces only items for personal or household use, jewellery, cups, and that sort of thing."

"I think what your father means, Richard," Bassett interjected, "is that if any coins from a hidden cache have been discovered, this silversmith—Tasser—has the means to melt them down in his workshop. Once that is done, who is to prove the silver was once part of a hidden cache? It would be an impossible task."

"Exactly," Gerard Camville confirmed. "And Tasser is just the sort of miscreant who would do so. He has never been averse to lining his own coffers with wealth stolen from others."

"Ernulf told me you found the corpse of Fardein near to the castle gate, lord," Bascot said. "Was it near enough to the gate tower that one of the guards might have seen him or the person that killed him?"

"The apprentice must have been murdered before this last fall of snow, for he was buried deep under it," Camville said. "That means he has been there for at least three, possibly four, days. The guards assure me that because of the weather, there was little traffic through the western gate during that time and only those who were expected came in or out; carters bringing loads of wood and a couple of charcoal burners with fuel for the castle braziers. The guards saw no one else nearby during the day, or at night either, and definitely not anyone carrying a torch or lantern. There are two small postern gates in the western wall of the city that are near the entrance to the castle; Fardein must have either walked to his death or been killed in the town and his body dragged to the spot."

Camville stopped in his pacing and cursed. "I am

certain Tasser had something to do with these deaths. He is too clever to have wielded the dagger that killed them, but I am sure he is behind the murders."

"Do you wish me to interrogate him, lord?" Bascot asked.

"I do," Camville grunted. "And you do not have to worry about the niceties of your questions, although I still want my suspicion of a trove kept privy. Take Roget with you. Search the silversmith's workshop and home; look for any item that may have doubtful provenance, especially coinage. You may be as rough as you like. Tasser has proved he rides a thin line between what is legal and what is not; you need not be concerned if you give him offence."

"If Tasser's apprentice was murdered a few days ago, and the silversmith was involved in the crime, any incriminating evidence will have been removed from his premises by now," Bascot said.

"I know, but I want you to put the fear of God, and my authority, into him. If you shake his bones enough, he may let something slip."

BEFORE HE WENT DOWN INTO THE TOWN TO QUESTION the silversmith, Bascot went to the castle chapel to examine the corpse of Roger Fardein. Camville had told him there was nothing on the body to indicate a possible reason for his murder; the dead man's scrip was still attached to his belt and had been empty except for two silver pennies, but the Templar wanted to inspect his wounds. In a previous case of murder, such an examination had provided an important guide to finding the perpetrator. He was hoping it might do so again.

After sending one of the castle men-at-arms into town with a request for Roget, the former mercenary soldier who was captain of the sheriff's town guard, to meet him near the silversmith's workshop on Mikelgate, Bascot went into the chapel. It was a small place of worship and, except for morning Mass, most of the castle household attended services at the church of St. Clement just outside the northwest corner of the bail, but there was an alcove in the chapel where a bier could be laid to serve as a resting place for any who died within the castle walls. It was here that Fardein had been laid to await removal to his coffin.

The silversmith's apprentice looked to be about twenty-four or twenty-five years old. He had a broad face with a nose that was slightly flattened and dark red hair. His high cheekbones gave his face an almost oriental cast and the skin was riddled with broken veins, giving him an appearance of dissipation. The flesh of his face and hands was a mottled white. His clothes were of poor quality—a dark brown tunic of fustian and hose of rough wool. His cloak was of cheap material and bore no clasp, only ties at the neck to secure it. It was wet and bedraggled. Bascot saw the rent in the front of Fardein's tunic and pulled the cloth apart to examine the wound. It was as he had expected from the sheriff's description, a deep and jagged hole between the ribs over the heart. The incision appeared to have been made by a blunter, and broader, instrument than the narrow wound inflicted on Brand. The flesh around the wound was covered with blood that had dried after he was stabbed but later become viscous from its covering of moisture-laden snow.

The Templar felt gently at the back of Fardein's head and found the place where a blow had fractured the skull. It was a shallow depression, and had it been the only injury inflicted, there was a good possibility the apprentice would have recovered. Nonetheless, the clout would have been strong enough to take him out of his senses for a time and make it easy for his attacker to stab him, just as could have happened to the clerk.

Fardein's possessions had been removed and laid beside him on the bier. Bascot first examined the scrip. It was of rough leather and still fastened to the dead man's belt. As the sheriff said, it contained only two silver pennies. Alongside it lay a dagger and a small cudgel, the latter made of solid hickory and of the type many men carried for protection. The Templar fingered it thoughtfully. Neither weapon bore any trace of blood. Why had the apprentice not used one of them to defend himself? Perhaps because he had known his attacker, or been assaulted from behind? These questions and more all needed to be answered, but it appeared that nothing likely to prove useful could be learned from the condition of Fardein's body or his few possessions.

Asking heaven's forgiveness for his intrusion, Bascot rearranged Fardein's clothing and left the chapel.

Roget was waiting outside the silversmith's workshop when Bascot guided his horse down Mikelgate to Tasser's manufactory. There were a few people about, but not many, even though the streets had been shovelled clear of snow. Piles of dirty slush lay heaped in intermittent piles alongside the thoroughfare. Thankfully, the temperature had stayed above freezing point and although the cobbles underneath his horse's feet were wet, they were not slick with ice. Bascot dismounted in front of the silversmith's door and, tying the reins of his horse to one of the posts placed at intervals along the street, greeted Roget.

The captain of Camville's guard had a countenance that would strike fear into the heart of any miscreant having the misfortune to encounter him. Blackvisaged, and with the scar of an old sword slash running from temple to chin, he had a powerful, rangy build and an aggressive stance. He gave Bascot a smile as the Templar came up, revealing strong white teeth that were gapped in places. The two men knew each other well and had become friends over the time Bascot had been in Lincoln.

"*Hola*, de Marins," Roget said. "I got your message." He looked up at the sign hanging above Tasser's door, a wooden board painted with a picture of a silver cup on a blue background. "I hope you want my help to interrogate this *chien*. It would give me great pleasure to beat some truths out of him."

Bascot laughed. "The sheriff told me that he is not the most honest of men. I understand his criminal activities have given you some trouble in the past."

"More than I care to remember," Roget replied. "Tasser is a thief of the worst kind. He lets others take the risk of stealing but ensures, by his slyness, that he garners the profit for himself. He is slippery, like an eel, and just as difficult to catch."

Bascot told him about the discovery of Fardein's body outside the castle gate. "What kind of man was the apprentice? I have examined his body but that does not give me his measure."

"He was an apprentice in more than silversmithing to Tasser," Roget said grimly. "As a child apes a parent, so did Fardein copy his master. He was often in one tavern or another, all of the lowest type, and huddled together with men who have had their noses clipped for thievery. I am sure he helped Tasser buy stolen goods but I have never been able to prove it."

Bascot considered this information and then said, "The sheriff thinks the body of the apprentice may have been taken outside the town through one of the postern gates. Either that, or Fardein walked through it willingly with his attacker before he was killed. How carefully are the gates watched by your guards?"

Roget thought for a moment. "There is no gateward on any of them, but my men ensure they are shut and barred at curfew." He shrugged, a Gallic movement of his shoulders. "But the gates are closed to keep intruders outside the city walls, not to prevent honest citizens from leaving. They are only sealed by means of an iron bar across the inside. It would be an easy matter to remove the bar and leave the gate open for a couple of hours without my guards noticing, then reenter the town and close it again. I will ask my men if they noticed anything untoward during their nightly rounds over the last few days, but I am sure they would have reported it if they had."

"Do that, Roget, but in the meantime let us see what Tasser has to say about the death of his apprentice. I

want to know why he didn't raise an alarm when
Fardein failed to report for work over the last few days.
Sheriff Camville has given his permission for us to be
as forceful as we like with our interrogation."

Roget's mouth split into a grin. "I am glad to hear it,
mon ami. It will make this task one greatly to my liking."

Eleven

✣

Within an hour of the finding of Roger Fardein's body, report of his murder had spread through Lincoln. The first to relate it was a chandler who had been in the castle ward when the guards brought the body into the bail. When the chandler left the bail, he related it to an acquaintance he met in Ermine Street. A few minutes later the chandler's acquaintance told the story to one of the flesh mongers in the market and the monger, in turn, repeated the news to every customer who stopped at his stall. After that, rumour of the death, like the heavy rain that had fallen on Lincoln before Christ's Mass, flooded through every street in the town.

Two hours later, in a large room on the upper floor of Helias de Stow's house, two women sat in company with each other. One of them, and the older of the pair, was de Stow's wife, Blanche; the other was the spouse of the assayer, Simon Partager, a vivacious young woman named Iseult. They sat in front of a roaring fire,

drinking watered wine heated with a hot poker.
Blanche was stitching on a tapestry while her companion sat idle, toying with an expensive bangle encircling
her wrist.

The two women were not much alike in appearance
or nature. The moneyer's wife was a plump woman
with plain features, but she had about her an air of
competence while Iseult, although very handsome with
long braids of corn-coloured hair and flashing eyes of
deep blue, had a petulant manner. As she sat sipping
her wine, there was a decided droop in her full red lips.

"You have heard there has been another murder in
the town?" Iseult said in an effort to make conversation
with the woman across from her. Although their husbands worked together, they had little of common interest to share, but Iseult was bored and had come to
the moneyer's house in the hope that Blanche would be
willing to engage in the gossip buzzing about the town.

"Yes," Blanche replied. "An apprentice to a silversmith named Warner Tasser, I believe."

Iseult nodded, becoming slightly more animated. "It
is said that Tasser is responsible—that his apprentice
became privy to the silversmith's nefarious dealings
and Tasser killed him to ensure his silence."

Blanche pursed her mouth in disapproval. Iseult had
come to Lincoln with her husband two days before and
was staying in the exchange while he assayed a quantity of coinage. The rooms above the exchanger's office
could be lonely while Simon was at work and Iseult
had come to Blanche for company to while away the
tedium. From prattle told to Blanche's maid by the girl
that served Iseult—which had in turn been repeated to
Blanche by her maidservant—the moneyer's wife

knew that Partager had only insisted on his wife accompanying him to Lincoln because he feared she would be keeping his place in their bed at Canwick warm with his employer, Walter Legerton.

Blanche flashed a glance from beneath her brows at the woman who sat across from her. Iseult was beautiful, it was true, but her prettiness was too bold for a married woman. Blanche was not sure if Legerton was the first man on whom Iseult had bestowed her adulterous favours in her short married life, but she was certain he would not be the last.

"Many things are carelessly said after someone is murdered," Blanche said reprovingly, "but that does not mean they are true. You would do well to remember, Iseult, that my husband's clerk was also murdered. Would you be so anxious to repeat gossip that accused Simon, or my Helias, of killing him?"

Iseult reared back in her chair, shocked. She did not particularly like Blanche and knew the feeling was mutual, but never before had the moneyer's wife spoken to her in such acerbic tones.

"There is no one who would dare accuse my husband of murder," Iseult said defensively. "He is a respected man."

"So is mine," Blanche said placidly. "But that does not mean they do not have enemies who would be only too pleased to spread gossip harmful to their reputations." She gave Iseult a piercing look. "You should be more careful of repeating rumours, mistress. The Bible admonishes us not to judge lest we be judged. Are you so free of sin you have no fear of finding yourself a target for malice one day?"

Iseult stood up, her nostrils flaring. "Any who

would say evil words about me are just jealous, that is all." She tossed her head and the heavy yellow braids under her coif slithered forward enticingly over her ample bosom. Her eyes narrowed as she reached for her cloak, which she had thrown over the back of a settle when she came in. "Women, especially *older* ones, always bear enmity towards those who are young and beautiful. Their comments do not interest me, nor do I take heed of them."

With this vituperative pronouncement, she flung the cloak about her shoulders and left the room. Blanche heard the outer door slam as Iseult left the house. The moneyer's wife smiled to herself and went back to stitching her tapestry. Now she would not have to endure the burden of listening to Iseult's inane chatter for the rest of the afternoon.

AT CANWICK, WALTER LEGERTON WAS SITTING IN the little chamber where he and Partager had spoken to Bascot. With him was his sister, Silvana. Together they were reviewing the household accounts.

"You have been too generous with the gifts you purchased for New Year's Day, Brother," Silvana said in gentle admonition. "There was no need to buy that costly jewelled comb for Partager's wife. The gold bracelet you gave her just a few weeks ago was surely enough to sate her hunger for expensive finery."

Legerton's florid face flushed an even deeper red. "Simon is a good assayer. Whatever I give his wife is merely my way of showing appreciation for his industry."

Silvana gave him a sceptical glance. "Or that you value his wife's company in your bed?"

"That will soon be over," her brother replied defensively. "It was amusing for a time, but my interest in her is waning."

"Then perhaps it is not wise to give her such an expensive trinket," Silvana said thoughtfully. "Otherwise she will believe she retains your favour."

Legerton sighed. "You are right, Silvana," he agreed. "I will give her something more in keeping with her position."

As her brother returned his eyes to the list of figures in front of him, Silvana felt a surge of affection smother her impatience with his lechery. She knew Walter was a weak man but she loved him dearly all the same. They had been together for many years now, ever since their father, a widower and a prominent silversmith in Lincoln, had died. Their sire, an upright and extremely moral man, had curbed Walter's excesses while he was alive but, soon after their father's death, her brother had sold the business he inherited and used the funds to buy the manor house at Canwick. Silvana had gone with him for, since the death of Walter's wife in childbirth some years before, she had taken over the running of her brother's household as well as the care of his two sons. It suited them both; Silvana had never had any desire to wed and enjoyed the position of a married woman without the onerous task of bedding a husband, while Walter was ensured that the person in charge of his domestic affairs was one he could trust. Their fortune in life was bound up in each other, tied securely by the bond of shared blood.

But lately Silvana had come to fear her brother was putting the financial security of their small family in jeopardy. She had advised him against selling their father's business, but he had not listened to her, his eyes too eagerly set on living a life of ease away from the hard work of toiling in the silver manufactory. Once he had been awarded the post of exchanger—which he secured only by paying a hefty fee to the royal official who held the gift of the office in his hands—Walter had believed the commission he derived from the post would provide more than enough for him and his family to live on. But it had not taken long for him to realise that his hedonistic inclinations were proving far too expensive for his means. Entertaining and feeding the number of guests at Canwick during the feast of this year's Christ's Mass was too costly by far and Walter knew it, but he had invited all of them just the same, fearing he would be seen as parsimonious if he did not. Only Silvana knew of the desperate measures he was in and that he had borrowed money from one of the Jewish usurers in Lincoln to replenish his empty coffers.

"Walter, you must curb your spending," Silvana said gently. "Once Epiphany is over, and our guests have gone home, we must try to live simply. There is no need to have expensive viands at every meal and strew the manor house with costly trappings. If you do not bring yourself to practice more thrift, we will soon be reduced to penury." The softness in her voice removed any sting from the rebuke.

Walter looked up at his sister, at the features so like his own. Silvana had the same thick dark hair, which she wore braided and neatly coiled under a close-fitting coif, and the identical rosiness of cheek. Although she was five years younger than he, Silvana had always seemed as though she were the elder, for she watched over his well-being as though she were their long-dead mother. From any other, the words she had just spoken would have invoked his wrath, but he knew her castigation was well meant and given only out of concern for him and her nephews.

"You are right, Silvana," he said with a groan of despair, his habitual haughtiness absent in the presence of his sister. "I promise that after Epiphany it will be as you say. I fear I do not have any choice in the matter."

At Tasser's manufactory on Mikelgate, Bascot and Roget were searching the silversmith's premises. They had gained entry easily enough, for Tasser made no objection when told they had come on the sheriff's behalf to enquire into the murder of Roger Fardein.

Tasser was a short fat man with an oily, obsequious manner and thick lips above a receding chin, a combination that gave him more than a passing resemblance to a toad. His hands were adorned with costly rings and around his neck was a heavy chain of meshed gold links. When asked why he had not reported the absence of his apprentice from his place of work, Tasser shrugged and replied that because it was the season of Christ's Mass he thought Fardein was indulging in a prolonged celebration of the holy days.

"Roger was a man who liked his wine cup," Tasser said in an offhand manner. "It was not the first time he failed to turn up for work. Had he not been such a competent apprentice, I would have dismissed him.

But"—and here he directed an unctuous smile at Roget, who had the reputation of being a womanizer—
"we all know what it is to be young and have an itch in
our loins. I thought he would turn up when his passion
was sated."

Bascot told him they wanted to question the other
men who worked in the silver manufactory, and Tasser
summoned his remaining employees. There were only
two: an accredited silversmith past his middle years,
and a younger man who fulfilled the function of general factotum.

Both of them, when questioned, denied keeping
company with their dead colleague in off-duty hours or
knowledge of his whereabouts around the time he was
murdered.

When asked where Fardein had lodged, Tasser took
them to a chamber at the back of the building and said
he had allowed his apprentice to sleep there. The silversmith made no demur when they informed him they
intended to search both it and the rest of the premises
for evidence.

Tasser, a knowing smirk on his wide lips that infuri-
ated both men, left them to their task and they searched
through Fardein's few belongings. The room did not
contain much in the way of furniture, and they found
nothing under the thin mattress that comprised a bed, or
in the leather satchel that hung from a peg on the wall.
Aside from an extra pair of hose which were grubby and
stained, and a couple of small tools used in his trade, the
apprentice seemed to have owned nothing apart from a
badly dented pewter mug that sat alongside an empty
wine flagon on a table beside his bed.

The pair then went upstairs, to the three large pri-

vate rooms that, along with the hall downstairs, consti-
tuted the silversmith's living quarters. One of the chambers appeared to be an office, for there were a number of
documents neatly stacked in an open-faced cupboard and
a desk laid with parchment and writing implements.
Around the desk were a number of comfortable chairs
with laddered backs. Next to the office were two sleeping
chambers, one containing a large bed fitted with a thick
mattress and overlaid with quilts of goose down and the
other appearing to be a guest chamber, with a smaller bed
and less extravagant bed linen. All the rooms were richly
appointed, with draught-excluding tapestries on the walls,
rugs of sheepskin on the floors, and beeswax candles in
finely wrought silver holders, but a thorough scrutiny
revealed nothing incriminating.

Bascot and Roget went back downstairs and
searched the hall. Although it contained a heavy oak
table and chairs of fine craftsmanship, neither it nor
any of the other furniture—a padded settle, two massive chairs with arms and an open-faced cupboard laid
with pewter platters and silver drinking cups—
contained any crevices that could be used as a hiding
place. Out back, in the yard, was a building housing a
small kitchen where an elderly woman was boiling a
hock of bacon in a cauldron hanging from a tripod over
the fireplace. She did not seem surprised when they
interrupted her chore; both men guessed she was in-
ured to the disturbance of authorities investigating her
master's activities.

When asked if she had any knowledge of Fardein's
personal life, she turned up her nose in disapproval. "I
never talked to that one any more than I had need," she
replied. "I'm sorry he's dead, but he thought himself

far above the likes of me 'cause of the confidence the master placed in him."

She had looked at both of them with wise old eyes. "I know the reputation Master Tasser has and I wouldn't work here if I didn't need the money, but I keeps myself to myself and only come in to cook the meals and give the place a clean once a week. I don't stay any longer than I have to, but goes back to my lodgings in Pottergate every night."

She stood by stoically while they searched the kitchen, but it contained only a supply of staples, some kegs of salted fish and rounds of cheese. Leaving her to resume her task of cooking the bacon, they went back to search the manufactory.

In the large chamber where the silversmith plied his craft, they paid special attention to the locked chests on the floor. In one was a number of newly made vessels Tasser claimed were items commissioned by various customers. After Roget gave all of these a careful examination, Bascot asked the silversmith to open the other chest. When the lid was lifted, it could be seen the coffer was half-filled with bags of coin that were, Tasser claimed, profits from his trade. Without telling Roget the reason for doing so, the Templar asked the captain to upend the leather satchels onto the floor. As the silver pennies spilled and rolled onto the ground, a quick glance was enough to ensure all were of recent minting and of the short cross design instituted during the reign of King Henry II. None of them bore the head of King Stephen.

During their search, Tasser stood complacently by and made no complaint at the disturbance of his trade or his premises. When they finally left, Roget was extremely angry.

"I hoped to find something that had been reported stolen," he growled in disgruntlement. "Then I could have arrested that *bâtard*."

"Fardein has been dead for a few days," Bascot replied. "If Tasser knew of it before times, he has had ample time to rid himself of any evidence connected to the murder or to a theft."

Roget nodded gloomily. "You are right, *mon ami*. But the day will come when I will find him out and, when I do, I will take great pleasure in seeing his right hand struck off for larceny."

Twelve

✛

IT WAS LATE IN THE AFTERNOON BY THE TIME BASCOT
met with Gerard Camville, Nicolaa de la Haye and
their son, Richard, in the sheriff's private chamber and
told them the search of the silversmith's premises had
not produced any gainful results.

Camville, as usual, was on his feet and striding back
and forth along the length of the chamber. "I am sure
there is a connection between the murdered men and
Tasser," he said angrily. "The death of Fardein con-
vinces me of that. And if a treasure trove is involved,
the silversmith is corrupt enough to kill for possession
of it."

"After speaking with the man, I am inclined to agree
with you, lord," Bascot said, "but I think Tasser is too
wily to wield the dagger himself."

"But if there is, as you say, a link between the two
deaths, Father, it is not likely that Tasser would even
have known the clerk, let alone had reason to kill him,"
Richard protested. "And there is still nothing to give

proof, other than the old coin found in the quarry, that a trove is involved in either slaying."

Camville glared at his son, but did not refute Richard's objections.

Nicolaa, who had been listening to the exchange in silence, asked Bascot for his impressions of the people who worked in the exchange and the mint. "Are there any among them that arouse your suspicion, de Marins?"

Bascot gave her question a moment's consideration before answering, "The moneyer, de Stow, was forthright in manner, but perhaps a little too much so. It could indicate he has nothing to hide, of course, but it could also mean he had foreknowledge of the crime and was well prepared for an enquiry. Of his employees, including the guards, all seemed slightly apprehensive but, again, that may not indicate guilt. They had just learned one of their colleagues had been murdered; that in itself is enough of a shock to cause fear.

"As far as the exchanger is concerned, I was not entirely satisfied with the attitude of either him or his assayer. Although both answered my questions readily enough, I had a feeling they were not telling me all they knew. Legerton's reluctance could be accounted for by the fact that he is, as you said, lord, an overbearing man and resented being subjected to your authority. As for Simon Partager, he may simply have been inhibited by his employer's presence during the questioning."

"I have heard Legerton keeps his manor house in a fine way," Richard said. "Is that true?"

The Templar nodded. "There were quite a number of guests when I arrived and the food and entertainments did not look as though they had been stinted. The building itself is well fortified and in good repair."

Richard looked at his father. "As far as I am aware, Legerton has no income except for the stipend and commission he derives from the exchange, nor does he have any land other than the manor house at Canwick. While his earnings would be a very satisfactory remuneration for a man who lived in the free lodgings on the exchange premises, it surely cannot be enough to support another property without a great deal of parsimony. How can Legerton afford to live in such grand style?"

"I remember that he sold his father's silver manufactory when the old man died," Nicolaa interposed. "Perhaps he is living off the profit he obtained from the sale, although he must have spent a good portion of the proceeds to purchase the manor house. It was in a bad state of repair when he bought it, I recall, and because of its condition, the Jewish moneylender who claimed the property in repayment of a debt after the owner died was willing to take a very low price. Nevertheless, it was built at least sixty years ago and must have cost a great deal to restore. It would appear Legerton has not only spent his inheritance but is living beyond his means." She made a moue of disapproval. "If that is so, he is a foolish man. Money should be used to provide the means of an income, not frittered away until it is no more."

"If the exchanger's coffers are empty, it would give him a motive for concealing a trove. But even if he has the wealth of Croesus hidden in his office, I need evidence of culpability before I can authorise a search of the building," Camville said.

"The two men hired to guard the exchange," Bascot said musingly. "I have yet to question them, since they were not on duty the day I went to the mint. If Legerton is hiding illicit monies on the premises, they may be privy to it."

The sheriff stopped in his pacing, his face resolute. "Go back and find them, de Marins, if you will; see if they know anything that will help us. Find me one small trace that Legerton has betrayed his oath to the king and I will tear the exchange apart stone by stone."

THE NEXT DAY WAS THE FIRST ONE OF THE NEW YEAR. In the morning, after everyone had attended Mass, Lady Nicolaa gave gifts of silver coin to all the household staff. Those of lowest station received one new penny, with the amount of the gift increasing accordingly up through the ranks of the servants and men-at-arms until it reached those of the highest station, such as John Blund and Eudo, who each received six shillings.

It was then Gerard Camville's turn to recognise, by the giving of a gift, his appreciation of his household knights. To each he handed a small leather bag containing a quantity of silver coins and they, in turn, extracted a coin from the bag and presented it to the squires and pages who attended them.

Once this yearly ceremony was completed, and while wine and ale were served to all the company, gifts of a more personal nature were exchanged. On the dais, Nicolaa and Gerard presented Richard with an eating knife decorated with a scrolled silver haft and gave Eustachia a cloak of deep red wool edged with squirrel fur. Gilbert Bassett's gifts to his wife and two daughters were delicate rings of gold filigree and Ralph of Turville gave Maud a small pair of scissors with ivory handles. His present to his son, Stephen, was an illuminated Psalter.

On the floor of the hall, servants also exchanged small tokens of affection as scullions from the kitchen brought in trays laden with individual cakes of mincemeat topped with marchpane and distributed them throughout the hall. In one of the cakes, the cook had placed a small piece of wood carved in the shape of a bean. The servant who had the good fortune to find the wooden bean in his or her portion of cake would be proclaimed Lord or Lady of Folly and allowed to preside over the festivities later that evening. The mock noble would be served food and wine as though they sat at the high table and have the extraordinary licence of making outrageous demands on the rest of the staff. These commands were usually frivolous in nature and had included, in years past, ordering a manservant to walk the length of the hall holding a wooden platter between his knees or standing on his head while his nostrils were tickled with a feather. Because Nicolaa de la Haye frowned on lewdness, usually only male servants were asked to engage in antics that might require a woman to lift her skirts. But the female servants did not escape taking part in the buffoonery. They could be ordered to push an inflated pig's bladder along the floor with their nose or submit to walking in circles with a bowl of greasy scraps on their head until the mess spilled over their clothes. All this lighthearted foolery would provoke helpless laughter in the spectators.

The wooden bean was, therefore, a much-coveted prize and each servant immediately searched his or her portion of cake in hope of finding it. Finally, a shout of triumph came from one of the varlets, a young lad responsible for cleaning the grate of the huge fireplace in the hall. As he held his trophy aloft, everyone clapped their hands loudly and two or three fellow menservants hoisted their fortunate companion up on their shoulders and carried him about the hall. The steward, Eudo, let them enjoy their merriment for a few moments before calling them to order and back to their duties. He reminded them all there were still some hours to go before the commencement of the evening's festivities and added a warning that any who did not complete their allotted tasks would be forbidden to take part.

At the first table below the dais, Bascot sat with the other household knights. He had again allowed Gianni to be seated and the boy had taken the same place as he had done on the feast of Christ's Mass, beside Lambert. That morning, in the privacy of their chamber, Bascot had given the boy a small pewter medal bearing the image of St. Genesius of Arles, a clerk who suffered martyrdom in the fourth century. When Bascot had given Gianni the medal, the boy had pinned it to his tunic with tears in his eyes. Now, as he watched the antics of the servants, his fingertips kept straying to the miniature pewter figure while his lips curled in a smile of happiness.

Once the morning ritual was over, the company began to disperse and Bascot and Gianni left the hall and went over to the castle barracks to spend the hours until evening. Ernulf, who had a gruff fondness for Gianni, had persuaded the castle cook to make a cake

of saffron and plum conserves as a New Year's gift for
the boy, parting with two silver pennies for the favour.

"Plums are Gianni's favourite fruit," Ernulf had told
the Templar. "I am sure he will enjoy it."

He had not been wrong. Gianni's face broke into a
wide smile and he clapped his hands together in appreciation when he saw the serjeant's gift. The serjeant
ordered a keg of ale broached for the enjoyment of all
of the men-at-arms who were not on duty and, as
Gianni happily munched on the cake, the soldiers began to reminisce of previous New Year's Days and the
splendid food they had eaten.

As the tales circulated, and the men-at-arms' memories grew more fanciful in recalling details of the quantity and quality of the dishes that had been served,
Bascot let his mind drift back to the day before and his
questioning of the two guards who worked in the exchange.

After his meeting with Gerard Camville, he had ridden immediately to the exchange and, finding it closed,
gone next door to the mint. He arrived just as de Stow's
employees were finishing work for the day. When he
asked if any knew the whereabouts of Legerton's
guards, one of the hammermen told him they lodged in
rooms above a nearby alehouse.

Bascot found the alehouse in a street called Walker-
gate, where the patrons were mostly dyers who plied
their trade close to the river Witham. The wattle and
daub walls of the building were badly in need of a
fresh coat of lime and the inside was just as ill-kept,
with rough tables and benches scattered about and
filthy rushes on the floor. The ale keeper, a shrivelled
individual with a hook fitted to the stump of his left

arm in place of a hand, answered Bascot's enquiry for the whereabouts of the guards with an anxious look, pointing his hook at a table in the corner where two men were sitting. Both were of a similar type to those employed by de Stow, former soldiers who had fallen on hard times and depended on their military skills to earn a living. They were dressed in boiled leather jerkins and plain dark hose and each carried a cudgel and short sword on their belts.

Respectful of Bascot's rank, neither guard gave any sign of apprehension when he told them he was investigating the death of Peter Brand and asked them the same questions he had put to de Stow's employees. They answered in a similar manner as the workers at the mint had done—both denied keeping company with the clerk outside of working hours and claimed he had not made any mention of going to the quarry on the day of his death.

As they made their replies, the older of the two, a hirsute man with a thick wiry beard named Jed, pulled at his lower lip thoughtfully and added that the clerk had seemed a little excited in the two or three days before he disappeared.

"How so?" Bascot asked.

"He were merry, like," Jed replied. "Not that he were ever glum. Mostly he seemed a friendly enough fellow—mayhap a bit too garrulous at times—and always gave a greeting in passing, but for those days 'twas like he was burstin' with happiness. We all knew he was lookin' forward to going home to see his sweetheart, and reckoned he was in high spirits at the prospect of bein' with her again. But mebbe we wus wrong; mebbe 'twas somethin' else that had nowt to do

with the girl." The guard looked at Bascot with sorrow
in his dark eyes. "Mebbe 'twas that somethin' else that
got him killed."

When Bascot added a question about money stored
in the exchange, both men were adamant that the only
time coinage was brought onto the premises was during transactions with customers.

"And then it's only there for as long as it takes to
exchange it," Jed assured him. "All t'other times the
money is kept in the mint, else we'd be on guard every
day and all night too, just like the men that work for
Master de Stow. 'Twould suit our purpose right enough
if it was, then we'd get our lodgings free and wouldn't
have to share a room in this hovel."

The Templar did not detect guile in either of the
men. They had answered his questions readily and
without evasion; if they had been privy to any criminal
activity in the exchange, Bascot was sure they would
not have been so candid. Disappointed, he bought the
men a pint of ale each and returned to the castle.

LATER THAT EVENING, AFTER HE AND GIANNI HAD
returned to the hall and were watching the Lord of
Folly command six of his fellow servants to spin
around in a circle until they could no longer stand, the
Templar felt as though his own senses were reeling.
The more he investigated the murder of the two men,
the more he felt as though he was caught in a maelstrom that was tossing him first one way, and then another. Again, he wondered whether the sheriff was
correct in his assumption that the deaths of Brand and
Fardein were connected. And, if he was, did the mur-

ders have a further link with a cache of silver coins, as Camville also surmised? If either of these suppositions was in error, he was following a false trail by giving them credence. In the case of Tasser's apprentice, and given the silversmith's penchant for larceny, the motive for Fardein's death could be associated with his employer's illegal acts. As for Brand, the exchange guard had said the clerk seemed excited during the few days before he was murdered. Lust was often a stimulant, especially in a young man thwarted by distance from the object of his affections—had Brand found a new love in closer proximity than Grantham, one that lived in Lincoln but whose affections were engaged elsewhere? Even though the quarry did not seem a likely place for a tryst, was it possible the clerk had been lured there by an irate husband, or even a jealous paramour, and subsequently murdered for his sexual trespass? But if that was so, and his love for the girl in Grantham had waned, why had a betrothal ring seemingly intended for her been among his belongings?

The Templar shook his head to clear it of his swirling thoughts. There could be many reasons for the slaying of either man, as there always were in instances of secret murder. He must be patient. Tomorrow, if the weather held fine, he would ride to Grantham and speak to Brand's mother and the girl. Perhaps one of them would have information that would help him.

Chapter 13

✛

At Walter Legerton's manor house in Canwick, celebration of the New Year's arrival was in full spate. There were about twenty guests in all; most of them acquaintances who lived in Lincoln, invited to stay for the duration of the holy days with their wives and children, along with a pair of elderly sisters, both spinsters, who were distant cousins of Walter and Silvana.

As at the castle, after the exchanger and his guests had broken their fast, Legerton distributed the customary small gifts of silver coins to his staff and then presented his two young sons with belts of chased leather. To each of his cousins he gave silver thimbles inscribed with their names and then instructed his steward to distribute inexpensive items of jewellery to the women guests—small brooches or cloak clasps of silver gilt. All of the recipients thanked him and praised his thoughtfulness—all except Iseult, the wife of Simon Partager.

Iseult's pretty mouth pouted with disappointment as she, like a few of the other women, received a brooch shaped in the likeness of a flower. The brooch was no more remarkable than the rest and Iseult threw her lover a barely veiled look of resentment as she cast it carelessly on the table in front of her.

Silvana, seated beside her brother at the table on the dais, noticed Iseult's glare of dissatisfaction and, leaning over to Walter, said in a whisper, "Your mistress is not pleased with your gift, Brother. What happened to the jewelled comb you showed me, the one you said was intended for her?"

"It is locked away in my chamber," Walter replied, "and will stay there until I can return it to the merchant from whom I bought it. I told you I was tiring of Iseult and I did not lie."

Silvana gave a small smile of satisfaction. Her brother was finally learning to curb his excesses and she was glad Iseult was among the first to be restrained.

Walter noticed his sister's gratification and felt guilty. If Silvana should find out he had far more to worry about than the resentment of a jilted leman, or even the small amount of money he had borrowed from the Jew, she would be horrified. He hoped he could find a way to solve his most pressing problem without his devoted sister ever being aware it existed.

Silvana Legerton was not the only one who noticed Iseult's displeasure. Her husband also saw her look of disappointment and, like Silvana, knew the cause. Iseult had taken barely any notice of Simon's own gift to her, an intricately embroidered girdle that had cost him almost half a year's wages. Anger surged up in Partager's breast as his wife thanked him distractedly, her eyes hot with indignation as she glanced up at Legerton. She then turned away from Simon and began to talk to the man seated on her other side, a young fellow who was the son of a Lincoln draper and had accompanied his parents to Canwick in response to the exchanger's invitation. He was a handsome youth with curly red hair, knowing blue eyes and an infectious grin. As Iseult laughed up at him, flirting outrageously, Simon knew she was doing so in an attempt to make Legerton jealous, but the exchanger took no notice, more interested in his conversation with his sister and two sons than in a woman that had briefly captured his fancy.

Partager toyed with a piece of manchet bread on the table in front of him, bile rising in his throat as he forced himself not to allow his anger to show on his face. He had been in Legerton's employ for a few years now and happily so until he had married Iseult on a bright day in the middle of last summer. He had met his future bride at Eastertide of that same year, just as the congregation attending the service was leaving the cathedral. Iseult's beauty had immediately captivated him. She had dropped her glove as she and her sister walked past him and, when he picked it up and returned it to her, he thought he would drown in the blueness of her eyes. She, with a tinkling laugh, had thanked him prettily for his courtesy and told him she was from Nottingham and was visiting a married sister, who lived in Lincoln. For days afterwards he had dreamed of Iseult's beautiful hair, like twin ropes of corn silk, and the lush fullness of her mouth. He had pursued her avidly until, a few weeks later, she consented to be his wife.

The joyous day of their wedding celebration was the last happy time that Simon remembered. As he recalled how eagerly he had brought his new wife to Legerton's house and installed her in the comfortable chamber he was allotted as part payment of his salary, bitterness engulfed him. That first night, as he led Iseult out to sit by his side at the evening meal, he thought his heart would burst with pride as he saw the admiring glances sent in her direction by all of the household, servants and Legerton's family alike. How foolish he had been, he reflected. Within just a few short weeks, the beautiful girl he had married was sharing his employer's bed at the manor house while he, her husband, was sent by Legerton to the exchange office in Lincoln for days— and nights—at a time.

The moment of revelation was struck into his memory just as surely as the image of the king was hammered into the surface of a new silver penny. One morning he returned to the manor house earlier than expected, prompted to do so by the sudden appearance of a gold bracelet on Iseult's wrist a couple of days before. She said it had been a gift from her mother on the occasion of their marriage but Simon did not believe her. Iseult would surely have shown him such a costly present as soon as she received it and she had not done so. Alone in the exchange office in Lincoln, his suspicions grew so large he could not concentrate on his work. Legerton's insistence that he remain overnight in the exchange when there was not enough work to require the extra hours fuelled his mistrust. Deciding to make an attempt to lay his disquietude to rest, he returned to Canwick well before dawn, tying his horse up outside the manor door so as not to disturb the stable servants. Stealing quietly into the house, he hoped to find his wife sleeping chastely alone in their marriage bed. As he made his way down the dark pas-

sageway to their chamber, Iseult was coming from the
direction of Legerton's room. In her hand was a candle,
and its light revealed that she wore only a thin summer
cloak over her naked body. Her features were flushed with
the aftermath of lovemaking. Partager had not revealed
his presence, nor spoken of what he knew, either to her or
to Legerton. Despite his wife's betrayal, the assayer was
still desperately in love with her. The knowledge that his
beloved young bride was nothing more than a wanton
burned in his gut like a canker, but he knew that if he accused her, the pretense of harmony between them would
be destroyed. However little was the happiness they
shared, he did not want to lose even the smallest jot.

He glanced at Iseult as she gave the draper's son a
suggestive glance from her entrancing blue eyes. Looking around, he saw the knowing looks the household
servants were casting in her direction. Not only he, her
husband, but all those in the hall were aware of Iseult's
proclivities, knew that now that Legerton's interest in
her had waned she would look for a new lover. Simon
had to get her away from Canwick, and Lincoln town,
somewhere where her reputation was unknown and
they could start afresh. Once he had accomplished that,
he would tackle her licentiousness, warn her that if she
strayed again, he would disown her and leave her to
whatever fate awaited a woman scorned by her husband for unfaithfulness. Iseult, for all her lechery, was
not a stupid woman. He was sure she would obey him
if he threatened to cast her aside. Although he had
made plans that would enable him to realise this goal,
the completion of a few minor details still remained
before he could bring them to fruition.

* * *

IN LINCOLN TOWN, HELIAS DE STOW AND HIS WIFE
were walking back to their home after attending Mass
at the cathedral. Even though the temperature had
risen, there were still treacherous puddles of slush scattered on the cobbles, and the moneyer's wife had a
secure grip on her husband's arm to aid her unsteady
steps. Behind them trailed their two daughters, girls of
ten and eleven, in the company of the young maidservant de Stow employed to tend to the needs of the fe-
males in his household. The family was looking
forward to getting back to their house and a warm fire-
side, but although they tried to step along Mikelgate
with a quick pace, the ground was too slippery to do
more than trudge slowly.

As her foot slid once again in the miry mess,
Blanche looked up at her husband. "We should have
gone to the service at St. Mary Crackpole, as you suggested, Helias. I am sorry for my insistence on going to
the cathedral."

Helias patted his wife's arm. "Do not be concerned
about it, Wife," he said. "The service was uplifting and
most welcome, especially as a consolation for the sadness brought on us by Peter's death."

"Do you know if the sheriff has any suspects for the
crime yet?" Blanche asked.

"I do not believe so," Helias replied. "The Templar
knight came back again to ask if we knew the lodging
place of the two men who guard the exchange, but he
said nothing to indicate he knew who was responsible
for Peter's murder."

Blanche did not attempt any more conversation until

her husband had manoeuvred her around a particularly dirty patch of melting snow. "You will have to engage a new clerk, Helias. Have you thought of anyone suitable?"

The moneyer shook his head. "I think I will have to carry on alone for a bit, even though it makes a lot of extra work. Once the feast of Epiphany is over, I will call on the head of the silversmith's guild and see if he can recommend someone."

As he said this, they were not far from the door of Warner Tasser's manufactory and, as their steps drew level with the entrance, the silversmith emerged, carrying a bundle in his hands. When he saw Helias and his family, his plump jowls creased into a smile and he made a low bow.

"Good morrow, Master de Stow," he said in a congenial manner, bestowing a friendly look on Blanche as well as the moneyer. "I hope this day finds you and your family in good spirits."

Helias nodded to the silversmith and made a civil reply but did not pause for further conversation. He could feel his wife's shocked gaze on him as they continued their trek down Mikelgate but she constrained herself from speaking until they were out of Tasser's earshot.

"How dare that man address you?" she demanded in outrage. "He is a thief and an embarrassment to his guild." When her husband made no response, Blanche's voice hardened. "I hope he has not forced his acquaintance on you, Helias. If he has, it will do your reputation no good, no good at all."

Helias again patted his wife's arm in a comforting manner. "Do not fret, my dear. It is only polite to respond to his greeting. We have just celebrated the season of Christ's birth, after all. At such a time, you would not have me disobey Our Lord's commandment to show goodwill to all men, would you?"

Blanche made no reply to her husband's mild reprimand, but the ambiguity of his response made her uneasy.

Fourteen

✦

IN THE EARLY HOURS OF THE NEXT MORNING, JUST AFTER Nocturn, the fire bell hanging from a pole on Mikelgate began to ring. Its insistent pealing soon had people running from their homes and out into the street. Captain Roget and the off-duty guards sleeping in the town gaol leapt from their beds and pulled on their boots. As Roget and his men ran towards the sound of the tocsin, one of the men who had been on night patrol met them just as they rounded the corner of Brancegate.

"The fire's in the casket maker's shop, just down there," he said, pointing to the end of the road.

His men at his heels, Roget ran towards the glow of flames flickering around the shutters of a casement on the ground floor. "The alarm was sounded by a sempstress who lodges above the shop," the guard told Roget as they ran. "She's a widow and got herself and her two children out safely, but she said she hasn't seen the casket maker since early yesterday afternoon. He must still be in there."

Shouting to two of his men to bring ladders and hatchets, Roget directed others to gather some of the emergency water barrels placed about the town and roll them to the site of the fire. A crowd of neighbouring householders were hauling buckets of water from a well in the middle of the street and Roget pushed past them to take stock of the situation. The casement was burning fiercely, flames licking up the walls of stout timber beams set in a crosswise fashion atop a low foundation wall of stone. The preservative tar painted on the beams was beginning to blister and pop with an ominous sound, as was the wattle and daub used as infill. Although there was only a slight danger of the tiled roof catching fire, it was imperative to prevent the wooden framework of the dwelling, and that of the adjoining houses, from igniting. Roget hoped the recent snow and rain had dampened the wood thoroughly enough to make it difficult for the flames to easily catch hold.

As the two men he had sent for ladders and hatchets came running with the equipment, the clatter of horses' hoofs could be heard as Ernulf and a half dozen men-at-arms from the castle raced down Mikelgate to give their assistance. Propping the ladders up against the walls of the adjacent houses, the soldiers clambered up and tossed buckets of water onto the beams at the top of the house's facade, while the men of the town guard tried to douse the flames at ground level. Roget ripped off his cloak and, soaking it with water from one of the emergency barrels, wrapped the dripping fabric around his arm and lifted it to shield his face as he took an axe to the burning casement. The wood of the shutter was almost burned through and fell quickly, but as soon as it lay smouldering on the ground, fierce flames from the inside of the window leapt greedily through the opening.

As townspeople ran forward with more buckets, Roget called to the sempstress, who was standing with her arms around her crying children at the edge of a crowd of frightened women. "The casket maker— where does he sleep?"

"In a room at the back," she replied. "But 'tis in that room"—she pointed to the burning chamber beyond the casement—"that he keeps cloths for lining the coffins. It must be those that are burning. Our room is just above and the smell of smoke woke me up."

"We can't get through the casement, the flames are too fierce," Roget shouted to Ernulf. "We'll have to go through the door."

The serjeant nodded and, as Roget had done, removed his cloak and dunked it into a water barrel. As the two men went towards the front door, which had been left slightly ajar by the fleeing sempstress and her children, the captain yelled to one of his guards. "Take two men and go down the lane behind the building. Make sure the fire has not spread to the back of the house."

As the men ran to do his bidding, he and Ernulf, their upper torsos and heads swathed in the dampened cloaks, kicked open the door. Inside, the passageway was filled with dense black smoke, but thankfully there were, as yet, no flames. Calling for his men to bring more water, Roget used it to soak the wood of the door that led into the burning room before cautiously pushing it open. There was a slight whoosh of hot air as he did so but, once they were inside, it was apparent the core of the fire was, as the sempstress had suggested, in a pile of burning cloth. The material lay directly underneath the open window and was fiercely ablaze. A coffin on a stand on the opposite side of the room had begun to char from the heat but, apart from that, the rest of the room was intact. There was no sign of the casket maker.

"Thanks be to *le Bon Dieu*," Roget breathed as his men extinguished the blazing material, sending up a cloud of smoke tinged with an acrid smell that caught in the throat and set them all to coughing. "Bring some sand and cover all the embers," he instructed the guards, "and make sure both the inside and outside of the walls are well damped down."

He and Ernulf, still coughing from the effects of the smoke, went out into the street. As he began to assure the crowd the danger was past, the guards he had sent to check on the rear of the house came around the corner. With them were two men, one stumbling along as though bemused while the other was being hauled along reluctantly.

"Found the casket maker asleep in his bed," one of the guards said with a grin. "Had to wake him up to tell him he was near to needing one of his own coffins."

Roget looked at the coffin maker. There was a strong smell of ale about his person and his gaze was uncomprehending as he stared at the charred wood on the front of his shop and the people gathered round. It was clear he must have been drunk when he went to bed and the effects of the alcohol had not yet worn off.

"Were you drinking in your shop tonight?" Roget asked him.

The man nodded, his eyes bleary. "Only a cup or two," he replied. "Helps me sleep."

The sempstress came forward, her eyes ablaze with anger. "'Tis more like you had a dozen," she yelled at him. "You're always drinking in there and it's not the first time you've left a candle alight. 'Tis only by God's grace that I and my children were not burned to death."

"No, no, mistress," the casket maker slurred. "I only had a few cups, I promise you. No more." His words ended in a prodigious belch, the smell of which sent them all reeling away from him.

Disgusted, Roget told one of the guards to take him to the gaol and keep him in one of the cells until he slept off the effect of the ale. The captain then spoke to the sempstress. "I shall report his drunkenness to the town bailiff," he told her. "If any of your property is damaged, he will ensure you are paid reparation."

Mollified, the sempstress turned away and a kindly neighbour offered to give her and her children lodgings for the night, which she gratefully accepted. Roget now turned his attention to the other man the guards had brought with them, and who was still held firmly in their grasp.

The captain stroked his beard and a smile curved his lips as he looked at the cringing figure. The guards returned his smirk. Their captive cowered under Roget's gaze as one of the guards held aloft a rough sack. It swung heavily from his raised fist.

"Found him with this, Captain," the guard said. "He was climbing over one of the fences in the lane."

"So, Cotty," Roget said, addressing the prisoner, "you are back in Lincoln and are once again trying my patience with your thieving ways."

"I found the sack on the ground, Captain Roget,"

the man whined. "I was just on my way to turn it in to you."

Roget regarded the thief. He was dressed in rags and was extremely dirty. Looped around his neck was a pair of old rope sandals tied together with string. Both sides of his nose had been slit and his left hand was still red and sore on the stumps of two missing fingers.

"I thought I told you never to come back to Lincoln," Roget said, gesturing to the thief's mutilated hand. "Did that punishment not teach you a lesson?"

"'Twas hard out on the road in this weather," the man snivelled. "I only come to town to get some alms from the church and then I was going to be on my way. I didn't steal anything, I promise you. I found that sack. It was just lying on the ground where someone must have dropped it."

Roget pointed to Cotty's bare feet; his toes, curling on the cobbles amid the churned-up mess of slush and ashes from the fire, were nearly as long as his fingers and almost as prehensile. "If you are lying, it will be your toes I take this time. Without them, you will no longer be able to climb through windows like a thieving squirrel." Roget thrust his hand into the sack. "Let's see what it is that Cotty claims he has *found*."

Ernulf and the guards gasped as Roget pulled out a leather pouch and upended it into his open hand. From inside slithered a heavy gold chain adorned with a ruby pendant and two men's silver thumb rings set with precious stones. As the captain gave the pouch a final shake, a cloak clasp of beaten gold tumbled out to join the rest. "*Ma foi*," Roget exclaimed, "you have struck on a pretty nest of treasure this time, Cotty." The captain glowered at the thief. "Which house did you steal this from?"

Cotty fell awkwardly to his knees, his arm still in the grasp of one of the guards. "I didn't steal it, Captain, I swear."

Roget looked up Mikelgate. The back of all the houses adjoining the casket maker's faced into the lane where Cotty had been apprehended. Among them was Warner Tasser's silver manufactory.

"I don't believe you, Cotty, and I have no doubt report of this theft will soon prove your lie." He motioned to the guard who held the unfortunate thief. "Take him to the gaol and lock him up. And give him some water to wash his feet. I have no wish to soil my sword on the filth that encrusts his toes."

With an evil grin, the guard dragged his captive away, Cotty still protesting his innocence. Roget turned to Ernulf. "Will you tell Sheriff Camville there is no longer any danger from the fire, *mon ami,* and also that I will be delayed in making my report until after I have found out who this jewellery belongs to?"

Ernulf nodded his compliance and, calling to his men, mounted his horse and rode back to the castle.

Fifteen

✦✦✦

IT WAS WELL PAST THE MIDDAY HOUR BY THE TIME Roget trudged up to the castle, the leather bag of jewellery firmly tied to his belt. He was tired and hungry and his clothes and hair stank of smoke. Before he went to make his report to the sheriff, he went over to the barracks, hoping to get a pot of ale and something to eat from the store Ernulf kept in the guardroom.

Once inside the building, he went to the room the serjeant used as his own, a small cubicle separated by a leather curtain from the large open space shared by the men-at-arms. Pushing the curtain aside, he went in and found Bascot and Gianni in company with the serjeant, the Templar having delayed his journey to Grantham in case the fire in the town spread and every able-bodied man in Lincoln was called out to fight it.

"I have come for a pot of that malodorous brew you call ale, Ernulf," Roget said to the serjeant, hooking a stool from the corner and sitting down heavily. "My throat is as dry as the sands of Outremer." The air in the tiny chamber was warm from the heat of a brazier burning in the corner and the captain began to relax as he took a pot of ale from the serjeant and downed it in one gulp.

"Have you found the owner of the jewellery?" Ernulf asked as he took the captain's cup and refilled it.

Roget shook his head and patted the scrip at his belt. "No. I still have it here. When I make my report to Sir Gerard, I will give it into his safekeeping."

"Ernulf told me about the theft and how the jewellery the thief had on him appears to be very valuable," Bascot said. "I would have thought that whoever owns it would have soon noticed it missing and reported their loss."

"So would I, *mon ami*," Roget replied. "But I went to every building along Mikelgate, including the one belonging to that *chien* of a silversmith, and asked them to check their valuables. All denied having anything taken while they were out in the street."

He took out the leather pouch and tipped it up so Bascot could see the contents. The ruby in the pendant gleamed richly in the light from the brazier. The Templar leaned forward and picked up one of the rings. "These are fine pieces. Their absence would not be easily overlooked."

Roget nodded. "When no one claimed them, I thought that maybe one of the Lincoln gold- or silversmiths would recognise the workmanship and, if they did, I could discover the owner through whoever made them. So I went to the head of their guild and asked if he could help me. But he could not. He said that even if the rings had been fashioned by a Lincoln smith, they would not have been by any who are living here now. The design is a very old one and whoever made the ring will have been a long time dead."

Roget pointed to the mounting on the shoulder of one of the rings. It was bevelled and etched with a pattern of curlicues and tiny feathery leaves. Set with a sapphire, the jewel seemed as though it was a flower nestling in a bough of greenery.

"The head of the guild said this design was popular just before the reign of King Stephen. It wasn't made after Stephen took the throne because it resembles the flower that Geoffrey of Anjou used as his symbol."

Bascot glanced over at Gianni. The boy had been studying a set of questions given him by Lambert that morning and was writing down the answers on his wax tablet. When Roget mentioned King Stephen's name, however, he looked up at his master in surprise. Geoffrey of Anjou had been married to Matilda, daughter of King Henry I and the heir her father had chosen to reign after his death. After Henry died, Matilda's cousin, Stephen, seized the English throne before she could come to England and claim it. His precipitate action had plunged the country into a civil war between the two contenders. Matilda's husband, Geoffrey, had always worn a sprig of *planta genesta* in his helm and the simple plant, which was the common broom, had become associated with him and his wife, and also with his son, who later became King Henry II. To wear such a likeness during the reign of King Stephen would indicate a partisanship for Matilda and would not have been wise.

"And the other pieces—the chain and pendant and the cloak clasp?" Bascot asked. "Did the goldsmith say they are old, too?"

Roget shrugged. "He made no mention of it. He only told me he didn't recognise the workmanship, and so it wasn't likely a member of the Lincoln guild who made them."

Bascot ran his fingers over the smoothness of the links in the heavy gold chain from which the pendant hung. The setting that held the jewel, like the unadorned surface of the cloak clasp, was plain and without design. These pieces, unlike the rings, would be hard to identify as to age, but could easily have been made many years before.

"What will you do with the thief?" Ernulf asked. "If you cannot find out who owns the jewellery, he cannot be punished for stealing it."

"Oh, he stole it, alright," Roget said with certainty. "Where he got the valuables from is a mystery, but I know he did not come by them honestly. I had one of my men knock him about a bit, but he will not admit to theft. He just keeps saying he found them." Roget shrugged. "If the sheriff thinks it worthwhile, I will question Cotty further, but if no one comes forward to claim the jewellery, Sir Gerard may be satisfied just to confiscate it and let Cotty off with a good flogging."

Bascot looked across at Gianni and the boy surreptitiously made a circle in the palm of his left hand with the forefinger of his right, then pointed at the jewels and meshed the fingers of his hand together. The Templar nodded. The same thought had occurred to him. The coin Gianni had found atop the cliff face and the jewellery were of the same period, that of the reign of King Stephen. If Gerard Camville was correct in his assumption that the coin was part of a hidden cache, it could be the jewellery had also been in the hoard. If that was so, whoever Cotty had stolen it from would be reluctant to claim ownership because it would be impossible to prove a legitimate provenance of the items. It was a tenuous link, but it was there. Even if the coin, or the jewellery, did not have any connection to the murders of Brand or Fardein, they could prove the existence of a cache of valuables that belonged, by right, to the crown.

"I think I would like to speak to this thief you are holding, Roget," Bascot said.

The captain gave the Templar a look of surprise. "I did not think you would be interested in such a simple crime, *mon ami*. There is unlikely to be any murder done in this theft; Cotty would never have the courage. He is just an insignificant little villain who climbs inside people's houses and steals whatever he can find."

Mindful of Gerard Camville's stricture to keep private the existence of the coin, Bascot did not want to reveal his true purpose for wishing to question the thief and so was careful with his answer to Roget.

"This jewellery is valuable—murder has been committed for items of much less worth. Even if Cotty is not responsible for the two deaths I am investigating, he may have stolen the jewellery from the person who did kill them, and if so, I want to know who it was."

A smile lit Roget's weary features as he fingered one of the rings. It was set with a large topaz and the jewel glowed like the eye of a cat. "You could be right. As soon as I have made my report to the sheriff, we will go to the gaol and question Cotty a little more zealously."

Sixteen

✦

BASCOT WENT WITH ROGET WHILE HE MADE HIS REPORT to the sheriff. Gilbert Bassett was with Camville, and both men listened attentively as Roget told of the fire and how Cotty had been apprehended. When the captain produced the jewellery found on the thief and related the guild master's opinion that the age of the rings dated from the reign of King Stephen, the Templar could see from the expressions on their faces they had formed a similar conclusion to his own.

Camville readily agreed to Bascot's suggestion that he accompany Roget to question the thief, and the two men set off down into the town. The town gaol was located near to the centre of Lincoln and not far from the casket maker's house where the fire had occurred early that morning. It was a squat rectangular building of thick stone housing four large cells and a small area furnished with pallets and a table where the guards slept or ate when not on duty. Cotty had been placed in a cell at the far end and was secured to the wall by a manacle around one leg. When Roget and the Templar entered, his face became fearful and he shrank back against the wall.

"I'm telling the truth, Captain Roget," he whined. "I found that jewellery. I didn't steal it, and may God strike me dead if I'm lying."

"Then *le Bon Dieu* will save me the trouble of slicing off your toes," Roget answered complacently. One of the guards had come into the cell with them, and the captain ordered him to fetch a stool. When it was brought, the captain grabbed one of Cotty's legs and, propping the thief's foot on the top, drew the short sword from his belt. The edge was sharp and reflected pinpoints of light from the flaring torch held by the guard. Cotty's long toes wriggled as he tried to extricate his foot from Roget's grasp.

"No, Captain, no," he screamed. "You ain't going to cut off my toes, I beg of you. I won't be able to walk."

"Nor will you be able to climb," Roget replied, "and that will save me a great deal of trouble." With these words, Roget lowered the blade until its edge rested on the joint of the thief's largest toe. Blood began to well from the wound. "If you tell me the truth about where you stole the jewellery, I might only take off one of these miserable worms," he said to Cotty. "But if you do not . . ."

The threat was enough. Cotty began to blubber and admitted that his tale of how he had come by the sack was only partially true. "I found it, Captain, just like I said, but not on the ground. It was in the wall of one of the houses, behind a stone that was loose. I found it when I was climbing up to get to a casement in the house beside it. . . ."

And so the thief's story came out. It required little prompting from Roget beyond a slight pressure on the knife he held against Cotty's toe. The thief said that in the late afternoon of the day before he had been in the lane behind the row of houses where the guard had found him and noticed that one of the windows on the top storey of a house appeared to be unlatched. He kept watch for the rest of the day and evening and, when no light appeared behind the shutters after darkness fell, he thought the room was most likely used for storage purposes and not a sleeping chamber. Aware the premises belonged to a clothier, Cotty said he thought he might be able to steal some better clothing than the rags he possessed. His only reason for doing so, he said, "was to keep my bones warm, Captain. I was perishin' from the cold." He said he thought the best way to climb up to the unlatched casement was to scale the stones of the building next door, which belonged to the silversmith, Tasser. "It's stone all the way up, Captain, as you know, and made that way for to keep his workplace safe from the flames of the forge."

When Roget had nodded at his explanation and eased the pressure of the knife a little, Cotty became more garrulous. "'Twas easy to scale it, Captain. There's some good toeholds on them stones 'cause the mortar's beginning to crumble. I was up it in a minute, intending to climb along a wooden beam that edges onto the stone on Tasser's building and get up to the clothier's casement."

He paused for a moment, his eyes glistening as he drew a deep breath and then went on. "But I never got onto the beam. I'd just got level with the floor of the top storey on Tasser's house when I felt one of the stones was loose. I pushed it and it turned sideways a little bit, like there was nothing behind it, so I put my hand inside and felt around. It seemed like there was some bundles in there, so I grabbed ahold of one and pulled it out. It was that sack you took off of me that came out in my hand, Captain, the one with the jewellery inside."

He stopped again, looking at Roget to see his reaction. When he got nothing but a slight increase of pressure on the knife, he winced and quickly finished his tale. "It was just then that the tocsin began to ring. I knew as how everyone would come out into the streets and maybe into the lane—for all I knew the fire could have been inside Tasser or the clothier's house and I'd be burned to death—so I shoved the sack inside my tunic and climbed down. I thought I'd hide in the silversmith's yard 'til I knew it was safe to come out."

He threw a hateful glance at the guard standing at the door. It was one of the men that had caught him. "Looks as how I should of stayed hidden a bit longer."

COTTY HAD HARDLY FINISHED SPEAKING BEFORE BASCOT and Roget were running from the gaol, Roget yelling at two of his guards to follow. When the little thief had spoken of "bundles" the Templar and captain had realised it was more than likely there were other sacks of valuables secreted in the hidey-hole Cotty had found. If Tasser had been alerted by Roget's questioning at the houses along Mikelgate about the owner of the jewellery, the silversmith would, by now, have had time to dispose of the rest of the cache.

With the guards following, Roget and Bascot went

immediately to the manufactory. The door was locked but Roget kicked it in. The blast of heat from the tiny furnace almost knocked them back as they entered. The silversmith's two employees—the old man and his lackey—were busy at the crucible. At their feet lay a pile of candlesticks, cups and plates, all fashioned of silver. In the small crucible a half-melted salt cellar was fast disappearing in a molten pool, while a square-shaped mould on a nearby table was already filled with liquid silver. Tasser was standing alongside it. When Roget and Bascot entered, he looked up at the intruders with a resigned expression on his face.

"You have been quicker than I thought, Captain," was all he said.

Ordering Tasser's employees to leave their task and stand to one side, Roget bent down and examined the items lying on the floor. "Every one of these pieces has been reported stolen within the last six months," he said to Bascot and then, to the silversmith, "You will not be able to convince either the sheriff or your guild you are innocent of conniving with thieves this time, Tasser."

The silversmith nodded. "I am aware of that."

Roget ordered his guards to take Tasser to the gaol and incarcerate him in one of the cells, but Bascot intervened and countermanded the instruction. "Take him to the castle and have Serjeant Ernulf place him in one of the holding cells. I think the sheriff will want to question him personally."

Tasser's face went ashen. Camville's reputation for brutality was well known.

"Why am I to be taken to the sheriff?" the silversmith asked fearfully. "I am a wealthy man; I can pay a surety to guarantee my presence in the sheriff's court."

"A surety is not allowed for a charge of murder," Bascot replied in a hard voice.

"Murder?" The word was a breathless squeak. "But I have killed no one."

"Have you so quickly forgotten that your apprentice, Roger Fardein, was murdered just a few days since?" Bascot said. "I think perhaps it was your hand that dealt the deathblow."

"No," Tasser said vehemently. "I did not kill him. Why would I do such a thing?"

"Perhaps because he knew of your dealings with thieves and wanted a share? Or because he threatened to tell the authorities of your criminality?" As the Templar spoke, he looked at the silversmith's two remaining employees. Both of them were edging away from Tasser, tripping over each other in an attempt to distance themselves from him.

"No, lord. It is not true," the silversmith replied, his voice shaking as sweat began to form in droplets on his forehead and run down his fat cheeks. "I did not murder Roger. I swear it."

"So you say, silversmith," Bascot replied laconically. "But I have heard such lies from the lips of murderers before." The Templar nodded to Roget's men. "Take him to the castle and tell Ernulf I shall be along directly."

As THE GUARDS HUSTLED THE SILVERSMITH AWAY, Bascot and Roget went out into the yard behind the manufactory and looked up at the rear wall of the premises. The masonry, as Cotty had said, was badly in need of pointing and the loose stone the thief had chanced across jutted out at an angle from the rest of the wall.

"If I remember correctly from the day we searched Tasser's premises," Bascot said, "the room behind that loose stone is the chamber where the silversmith keeps his records."

Roget nodded. "There was nothing of value in there, just rolls of parchment and some writing implements."

"And therefore no reason to believe the room contained anything of value."

They went back into the house and up to the chamber on the second storey. One of the stones along the edge of the floor swivelled out easily when pressure was applied to a corner. Behind it was a cavity of capacious size, lined on the bottom with wood that rested on the infill of rubble between the inner and outer stones of the wall.

"If Tasser had been more conscientious about repairing the outside of the building, Cotty would never have discovered this hiding place," Roget said.

Bascot shook his head. "Tasser could not take the chance of hiring a mason. Any good workman would have found the hole while repairing the mortar, just as Cotty did. Once it was known to be there, it would lose its security."

Roget nodded his agreement. "Do you really think the silversmith murdered Fardein?"

"I do not know, but if he did not, it is likely he knows who did," Bascot replied.

Seventeen

✦—✦

As the silversmith was marched up Mikelgate by Roget's guards, people on the street stopped and stared. Most of the bystanders were goodwives shopping for meat, fish and poultry at the markets near Bailgate, but a few were strolling along looking at the wares displayed in the open-fronted shops along the thoroughfare. One of these was Iseult Partager. She had begged her husband to allow her to come to Lincoln early that morning with him and Legerton, hoping to renew the exchanger's interest in her once they were away from Canwick and the eagle eye of his sister. But all her efforts to coax a smile from her lover proved of no avail. He had ignored her throughout the short journey, his only conversation being with Simon as they discussed the various merchants with whom they were to meet that day and whether they had enough new coinage to exchange for the silver pennies the burgesses would bring. Even Simon, usually so attentive, had barely spoken a word to her since they had risen from their bed that morning.

Once the small party arrived at the lodgings above the mint, the two men went downstairs to confer with de Stow and see how his production of new coinage was faring. Unused to being ignored, and left with only the company of a young serving maid, Iseult quickly became bored. As the morning passed, she gave up hope that Legerton would return and seek out her company while her husband was engaged in his duties. He had done so once or twice in the past, and her lush mouth smiled in remembrance of the rollicking hour they had spent together in the bed in Legerton's chamber while her husband toiled on the floor below. But now she had to face the fact that the exchanger was no longer interested in sampling the delights of her body. It was time, she thought, to find herself a new admirer.

She had gone into the town, ordering the young serving maid to accompany her, with the intention of visiting the shop of the draper that had been one of Legerton's guests at Canwick over the holy days. The draper's son had been most attentive to her and was a handsome lad, with strong muscles rippling at the neck of his tunic and a smile showing teeth that were even and white. Iseult gave no thought to her husband. She had only married Simon to get away from the threats of her father who, when she lived under his roof in Nottingham, had sworn he would confine her in a nunnery if she did not mend her wanton ways. It had been in order to remove her from the scandal of bedding a neighbour's husband that her father had sent her to Lincoln for a prolonged stay with her sister, knowing his eldest daughter would keep a vigilant eye on her younger sibling. Soon after she arrived in Lincoln, Iseult had met Simon. From the first moment of meeting him, she knew the diffident assayer was besotted with her and would, she thought, be a biddable and complaisant mate. In that opinion she had been proved correct, and she gave no thought to the hurt she inflicted on him, nor would she have cared if she'd been aware of it.

Her trip to the draper's shop had not been fruitful. Although the merchant had greeted her civilly enough, he had been very curt in his response to her request to speak to his son, informing her in icy tones that his offspring was not in Lincoln at the present, having left their home almost as soon as they had arrived back in town. His son was, he said, visiting a family member who lived just to the north of Lincoln, in Riseholme, and not expected back soon.

Annoyed with the draper's attitude, Iseult left and wandered among the shops on Mikelgate. The weather had stayed reasonably warm and the streets, except for the odd slushy pile lingering by the roadsides, were almost devoid of snow. But as the short winter day drew towards time for the evening meal, and the sky began to darken, she decided she had no choice but to return to the mint and the company of the inattentive Legerton and her dull husband. It was just as she was on her way down Mikelgate that she caught sight of Tasser being hustled up the street by two of the town guards. Along with the other people on the street, she stopped and stared. The remarks of the spectators buzzed around her. Some opined that the silversmith's illegal trading in stolen silver had finally been proved while others, more pragmatic in nature, said it was more likely Camville had discovered that Tasser had murdered his apprentice, Roger Fardein.

Iseult felt a thrill of excitement as opinions were bandied about. To think that she may actually have seen a murderer being taken to the sheriff's gaol! The thought brightened up her mood considerably. She couldn't wait to get back to the mint and tell her news. Perhaps now Legerton would show a spark of interest in her conversation and, ultimately, in her.

ONE OF THE OTHER BYSTANDERS ON MIKELGATE had been Blanche de Stow. Having noticed Iseult ahead of her in the crowd just before the guards thrust the silversmith out the doorway of his manufactory, the moneyer's wife slowed her steps, not wanting to be caught up in conversation with Partager's wife. She, too, had watched Tasser's arrest with astonishment, but her reaction to the spectacle had not been the same as Iseult's. Blanche remembered her husband's vague reply to her question about his familiarity with the ill-reputed silversmith and wondered now if Helias had deliberately misled her. As some of the crowd around her mentioned Tasser's name in connection with the murder of Fardein, she refused to consider that her husband could be associated in any way with such a terrible crime. But murder was not the only offence the bystanders were linking to the odious silversmith, they were also speaking about his involvement in thefts of silver. She shivered slightly. It had not been long ago that Helias mentioned his need for money and his fear that the profit from the latest consignment of coins would not cover the cost of replacing some worn-out equipment in the mint. Then, just before Christ's Mass, the new bellows and tables he needed were delivered. When she had taxed him about the cost, he gave a tut of dismissal and told her not to worry, that a good discount from the supplier had enabled him to afford the new gear. She had thought no more of the matter until now. As she recalled how friendly Tasser had been on the day they passed his shop, she wondered if her husband was telling the truth.

AFTER TASSER WAS BROUGHT INTO THE CASTLE BAIL and his incarceration supervised by Ernulf, the serjeant returned to the barracks in high spirits. Gianni, who was waiting for his master in Ernulf's cubicle, saw the smile on the serjeant's face and gave him an inquisitive look.

"Well, lad, your master has done it again—caught a murderer. The town guards just brought in Warner Tasser and said he is to be interrogated about the murder of his apprentice. I warrant it won't be long before the Templar has caught the miscreant that killed the clerk as well."

Gianni clapped his hands together in delight at the news, but his jubilant mood was not wholly derived from his master's success. As soon as the evening meal was finished, he was due to give another lesson to Stephen Turville and demonstrate some of the more complicated gestures. While Gianni was more than happy to help the young nobleman, his main interest in giving the lessons was that Lucia would be in her cousin's company.

There had been one further learning session since the initial one and, as before, Lambert fulfilled the role of interpreter. John Blund had decided, after discussing the matter at some length with his clerk, to compile a book outlining the gestures, one that could be copied and used as a manual for pedants attempting to teach students stricken with similar difficulties to Stephen and Gianni. Both men were extremely excited about the project; Gianni merely looked forward to being in the company of the entrancing Lucia.

The boy knew the object of his admiration would never regard him in any other capacity than that of a lowly servant, but she nonetheless filled his dreams at night. When he was in her company, and close enough to see the luminous texture of her skin and smell the delicious scent of her gillie flower perfume, he thought himself in heaven. As she listened intently to Lambert's interpretation of the gestures, tiny lines of concentration formed on the delicate arch of her brow and Gianni longed to smooth them clear with his fingers. Once the lesson was over, she would smile at him warmly and use her hands to make the gesture that said "thank you." How Gianni wished he were older and handsome enough to make her look at him the way she did at Thomas, one of the squires. But even if he were, he would still be no more than a servant. Never would he be able to dance with her the way Thomas did or sign to her the gesture that said "I love you." But in his dreams he did these things and when he awoke, his body was tingling with unfamiliar sensations, pleasurable ones that left him aglow with happiness. At the moment, the news that his master had caught another murderer was not uppermost in his mind nor, in fact, was John Blund's manual.

Eighteen

✦✦

THE EVENING MEAL WAS BEING SERVED AS BASCOT AND Roget arrived back at the castle. When they entered the hall the sheriff, having been informed of the silversmith's arrest, rose from his seat on the dais and motioned for them to follow him up the stairs of the north tower to his private chamber. Once inside, he asked the captain for his report.

Camville listened in silence as Roget related how, after their interrogation of Cotty, they found stolen items of silver on Tasser's premises and subsequently discovered the silversmith's hiding place.

"It is also possible Tasser is involved in the murder of his apprentice," Bascot added. "If Fardein colluded with Tasser in his illicit trade of buying stolen silver, they may have had a disagreement connected with the thievery—how the profits should be shared once it had been resold, for example—and so the silversmith felt his apprentice was a threat which needed removing. It may not have been Tasser who dealt the deathblow, but the silversmith is a man of wealth; he could have hired an assassin. If he is questioned harshly enough, we may learn whether or not he is responsible."

Camville gave him a nod of understanding. For the moment, it was best if Roget was not made aware of their attempt to discover whether an unreported trove was implicated in the crime. They both knew the captain could be trusted implicitly with any confidential information he was given but, until it was made certain a cache existed, it was best as few people as possible knew of their suspicions.

Camville ruminated on what he had been told for a few moments, pacing the length of the room once or twice while he did so. Finally, he commended Roget on his quick action with regard to the fire and also to the apprehension of Cotty.

"You may return to the gaol now, Roget," he told the captain, "and get some well-deserved rest." As Roget turned to leave the room, Camville called after him. "On your way through the hall, tell the butler to give you a keg of wine from my personal store. You have earned it."

Roget's eyes, bloodshot from the effects of the fire and lack of sleep, lit with appreciation as he thanked the sheriff and left the room. Gerard Camville may be despotic, but the men under his command were well aware that while his punishments could be brutal, his largesse was just as unstinting. This equitability was one of the reasons they gave him their unswerving loyalty.

Once the former mercenary had left the room, Camville motioned for Bascot to be seated and poured them both a cup of wine.

"I am certain the coin found in the quarry and the jewellery are part of a hidden cache," the sheriff said as he resumed his pacing up and down the room, eschewing the comfort of a sturdy chair covered with padded lamb skin. "The silversmith must know its whereabouts. Are you certain there are no more valuables hidden on his premises?"

"Not completely, lord," Bascot replied. "The first time we went there, we only searched the rooms, and today, with the failing daylight, we could not examine the fabric of the building in any detail. I would like to return tomorrow morning with my servant. He has sharp eyes and, in previous investigations, has noticed details I have missed. It was he who found the coin."

"Do so, Templar," Gerard said. "Pinchbeck, the coroner, has not yet returned to Lincoln but if he does, and learns of my suspicion that an unreported trove is involved in these crimes, he will take the matter out of my hands and leap to the chase like one of my deerhounds. I would prefer he remain in ignorance until I am certain of all the facts. Report to me after you have searched the silversmith's dwelling. His interrogation can wait until you have done so. Perhaps a few hours of confinement will loosen his tongue."

"Even if Tasser has knowledge of a cache, I am not certain he is guilty of Fardein's murder. His surprise when I charged him with the crime seemed genuine."

"Nonetheless, he knows where that jewellery came from. Get him to reveal the provenance of it, de Marins, and the identity of the murderer may also be unmasked."

*   *   *

THE NEXT MORNING BASCOT WAS UP AND HAD PULLED
on his boots by the time the cathedral bells rang out the
hour of Matins at daybreak. Rousing Gianni, the pair
went down to St. Clement to attend Mass and then
back to the keep and up the stairs to the scriptorium.
Gianni, still slightly bemused from having spent an
hour in close proximity to Lucia the evening before,
tried to focus his attention on the errand his master had
told him they were to perform today. The night before,
the Templar had told Gianni he was to accompany his
master to the silversmith's manufactory the next morning and conduct a thorough search of the premises. He
also related the purpose of the scrutiny. Well aware of
the importance of the errand, and the privilege of being
in the confidence of his master and the sheriff, Gianni
knew it was important to show diligence. Resolutely he
pushed his reveries of Lucia aside as they went to tell
John Blund that Gianni would be absent from his duties for the day.

The chamber that housed the scriptorium was a
large one, with high casements along the outside wall
to admit the morning light. When Bascot and Gianni
entered the room, Blund and Lambert were poring over
some pages laid on a lectern.

They both looked up at Bascot's entrance and a
welcoming smile spread over the secretary's genial
features. "Sir Bascot! You are well come. I am just
inspecting the work Lambert has done on the book I
told you about, the one describing Gianni's gestures.
Lambert has done a fine job. Perhaps you would like to
see it."

He passed the sheets of medium-grade vellum to the Templar, and Bascot saw that Blund's praise was well merited. On each page there was a drawing of one or both hands, the fingers curved to depict the motion to be used. Underneath was a notation in Latin of how the hands should be held—whether palm outward, upward or in conjunction with each other—and the meaning of the signal. The drawings had been outlined with a quill sharpened to a fine point and the inscriptions were in clear and careful script. Bascot added his praise of the work to Blund's, and Lambert flushed with pleasure.

"Since Master Stephen will only be here until after the betrothal ceremony, I have asked permission from Lady Nicolaa to give him another lesson tonight," Blund said, "and one again tomorrow, perhaps in the daytime. Milady is most impressed with the book and asked Lambert to make an abridged copy of the work so the youngster can take it with him when he returns home." A frown creased the secretary's brow as he looked worriedly at the Templar. "I should also have asked your permission, Sir Bascot, for Gianni to attend the extra lessons. Please forgive my negligence, I beg of you."

Bascot smiled and quickly allayed Blund's fear of giving offence. "I am more than willing for Gianni to assist in the task. If his efforts, and yours, can benefit others such as Stephen, it is my Christian duty to aid you in the enterprise. You may avail yourself of Gianni's help as often as you like."

As Blund began to express his gratitude for the Templar's offer, Bascot interrupted him. "I fear, having given my assent, I must make one exception to the use of Gianni's time. I have need of his services this morning but will ensure he is available for this evening's lesson."

"Of course, Sir Bascot," Blund replied. "You have my thanks for your generosity."

Noting the broad smile that lit Gianni's face at mention of a few more hours in Lucia's company, the Templar and the boy left the scriptorium and went down into Lincoln town.

Nineteen

✛

As Bascot and Gianni were making their way to the silversmith's manufactory, Iseult lay beside her husband in the small sleeping chamber they shared in the cramped lodgings above the mint. The room was cold and she shivered as she tried to find some warmth in the heavy layer of quilts covering her. She had not slept well, too irritated by the memory of the dismal reception her story of Tasser's arrest had elicited from both Legerton and her husband.

It had been almost time for the evening meal to be served when Iseult and the maidservant returned. Not able to contain her exciting news, Iseult blurted it out as soon as the men came upstairs from the exchange, not even waiting until the servant girl had a chance to pour them each a cup of wine. Iseult had expected that Legerton, at least, would pay attention as she told of how fearful Tasser had looked and repeated the comments she had heard from the bystanders, but the exchanger's only response had been a tightening of his lips and a pretense of disinterest. Even her husband, Simon, had paid her words no mind; merely gave a nod to signify he had heard and turned away.

Frustrated by their attitude, Iseult went next door to the moneyer's house, hoping that Blanche de Stow would be willing to engage in gossip about the silver-smith's arrest. But when she was ushered into de Stow's hall, she found that Blanche had, like herself, been among the crowd of spectators that witnessed Tasser's downfall. Just as disappointing was that nei-ther Blanche nor her husband seemed interested in speculating about his crimes and had even gone so far as to show a disinclination for her company, begging her to excuse their lack of hospitality by claiming to be tired and intent on retiring early.

Iseult found it all most confusing. Later, after en-during an evening of dull conversation between Leger-ton and Simon about work in the exchange, Iseult snuggled up to her husband in bed, hoping to enjoy a marital romp to relieve the tedium. But he turned his back on her, feigning tiredness. It was an excuse he had lately begun to use, but Iseult was not completely surprised. He had proved to be a disappointing lover right from the first days of their marriage. Their wed-ding night had been the only time Simon seemed greedy for her body, and even then he had been reti-cent, especially after she made a pretense of pain when he supposedly ruptured her maidenhead.

All these thoughts had caused her to toss and turn restlessly, angry there was no one interested in her news, or her charms, annoyed by the coldness of the weather and the chamber, and disappointed by the ab-sence of the draper's son when she had gone to his father's shop. She was bored beyond her patience and knew the only remedy for it would be to visit her sister, Lisette. She was not close to her elder sibling—Lisette was cut in the mould of their father, sanctimonious and disapproving of what she called her sister's "ill-advised behaviour"—but at least she would be interested in a firsthand accounting of Tasser's arrest. Even though Lisette was a prig she did, for all that, like to indulge in a bit of gossip.

BASCOT AND GIANNI SPENT MOST OF THE MORNING searching the silversmith's premises. The manufactory was locked when they arrived, with a guard at the door, but the sheriff had given Bascot the keys confiscated from Tasser when he was arrested. The silversmith's two remaining employees had been ordered to go to their homes and stay there until they were deemed innocent of connivance, or otherwise, in the theft of the stolen pieces of silver, so there was no one on the property to hinder their search.

Once inside, they went up to the floor above the manufactory and into Tasser's office. Since access to the hidey-hole was in this chamber, it was here the pair began their search. When a careful examination of each of the stones in the rear wall revealed none loose in their setting except the one screening the hiding place, they turned their attention to the floorboards, carefully knocking on each one to ensure the space beneath was not hollow. When the search proved fruitless, they carried out the same procedure in Tasser's sleeping chambers.

Bascot then hoisted Gianni up onto his shoulders so he could crawl into the small space under the roof of the building, gaining entry through a trapdoor in the ceiling of the main bedchamber. The Templar waited hopefully as he heard the boy scamper across the boards above him, prying into every corner. When Gianni reappeared and shook his head, they went downstairs to the hall and carried out the same procedure there and also in the kitchen. Still finding nothing, they went into the manufactory. This was a much more difficult area to sift through, as there were shelves closely packed with the implements of Tasser's trade and numerous boxes containing everything from strands of fine silver wire to the lumps of tin used to make an alloy with melted silver.

Leaving Gianni to examine the stones of the forge—which were now cold—Bascot turned his attention to the locked chests on the floor. Although he and Roget had examined the contents a few days before, Bascot wanted to make sure the silversmith had not, in the interim, added coins previously hidden in the wall. Again, their efforts proved useless. No more secreted items were found, nor did any of the coins in Tasser's money chests bear any image other than that of King John, his brother Richard, or their father, King Henry.

Tired and frustrated, their hands and faces begrimed from their efforts—especially Gianni's—the pair went into the tiny room that Roger Fardein had used for sleeping. It was as bare as the Templar remembered, the scuffed leather satchel still hanging empty from a peg on the wall and the dented pewter mug and empty flagon sitting on the small table beside the apprentice's thin mattress. Nonetheless, Bascot asked Gianni to search the room again and watched as the boy ran his nimble fingers over the straw of the pallet and around the plank on which the bed rested. He then examined every crack and crevice he could find, both where the floor joined the wall and along the wood of the doorway, ending his search by making a gesture asking the Templar to hoist him aloft so he could run his fingers along the top of the lintel above the door. The boy was extremely thorough and Bascot knew Gianni hoped to repeat a previous triumph when he had found a scrap of red cloth that had proved instrumental in discovering the identity of a murderer, but this time his endeavours were in vain. At last the boy turned to his master with a doleful expression and shook his head, reluctantly admitting defeat. The Templar was disappointed, and knew the sheriff would be also, but was certain that if there were more valuables to be found, their search had ensured they were not hidden on Tasser's property.

Clapping Gianni on the shoulder and assuring him that even if his efforts had not been fruitful, they had been worthwhile, he gave the boy two silver pennies from his scrip and told him to go and purchase a couple of meat pies from the nearest bake shop and a jug of ale from an alehouse farther up Mikelgate.

"There are only the silversmith's records left for us to go through," he said. "I doubt whether he was foolish enough to make a record of his illegal transactions, but we must be sure. The task will take some time and it is nearly midday. Once you return and we have eaten, we will begin."

As Gianni hurried away, Bascot returned to the upper storey of the dwelling and back into the room Tasser used as an office. A chill was beginning to creep over the building now the forge had gone out, and the Templar

pulled his cloak closer around him as he looked for, and
found, a tinderbox to ignite the charcoal lying in a brazier. He also touched the flame to a couple of beeswax
candles standing in handsome silver holders. While he
waited for Gianni to return, he pulled some of the rolled
sheets of parchments from the pigeonholes of a large
open-face cupboard and looked at the dates appended on
the outside. The ones he had taken out were from several
years before so he searched until he found those that
pertained to the last few months and placed them on the
table alongside some blank sheets of parchment, an inkpot and a sheaf of quill pens.

After Gianni returned and they had eaten their
makeshift meal, it had not taken long to determine
that Tasser was a careful record keeper, even if his
literacy seemed to be limited to an odd combination
of words in Anglo-Norman, French and Latin. One of
the items described in the lists, a silver saltcellar, was
entered as a *saler*, which was an Anglo-Norman word
derived from the Latin *sal* for salt, while the word
used to describe the silver gilt overlaying the cellar
was a French word, *argent*. Spoons were listed in
French as *cuiller* while a paten made for the nearby
church of St. Peter at Arches was described by the
Latin word *patina*. Tasser's writing was not scholarly,
but it was legible, and the figures noting monetary
amounts precisely limned. Most of the sheets seemed
to be a recording of pieces made in the manufactory,
with a list of purchasers down the left-hand side of
the page, and a description of the item and date
alongside. Every entry had three amounts arranged in
columns on the right-hand side. The first number appeared to denote the cost of manufacturing the item,

the second the amount for which it had been sold and the third the profit gained from the transaction. Bascot and Gianni went through each one, but could find nothing untoward.

They turned next to a pile of scrolls tied in a bundle with a silk ribbon. Most of these gave the delivery date and cost of supplies but a few were lists of items bought for resale. All of the latter were purchases from local citizens, the names of some of them familiar to Bascot, and recorded the customers' placement of an item either as a deposit on the commission of a new piece or as a sale for cash money. There was no record of the jewellery Cotty had discovered, or of the pieces of stolen silver found in the manufactory the day before, but Bascot had not dared to hope there would be.

Only one list defied an understanding of its purpose. It merely had a column of single letters down the left-hand side of the page—a half dozen altogether—each letter different except for the appearance of *L* twice, and beside each letter was an amount. Two of the sums were considerable, but all of them above one hundred shillings. Gianni and Bascot pored over it for a time, but it seemed to bear no relation to any of the other records or have any obvious meaning. Finally they pushed it aside in frustration.

The Templar again scrutinised the records relating to the industry of the manufactory. The silversmith's profits from his legitimate business were considerable. Tasser was a very rich man. That being so, why did he feel the need to have dealings with thieves? Not only was he risking prosecution under the law but also the loss of membership in his guild. Was it simply greed? Was Tasser, like the fabled King Midas of Phrygia, so consumed with his love of wealth that he would risk all, and perhaps even commit murder, to slake his lust for money?

Bascot shrugged. The impulses that drew men to break God's commandments were varied and complicated. The reason why one man committed a mortal sin could be quite different from the urge that prompted another to the same terrible act.

With resignation, and an unwarranted sense of failure, the pair rose from their chairs and doused the candles. After covering the brazier with a metal cap to extinguish the burning embers, they locked the door securely and made their way back to the castle ward.

Twenty

✠

As Bascot and Gianni walked through Bailgate, they could see a sturdy cart trundling through the castle gate, laden with small pieces of stone. The rubble was purchased from the cathedral quarry on a regular basis during the winter season, and used to fill in the shallow holes pitted in the bail by rain or snow. Just as the tail end of the cart disappeared under the archway, they heard a rumbling noise and the sound of voices raised in anger. Hastening their steps, they saw that the hinged gate at the back of the cart had come unpinned and part of the load had spilled into the castle entryway.

"Get that bloody lot cleared up, and fast! You're blocking passage into the ward." It was Ernulf who was shouting at the unfortunate carter, running across the bail in the direction of the gate as he did so.

The driver stepped down from his seat and Bascot was surprised to see it was Cerlo, the mason who had reported the finding of Brand's body. Surely, the Templar thought, delivering a load of broken stone was a

chore beneath the talents of a journeyman mason. Ernulf, too, pulled up short when he recognised the driver.

"I'm sorry for yelling at you, Cerlo," Ernulf apolo-
gised. "I thought you were that dozy cowson who usually
drives the cart. Why are you doing such a menial task?"

The mason mumbled something Bascot could not
hear and Ernulf sent the gateward running for a couple
of shovels and gave him instructions to help clear up
the mess. The Templar waited until all the pieces of
stone had been shovelled up and then he and Gianni
walked through the entryway. As he passed the cart,
the mason saw him and raised a hand to his brow respectfully, his eyes downcast. The leather apron with
capacious pockets at the hem that Cerlo wore was covered in stone dust, and the mason mopped his brow
wearily as he clambered back onto the wagon.

Sending Gianni to wash his grimy face and hands at
the well in the castle bathhouse, Bascot walked across
the bail with Ernulf.

"Sad to see a man brought so low," the serjeant remarked.

"Are you speaking of Cerlo?" Bascot asked.

Ernulf nodded. "Aye. Alexander, the master builder
at the cathedral, told him today he'd be out of a job
come spring. 'Tis Cerlo's eyes that are the cause.
They're failing, and he can no longer see well enough
to use his chisel. He's been overseeing the quarry for
the last few weeks while the quarry master was laid up
in town with a broken leg, but the master is now fit
enough to return to work and Cerlo is no longer
needed. That's why he was drivin' the cart. Alexander
promised he'd try to keep him busy throughout the rest
of the winter if he could, but not beyond that."

Bascot remembered the odd way the mason held his head. The reason for it was now explained. "Can nothing be done to heal his eyes?"

Ernulf shook his head. "He went to see Brother Jehan at the infirmary but the monk told him there wasn't any remedy and warned he'd soon be blind." The serjeant's face was grim.

"Surely the mason's guild will help him?" Bascot said.

"They'll give him a bit of money to see he doesn't starve—that's what the guild members pay their dues for, after all—but it won't be enough to keep him and his wife indefinitely," Ernulf replied. "He'll lose the house they live in, too. It's on cathedral property and is only for the use of those employed by the Minster." Ernulf shook his grizzled head. "'Tis a hard thing to grow old and lose your abilities."

Bascot nodded in agreement, his own impaired vision inspiring commiseration for Cerlo. The Templar thanked God the sight in his one remaining eye was still sharp and prayed it would remain so.

Bascot waited with Ernulf in the barracks until Gianni returned from the bathhouse, and then told the boy he was going to report to the sheriff that, unfortunately, they had not found anything in the manufactory to provide evidence of Tasser's involvement in an unreported treasure trove.

IT WAS LATE IN THE AFTERNOON BY THE TIME BASCOT went to interrogate the silversmith. The winter day was already darkening and spatters of rain were beginning

to fall, driven on their course by a rising wind. Tasser
was in a distraught condition when the Templar entered
the cell. His squat body was curled up on a straw pallet
in the corner and the posture enhanced his unfortunate
resemblance to a toad. The fine tunic the silversmith
had been wearing when arrested was soiled and his
embroidered silk hat lay on the floor.

When the guard opened the door and Bascot came in,
Tasser struggled to his knees, his bulbous eyes fearful.
"Sir Bascot," he pleaded, hands clutched together in
supplication, "please, for the love of God, tell me you
have come to release me from this hellhole."

"No, silversmith, I have not," Bascot replied. "You
are to be charged with the murder of your apprentice,
Roger Fardein, and will remain here until Sheriff Camville convenes his court and tries you for the crime."

"But I did not kill Roger, I swear to you," Tasser
said, his fleshy lips quivering. "Why would I do such a
thing?"

Bascot shrugged. "We have proof you are a criminal. Perhaps your apprentice threatened to report you
to the authorities."

Tasser shook his head dolefully. "Since you found
stolen items in my possession, I have no choice but to
admit I have consorted with thieves, but that is all I
have done. I have murdered no one."

"Fardein knew of your illegal dealings, did he not?"
Bascot asked.

The silversmith gave a forlorn nod. "But Roger was
not a threat to me. He was a willing partner in the transactions. It was through him that contact with the thieves
was made. Whenever one of them had something to sell,
they would come to the alehouse where Roger drank and

tell him what they had to offer. If a piece seemed valuable enough to interest me, Roger would bring the item to the manufactory and we would decide together how much we would offer for it."

Tasser turned his sorrowful gaze on his inquisitor. "I paid Fardein a commission for each item I bought and I have no doubt the thieves paid for his services as well. He also took some of the stolen items to silversmiths in other towns, men who, if the price was low enough, were not overnice of how he had come by them. I paid Roger a further commission for that service. He was more than content with the arrangement and had no reason to threaten me with exposure." Tasser gave a great sigh. "I am sorry to say that Roger drank and whored away most of the money he earned, but he was a man with powerful urges and the extra income provided him with the means to satisfy them."

He paused for a moment, and then added, "It was Roger who persuaded me to have commerce with thieves in the first instance," he said. "Why would he wish to lose what was, to him, a lucrative source of income by reporting me to the sheriff?"

"Perhaps because he wanted more than just a small commission for selling the jewellery found in your hiding place," Bascot replied. "They are costly items; worth far more than the other pieces you had stored there. Perhaps he wanted a larger cut and you murdered him in order to keep it all for yourself."

"That jewellery was not stolen," Tasser burst out. "I bought it in good faith."

Bascot felt his pulse race a little. "It is not listed in the records you keep of such transactions," he said harshly. "I have been through them all. There is no mention of the chain and pendant, rings or cloak clasp."

Tasser clamped his fleshy lips shut tight and looked away.

"Well, silversmith, what do you have to say?" Bascot demanded. "If you bought them, as you say, in good faith, there should be a record of the purchase. I think they, like the other items, were stolen and you killed your apprentice in order to keep all the profit for yourself."

"No, no, I . . ." The silversmith swallowed hastily, and then said, "I purchased those pieces of jewellery recently, just before Christ's Mass. I had not yet had time to enter them in my records."

"Then tell me from whom you bought them. I will go to the original owner and verify your claim."

Tasser shook his head in agitation. "Even if I tell you, it will not help clear me. The man who sold me the jewellery is dead."

"What is, or was, his name?"

"Peter Brand," the silversmith replied.

"APPARENTLY, BRAND CAME TO TASSER WITH THE jewellery and claimed it was part of an inheritance left by his father," Bascot told the sheriff, Richard Camville and Gilbert Bassett later that evening.

"Brand also told the silversmith that while he was reluctant to sell the pieces, he needed money to enable him to get married and set up a home for him and his bride," the Templar added. "Tasser admitted he thought the story had a false ring to it but because Brand was a respectable clerk in the mint, he had no basis to doubt it. Tasser also said he did not have any means of checking whether Brand's claim was true since the clerk was from Grantham and not a local man whose family, and possible wealth, were known in Lincoln. The silversmith said he agreed to the purchase and had been intending to record the items in his inventory, but when Brand was found dead in the quarry, he became alarmed, worrying the jewellery was connected in some way to the clerk's death. Tasser claims he then decided to hide it away with the other stolen items until he could be sure it was safe to dispose of it."

"Do you think the clerk's claim of inheriting the jewellery is genuine?" Gerard Camville asked.

"I doubt it, lord," Bascot replied wryly. "De Stow told me Brand's father was a tanner and left his widow destitute. It is not likely he would have owned such costly adornments."

"And Tasser's tale—do you think he is telling the truth?" Bassett asked, scepticism written on his face.

"I believe so," Bascot replied slowly. "But only for the fact that if Tasser had come by the jewellery in some other way—especially if it was part of a trove—he would not have mentioned Brand at all. It would not have been hard for him to make up some tale that sounded plausible, such as buying them, through Fardein, from a thief whose identity he didn't know."

Camville's face was dark with anger. "Or he killed the moneyer's clerk and, by saying it was Brand who sold him the jewellery, he is providing an explanation for his link to the dead man. If Fardein found out what his employer had done and was trying to extort payment for keeping silent, it would explain Tasser's need to kill his apprentice."

"It is possible, I suppose, lord," Bascot admitted reluctantly but, as he recalled the soft body of the silver-smith, added, "but somehow I cannot see Tasser having the physical strength to creep up on two much younger, and stronger, men and kill them. Cunning he may be, but that type of bravado requires stealth and courage. I do not think Tasser possesses either."

Gerard snorted in derision but, well aware of Tasser's physical weakness, accepted Bascot's opinion could be valid.

"You will either have to charge the silversmith with Fardein's murder or let him go, Father," Richard said. "Despite having been found in possession of stolen goods, he is a prominent citizen of Lincoln, not some wolf's head captured in the greenwood. Even if he is not popular with other members of his guild, it is their duty to enquire after his welfare and ensure he is fairly treated. They will ask why he is being kept in the castle gaol and has not been allowed to stand surety for his appearance in your court."

"Richard is right, Gerard," Bassett agreed. "If there is no evidence to prove that Tasser killed Fardein or Brand, you cannot keep him penned up indefinitely. It would be best to release him and let the possibility of a trove lie fallow for the moment. From what you have told me of Coroner Pinchbeck, he will be satisfied with a resolution of 'by a person or persons unknown' as a result of your investigation into the murders, and consider that an end to the matter. If further information comes to light about a cache of valuables, you can pursue it later, and at your own discretion."

Camville reluctantly accepted the wisdom of his friend's advice, but added, "I will keep Tasser confined for a few days longer, at least until Epiphany. After that, de Marins, I would have you question him again before I order his release. A few more days in the discomfort of the castle gaol may prompt him to reveal something he has so far kept hidden."

"As you wish, lord," Bascot replied and then, since the road to Grantham was now reasonably clear, asked the sheriff if he wished him to go there and speak to the clerk's mother and the girl Brand had hoped to marry.

Camville shook his head. "No. I received a message from the town bailiff this morning. As soon as de Stow learned of Brand's death, he sent a messenger to Grantham with a letter for the clerk's mother. The courier was prevented from immediate return by the recent snowfall and just arrived back in Lincoln yesterday, but he told the moneyer—who passed the information along to the bailiff—that the mother and girl had made arrangements to travel to Lincoln and will arrive shortly. It is the mother's intention, apparently, to take her son's body back to Grantham for burial. You can speak to them both when they arrive."

Twenty-one

✦❦✦

ON THE FOURTH DAY OF THE NEW YEAR, NICOLAA DE la Haye rose early and sent for Eudo, her steward, to discuss the arrangements for the festivities to be held after the betrothal ceremony. After speaking to Eudo, she summoned the rest of the senior household staff. One by one, the cook, butler, table clothier, head usher and chandler reported on the sufficiency of supplies and the stage of their preparations. When she was confident all were carrying out their duties in a competent manner, she called John Blund and dictated some urgent letters, including one to the king, thanking him once again for allowing a liaison between her son and Gilbert Bassett's daughter. The letter would take some time to reach the monarch, for King John had spent the season of Christ's Mass at Argentan in Normandy, but Nicolaa knew that however long it took to reach him, it would please John to be reminded of her gratitude and loyalty.

Before Blund left her chamber, Nicolaa asked how Stephen of Turville's lessons were progressing.

Blund's faded blue eyes lit up with pleasure. "Very well, lady. Lambert has taken a great many notes and has already started work on the book of instruction I mentioned to you. We have great hopes of its efficacy. And Mistress Lucia told me that Stephen's mother, Lady Maud, has now become most enthusiastic about the project and has, in turn, learned some of the movements. She is, apparently, most gratified by her new ability to communicate with her son, even if it is only in a limited fashion."

The secretary went on to tell Nicolaa that although Lambert was preparing an abridged copy of the manual for Stephen, Lady Maud had asked that a copy of the entire book be sent to the Turville household once it was completed. "I am sure there will be others who want a copy, lady," he said and then became embarrassed for a moment before he added, "Lambert and I had thought to call it 'A Manual of a Silent Language for those Afflicted with Muteness and Difficulty in Speaking' and with your permission, we would like to dedicate it to you."

Nicolaa gave her faithful secretary a smile. "I would be honoured, John, although I fear I do not deserve such a compliment. I have had little to do with the compilation of the book."

Blund earnestly dismissed her objection. "Without your gracious permission for Lambert to spend time away from his duties to gather the information, lady, the manual would not have been possible. It is only right that your act of compassion be recognised."

Nicolaa thanked him and Blund left the room. Once he had gone, she poured herself a cup of hot spiced cider and sat down to enjoy a few moments of solitude.

Such quietness had been rare these last few days for her time had been taken up with her guests and preparations for the betrothal. As she sipped the cider, she tried to mentally review the arrangements she had made but found that her conversation with Gerard the night before kept invading her thoughts like an unwanted guest. She had shared her husband's frustration when Gerard told her that although the silversmith admitted he had bought the jewellery from Peter Brand, there was no evidence to link him to the clerk's murder or discovery of a trove.

"I am not convinced Tasser is uninvolved in either of these matters," Gerard had said, "and I have asked de Marins to question him again in a few days, after the betrothal ceremony has taken place."

While they had not spoken of the ramifications that could devolve on Gerard if a trove was implicated in the deaths, it was on both of their minds. If King John learned that such important information had been suppressed by his sheriff, only the basest of motives would be attributed to keeping it a secret. She could only hope the Templar would, as he had done in the past, get to the truth of the matter and, in doing so, prove Gerard's suspicions were without foundation.

IN THE HALL BELOW, THERE WAS A GREAT DEAL OF activity as servants ran to and fro preparing the huge chamber for yet another round of feasting. Fresh rushes were placed on the floor, musicians tuned their instruments and casks of wine were trundled up and placed in the buttery to replenish those used over the preced-

ing days. The chandler ordered his minions to remove
all the candles that had burned down low and replace
them with new ones while maidservants carefully laid
freshly laundered cloths on the tables.

In the midst of the hubbub, Ralph of Turville sat at a
small table on one side of the hall, idly tossing a pair of
dice over the chequered Quek board. He was bored—
Gerard Camville had proclaimed himself too busy with
the duties of the shrievalty to arrange another hunt,
Gilbert Bassett seemed content to keep his old friend
company while he attended to these matters, and Richard Camville had gone off to ensure the betrothal ring
he had ordered for Eustachia would be ready for the
ceremony. Ralph's wife, Maud, was ensconced in
Nicolaa de la Haye's solar with her female relatives
and his son, Stephen, was busy practising the gestures
he had been taught by the Templar's mute servant,
wanting to be well prepared for the lesson he would be
given that afternoon.

As Ralph cast about in his mind for some activity
that would be entertaining, one of the sheriff's retinue,
a knight named Miles de Laxton, came walking toward
him across the hall. They had played a few games of
Quek together on the day of Christ's Mass and quickly
discovered they shared a passion for games of chance.
Although the stakes had been only hazelnuts, they had
both played as earnestly as if there were a pile of silver
pennies to win, and had bemoaned the fact that Lady
Nicolaa had disallowed richer stakes to be risked.

Miles sat down on the other side of the Quek board,
bid Ralph good morrow, and asked if he cared to spend
a few hours in town. "There is a wine house near the
Guildhall that serves an excellent vintage and offers

patrons a variety of games of chance," Miles said. "There are tables for Hazard, Bac Gamen, chess and Quek, as well as plain boards with seven- or eight-sided dice."

Ralph felt his spirits lift at the prospect, and then frowned as he remembered his promise to Maud that he would never gamble again. It had been only a few months before, and in just such a gaming house as Miles was suggesting they visit, that he had lost the whole of the money gained from the spring sheep shearing on their demesne. Since then, they had been almost in penury. Maud had sobbed uncontrollably when she found out what he had done, fearful he would lose not only their livelihood through his gambling, but also provision of any inheritance for Stephen. So far, he had kept his promise to her, but it had not been easy, and now the temptation to break his word was almost too much to resist.

Miles, seeing his hesitation, thought it due to concern that the wine house might be a rough type of establishment and not seemly for a knight to patronise.

"I can assure you those who frequent this wine house are not of low station," he said. "The customers are mainly wealthy burgesses from Lincoln, but members of the local nobility also go there." Miles gave a wide grin and added, "There are toothsome harlots available in the rooms above, if such should be your fancy."

Ralph returned his smile, and his resolution wavered, but not because of the mention of prostitutes. "Bawds may be had anywhere," he said, "but it is not often one can find a place where such a variety of games are offered."

"You will come, then?" Miles asked. "Sir Gerard has no need of my services at the moment and none of the other household knights take such pleasure in a game as you do."

Ralph thought of the meagre amount of silver coins he had in his scrip. They were all he had left after his disastrous losses of the previous summer. But, he reasoned, if fortune was with him, he might double, or perhaps even treble, their number, and if he did, Maud need never know he had not kept his word to her. He stood up and called for a page to bring his cloak.

"Your suggestion is most welcome, Miles. I gladly accept your offer."

THAT AFTERNOON, WHILE BASCOT WAS WATCHING SOME of the squires at practise in the bail, a Templar man-at-arms came to the castle with a message from d'Arderon, requesting Bascot's presence at the enclave. The son of a local knight had arrived at the preceptory requesting admission to the Order, and d'Arderon would appreciate it if Bascot would come today to meet the young knight and assist, the next morning, in testing the supplicant's dedication.

The ritual for initiation into the Templars dictated that the postulant be judged as to the sincerity of his desire by brothers of equal rank. This enquiry was held during a chapter meeting and it was preferable there were as many brothers present as possible. At present, there were only two men of knight's rank in the commandery, d'Arderon and Emilius, a brother who fulfilled the function of draper. The preceptor wished Bascot to attend and add to their number.

Bascot felt a strong desire to participate in such an important conclave. He remembered his own initiation in London; the stern faces of the Templar knights as they asked him questions concerning the constancy of his faith and readiness to take up his sword to protect pilgrims. It had been a rare moment, with an aura of sanctity surrounding it, and that feeling had never completely left him, even during those terrible moments when he had returned to England from the Holy Land and learned that his family had all perished while he had been a prisoner of the Saracens. Every supplicant knight deserved to have the full support of as many brothers as possible on such an important occasion.

He was certain his presence would not be required in the castle for the next twenty-four hours. The investigation into the murders had come to a standstill and Lady Nicolaa was busy with preparations for Richard's betrothal. Gianni would be busy giving Stephen of Turville his lesson that afternoon and the boy could spend the night in the barracks under Ernulf's protection as had done once or twice before. Tucking the message from d'Arderon in the front of his tunic, he went to the keep to speak to the castellan.

Twenty-two

❖

OVERNIGHT THE TEMPERATURE ROSE AND LARGE drops of hail fell, each globule as big as a pea, followed swiftly by a downpour of drenching rain. By daybreak the cloudburst had ceased, replaced by a stiff wind that pushed the black clouds away to the east and allowed a few pale rays of sunshine to brighten the sky.

Gianni, asleep on his pallet in the barracks, was roused from his slumbers by the return of the guards who had been on night duty. Hastily relieving himself in a bucket in the corner of the huge room, he pushed a hand through his tangled curls and ran out into the bail, heading for the scriptorium to report for his morning duties. He was late, the bells for Matins having tolled some half hour before. As he skipped across the shallow pools left on the ground by the rain, he rubbed his eyes and tried to clear his fuzzy consciousness of the last vestiges of sleep. His night's rest had been uneasy, punctuated by disturbing dreams. Not even an attempt to concentrate on memories of the previous afternoon and Lucia's company enabled him to prevent the nightmares from returning.

He knew the source of his terrible dreams was the absence of his master. Although he had passed a night on his own in the barracks before, the arrival of the New Year had made him disturbingly aware of the passage of time. In only a scant four months' time, his protector would be gone from his life forever, sent to join other Templar knights in some far and distant land.

Well aware he must prove his worthiness to be a clerk before it was time for his master to leave, he was riddled with guilt for his slackness over the last few days while he had succumbed to his preoccupation with Lucia Bassett. Twice yesterday morning Lambert had given him a mild reproof for mistakes he had made in copying documents and now, to compound those errors, he was late in reporting to the scriptorium. He raced up the steps of the forebuilding and darted through the servants dismantling the maze of trestle tables used for the morning meal. Slipping through the door of the north tower and up the stairs to the scriptorium, he hoped Master Blund would not be too angry at his tardiness.

Gianni's passage was so hasty he did not notice Lucia was one of the people seated on the dais, or the enthusiastic manner in which she was describing to Stephen's parents, Ralph and Maud, the new movements she and her young cousin had learned the day before. Stephen was sitting beside her, his silken muffler drawn across his mouth and chin as usual, nodding at her explanations and making the sign for each gesture as she told of them. Nor did Gianni observe that Stephen's father was listening to Lucia with only an abstracted interest, a smile of self-satisfaction spreading across his face as his hand intermittently strayed to the full purse at his belt.

Fortune had smiled on Ralph when he had gone to the wine shop the day before with de Laxton. The place had been all that Miles had promised; the patrons, from the richness of their dress and distinguished air, had been men of means and the wine of superior vintage. There had been a variety of tables and games, and all the boards were of good quality and the dice unweighted—this last having been one of the first things Ralph checked. Even the prostitutes had the look of gentlewomen as they sat at tables near the back of the large room gracefully sipping wine from pewter goblets. Ralph had been very glad he had taken Miles up on his suggestion.

Play had been desultory at first as the regular patrons took the measure of the unknown knight de Laxton had brought into their company. After a few rounds of Hazard with three other players, Ralph had not gained any substantial winnings, but everyone was more relaxed in his company. The wine flowed freely and the conversation was genial.

It had been about an hour later that a man he surmised to be one of the wealthier merchants of the town invited him to play Bac Gamen. This game was a particular favourite of Ralph's and one at which he excelled. It had not taken long for him to realise that his opponent was not a strategist and far too eager to bear his men off the board without taking advantage of the positions of the pieces. Ralph let him win one or two games, and a small amount of silver, and then, when he felt the moment was right, suggested they use the doubling counter. The merchant, flushed with his small victories, readily agreed. It was only a short time before Ralph won all but one lone silver penny from the pile in front of his opponent.

Noting the merchant had become increasingly distressed by his losses, Ralph decided to call a halt to the game.

"That was my last throw," he said and laid down the leather cup that contained the dice.

"Damn your soul," his opponent muttered in a threatening fashion. "You had scant more when you sat down and I staked against it."

"And you lost," Ralph replied flatly, "more than once."

"I will give you a note of promise for another stake," the merchant said eagerly, his fingers trembling slightly. "Just one more game," he pleaded. "If I lose again, you will be that much the richer."

Ralph stood up; the man's overt display of desperation was distasteful. "I think not. The hour grows late and I am tired. I bid you good evening and wish you better fortune the next time you play."

Turville felt a fleeting twinge of guilt for winning so much money from his richly dressed opponent, having often been in the position of losing more silver than he could afford himself, but his conscience was quickly assuaged by thought of the amount of money he had won. It would alleviate a large part of the financial distress he and his family were suffering. He had returned to the castle in exceedingly high spirits. Now, sitting at the table with his family and listening to his son describe his new accomplishments, his contentment was unbounded.

IN THE TOWN, A SCANT HOUR LATER, ISEULT LEFT THE lodgings above the mint and, the maidservant in tow, went to visit her sister. Although she had been intending to visit Lisette for a good gossip about the silversmith's arrest, all thoughts of Tasser's incarceration had been chased from her mind by news that her husband, Simon, had given her that morning. She needed to discuss it with someone and hoped that her elder sister would prove a sympathetic listener.

Lisette was married to a harness maker and, with their four children and her husband, lived above his shop in a house on a side street just off Danesgate. Although she loved Iseult she, like their father, was shocked by her sister's licentiousness and thankful to see her safely married to an upstanding man of good repute. Lisette's relief had not lasted long, however, for a spiteful neighbour had been quick to repeat gossip about Iseult's wayward behaviour with Simon's employer. When Iseult knocked at her sister's door that morning, she was greeted with a scathing glance, for Lisette was quite ready to take her younger sibling to task for her outrageous behaviour, but her anger was quickly dispelled when she saw the downcast look on Iseult's face.

"Oh, Lisette," Iseult said when they were ensconced in the tiny hall of the harness maker's house, "Simon has just told me he has accepted the post of assayer at a mine in Tynedale. I do not want to go to some village in the wilds of Northumbria where there are only brutish miners and their be-draggled wives for company."

"Has your husband said why he has taken such a drastic step?" Lisette asked, confident she already knew the answer to her question. When Iseult had taken off her cloak, Lisette could not help but note the handsome girdle her sister was wearing. It was made of exquisite embroidery decorated with tiny gems and had fine silk tassels with which to fasten it. Simon could never have afforded such a costly gift, so it must have been a present from Iseult's lover. Was it any wonder her sister's husband was seeking a way to remove his beautiful young wife from the close proximity of her paramour?

Iseult shook her head in her response to Lisette's question. "No. Simon only said the position is a good one and he has a fancy to live farther north."

Lisette regarded her sister thoughtfully for a moment. "Perhaps he is not telling you the true reason, Iseult. It may be he has learned of your adulterous liaison with Master Legerton and wants to escape the shame you have brought on him."

Iseult waved her hand in dismissal. She was not surprised at her sister's knowledge of her lover; she had never been overcareful of concealing her attraction to handsome men and, as far as her husband was concerned, she had no care that he suffered dishonour through her actions. "I have finished with Legerton," she said airily. "He no longer interests me."

Lisette, remembering how their father's neighbour had lost affection for Iseult once he had tired of her body, gestured towards the belt Iseult wore and said caustically, "Is that expensive girdle his parting gift to you, then?"

Iseult looked puzzled for a moment and then, fingering one of the bright tassels lying in her lap, said, "Oh, no. This was Simon's New Year present to me. Legerton only gave me a paltry brooch. It was not even solid silver, merely gilt."

Her answer took Lisette by surprise. She had not thought Simon able to afford such an expensive piece of frippery. Despite Iseult's unfaithfulness, the assayer must still love his wife a great deal if he was willing to spend a good portion of his income on such a costly present. She regarded her sister and thought how self-centred Iseult was, how she did not realise there was many a husband who would have denounced such a flagrantly unfaithful wife and meted out the punishment proscribed by law. How would Iseult react, she wondered, if Simon were to order her beautiful hair shaved off and then drag her through the streets of the town for all to see?

At these thoughts, Lisette's patience finally snapped. "You should give thanks to God that Simon is such a caring husband, Iseult. Much as it pains me to say it, you behave like a harlot. I am ashamed to admit we share the same blood."

Never before had her sister spoken so harshly, and Iseult stared at Lisette in dismay. Her discomfiture lasted only a moment, however, before her innate self-absorption resurrected itself. Rising from the stool on which she had been sitting and tossing back her head arrogantly, she said, "You have always been jealous of me, Lisette, and I see you have not changed. Since you are embarrassed to have me for a sister, I will not trouble you with my company any longer."

So saying, she called for her maidservant and left the house.

IN THE MINT, DE STOW'S WORKMEN HAD ALMOST completed the manufacture of silver coins for the consignment ordered by Legerton. Helias had promised his employees that if the order was finished today, they could have a paid day of rest on Epiphany.

The air rang with sounds of industry as the hammermen struck the king's image on the last few coins. The furnace had been allowed to go out, but the odour of molten metal still lingered. De Stow was busy inspecting the work his men had done, stacking the coins in neat piles of twelve ready for inspection by Simon Partager, who would reweigh them and use his touchstone to ensure the silver content was as required by the king's ordinance.

As he worked, de Stow's brows were drawn down into a frown and his manner impatient. Usually of equable temperament, his men had noticed his foul humour for the last two or three days and been surprised when he railed at them for the slightest laxity.

One of the hammermen had opined that the moneyer's testiness was due to their employer having to cope with extra duties since the death of his clerk, and the other workers had agreed. Only de Stow's wife, Blanche, noticed that her husband's ill humour had not evidenced itself in the busy days just after Brand's murder but had, instead, coincided with the arrest of Tasser. With great effort, she kept her misgivings to herself and fervently prayed her husband was not involved in the silversmith's illegal dealings.

Twenty-three

·⚬·

Oɴ Epɪᴘʜᴀɴʏ, ᴛʜᴇ ᴅᴀʏ ᴄᴇʟᴇʙʀᴀᴛɪɴɢ ᴛʜᴇ Mᴀɢɪ'ꜱ adoration of the infant Christ child, the sky above Lincoln dawned clear and diamond bright. Long before the hour of Matins rang, the castle servants were astir and setting up tables in the hall for the morning meal, laying extra places with trenchers and wine goblets. Additional guests had arrived in Lincoln the day before, local knights of Gerard and Nicolaa's acquaintance invited, along with their wives, to witness Richard and Eustachia pledge their intention to wed. Most of the guests had taken lodgings within the town, for quite a few maintained homes of their own in Lincoln, but those who did not have such amenities had been invited to spend the eve and day of the betrothal in the castle.

Neither Richard nor Eustachia appeared in the hall, food having been taken to their chambers for them to eat while they dressed for the momentous occasion. Lucia was also absent, joyfully helping her sister's maid arrange Eustachia's hair and gown.

On the dais, both Nicolaa and Gerard, neither of whom was usually given to ostentation in their dress, were sumptuously attired, as were Gilbert and Egelina Bassett. Both barons were wearing tunics emblazoned with their respective emblems; Camville's that of two silver lions passant, and Basset his insignia of three gold chevrons. They chatted amicably with the guests seated alongside them as slices of cold viands and cups of small ale were served.

Once the meal was over, and the trestle tables and platters cleared away, Camville gave a signal to Eudo, and the steward motioned for a group of musicians waiting at the back of the hall to commence playing. As the strains of a popular hymn swelled above the heads of the company, Eustachia came through the door of the western tower of the keep. There was an appreciative gasp as she appeared. Her dark hair and pale olive skin glowed in contrast to the ivory silk of her kirtle and the creamy lace that covered her hair. Behind her came Lucia, dressed in a gown the colour of harebells.

As the two young women moved farther into the hall, the assembly noticed that Richard Camville had unobtrusively entered the huge room from the opposite side of the hall and was waiting for Eustachia in front of the dais. He wore a tunic and surcoat of vibrant green, and his flaming red hair, the colour of copper, shone beneath a silken cap of the same colour. His eyes were alight with pleasure as Eustachia moved forward to join him and, as he draped a magnificent cloak trimmed with vair around her shoulders, it was obvious he was well content to give his promise to wed the woman standing by his side.

The couple walked the length of the hall and out onto the steps of the forebuilding, followed by their parents, Lucia and guests. After descending the steep flight of stairs down into the bail, Richard assisted Eustachia onto the saddle of a gentle white mare caparisoned in the Bassett colours of red and gold and then mounted his own steed, a handsome roan whose tossing head set the bells attached to its harness jingling.

Once their parents and the other guests were mounted, Richard slowly led the entourage out of the eastern gate of the ward, across Ermine Street and into the grounds of the Minster. Behind them came the knights and upper servants of the Haye and Camville retinues, walking at a measured pace, followed by the rest of the household servants.

In the Minster, there was a great crowd of people. While the ill-tempered sheriff was not popular with most of the citizens in Lincoln, Nicolaa was held in high esteem and the townspeople had gathered as a mark of respect for her and her son.

At the main entrance to the cathedral, the archdeacon was waiting to add his official witness to the solemn vows Richard and Eustachía would exchange underneath the lintel of the massive doors. After they had given their pledges, the priest would give his blessing on their future union. The couple were to make the vow of *verba de futuro*—a promise to marry at some time in the future—but it was considered to be as binding as the pledge of *verba de praesenti*—a consent to be wed at that moment.

Once the vows were said and the blessing over, the archdeacon preceded the pair inside the cathedral and conducted Mass before the high altar. Richard and Eustachia knelt at the door to the chancel during the service and the witnesses stood in the nave behind the huge carved screen that separated them from the inner sanctum. As the service progressed, the church filled with the sweet smell of incense and at the end, when the choir lifted up their voices in praise of the Lord of heaven, a feeling of exultation descended on the assembly.

LATER THAT AFTERNOON, A MEAL FULLY AS SUMPTUOUS as the one served on the day of Christ's Mass was placed before the company. Bascot sat at his customary seat among the household knights while Gianni stood behind him in attendance.

As on similar occasions over the holy days, tumblers were cavorting among the tables, spinning coloured balls as they turned somersaults, and musicians were playing softly at the back of the hall while a troubadour stood in front of the dais and sang a romantic ballad to the newly betrothed couple.

The Templar tried to enter into the happy spirit of the occasion and, while he was pleased that Richard and Eustachia seemed truly happy with each other, he could not keep his thoughts from the night he had just spent at the preceptory and his conversation with Emilius, the Order's draper.

On his arrival at the enclave the day before, Bascot had met the supplicant knight, a young man named Hugh of Sturton, and spent some time in conversation with him before going to join the rest of the brothers in the refectory for the evening meal. The Templar had been favourably impressed with Sturton; the young

knight's desire to serve Christ seemed earnest and he
comported himself in a seemly manner. As they ate in
the silence demanded by the Order's Rule, Sturton had
listened attentively as a Templar priest read a passage
from the Bible.

Afterwards, in the hour allowed for a period of rec-
reation, the situation in Tomar was discussed and how it
was vital that the attempted encroachment of the Mus-
lims into Portuguese Christian territory be stemmed.
Emilius, who had spent some years in Portugal before
being sent to Lincoln to fill the office of draper—a post
which made him second-in-command to the preceptor
and involved the important duty of ensuring all brothers
in the enclave conformed to strict rules of dress and appearance—told the others a little of the history of the
region.

The castle at Tomar had been built about thirty
years before, on a grant of land given to the Templar
Order by a member of the monarchy of Portugal, together with another stronghold twelve miles south at
Almourol. The two fortresses formed the first line of
defence against repeated infidel attacks from the south.
Emilius related some of the atrocities the heathens had
inflicted on Christian villagers in the area—babies
impaled on the point of a sword, women raped, and
men disembowelled and left to die a lingering and
agonising death. As Bascot listened to the draper's
report, his heart flooded with anger.

His blood had cooled somewhat by the following
morning when he attended the chapter meeting and
listened to Sturton's quiet but resolute responses to the
questions put to him by d'Arderon, Emilius and himself, but the sentiment that fostered it had not dimmed.

Senseless killing, whether perpetrated by an enemy on helpless villagers or by means of secret murder, always inflamed outrage in Bascot's soul. It was God's right, and His only, to take the life of another without just cause. By the time he returned to the castle, he decided he would not wait until the morrow to question Tasser again, but do so as soon as the betrothal celebration was over.

THE SILVERSMITH BORE THE FULL BRUNT OF THE Templar's pent-up anger when Bascot went into the holding cell. Tasser was in an abject state; his cheeks were dark with days-old stubble and his fine clothes stained beyond cleansing. Confronted by the ice-cold gaze of the knight's eye, he quailed in Bascot's presence before the Templar spoke even one word.

"Sheriff Camville is out of patience with you, silversmith, and so am I," Bascot said menacingly. "If you did not, as you claim, kill Brand and your apprentice, then you know who did. If you do not give me his name, you will stand in judgment of the murders in his place."

"As God is my witness, lord, I do not know who it was. If I did, I would tell." The silversmith was almost crying.

"You lie," Bascot said and, stepping forward, grabbed Tasser by the front of his tunic and slammed him into the wall. The back of the silversmith's head struck the hard stones with a sickening crunch and his eyes rolled back in his head.

"I am telling the truth, lord, I swear it," he screamed as Bascot raised his arm and gave the prisoner the full force of a backhanded slap across the mouth. Blood gushed from Tasser's mouth and he screamed with pain as Bascot released his grip and let the silversmith fall to the floor.

Bascot stepped back a pace, appalled by his own brutality. He had let the deadly sin of anger lead him into the very behaviour he decried in the infidel Moors. Never before had he struck an unarmed foe, nor used force on a man who, even if he had not been manacled, would be no match for Bascot's youth and strength.

He was about to step forward and assist Tasser to his feet when the silversmith spoke, his words barely audible through the blood that welled from the split in his lower lip.

"I think ... I think ... Roger knew who killed Brand," he mumbled.

Bascot willed himself to stillness. "How so?" he asked.

Tasser lifted eyes full of resignation. "Roger was following the clerk, at least ... I think he was." Raising the arm that was not manacled, Tasser dabbed at the blood on his chin with the filthy sleeve of his tunic. "It was the day after I bought the jewellery from Brand. The clerk was passing my shop and Roger ... he made an excuse to leave his work. I saw him go after Brand, keeping a little distance behind him." Tasser dabbed again at his mouth. "There were other times, too. Over the next couple of days, Roger disappeared for an hour or two and, in the evenings, he would return to his room sober instead of cupshotten. He was up to something ... and I think it involved the clerk."

"Did you ask him whether he was following Brand?"

The silversmith nodded. "He wouldn't tell me if he

was or not, just laid his finger aside of his nose in a knowing fashion and would say no more."

"What about after Brand was killed? What made you think he had witnessed the murder?"

Tasser gave a sigh. "Because even before the clerk's body was found, Roger knew he was dead. He told me I had better lock up the jewellery I had bought from Brand lest I be implicated in a serious crime. When I asked him what he was talking about, he said only that I had better pay heed to his warning. But even though I did as he said, it doesn't look as though it was enough to save me, or him, from danger."

THE TEMPLAR WAITED UNTIL LATER THAT EVENING, when the festivities were almost at an end, before he approached Gerard Camville and asked if he could have a few moments of private speech with him. The sheriff raised his eyebrows at the request, but excused himself from his guests and took Bascot upstairs to his chamber. He gave his undivided attention to Bascot's words and, when the Templar finished speaking, began to pace.

"So it appears that Fardein saw the murder of Brand and was then murdered to ensure his silence."

"I believe so, lord," Bascot replied. "I think the apprentice, just like Tasser, was suspicious of the provenance of the jewellery the clerk brought to sell and wanted to find out if Brand had any more and, if so, where he had it stored. So he followed Brand hoping to confirm his supposition. What Fardein intended to do once he had uncovered the clerk's secret, we shall never know. It may be he planned to make an offer to buy the additional valuables without involving Tasser or he could have simply intended to rob Brand. Whatever his purpose, since he knew the clerk was dead before his body was found, it seems certain Fardein must have seen the murder."

"So you believe that whoever killed Brand also despatched the apprentice."

"It seems logical."

Camville paced the length of the room once or twice. "I agree," he finally said. "But even though it gives us proof the two murders are linked, we still do not have the name of the perpetrator, so are no further forward."

"We are now reasonably certain that at least three men were in the quarry on the night Brand was killed—the clerk, Fardein and the murderer," Bascot said. "It seems inconceivable that no one saw at least one of them either entering the quarry or leaving it, and earlier today I recalled I may have missed a possible witness."

"Go on," Camville directed.

"When I went to the quarry on St. Stephen's day, I met a stone worker who told me he did not work in the pit, but had been labouring in the workshop at the end of Masons Row. Cerlo assured me the quarry was deserted on the day the clerk was murdered, but the workshop does not fall within the quarry master's jurisdiction and the mason may not have been aware of anyone at work in the building. There could have been someone there."

He shrugged his shoulders. "It is only a slim chance, lord, but one worth checking all the same. If one of the stone workers was coming up the road—

as was the man I met on the day I went to see the mason—they may have seen the clerk's killer near the city gate and be able to identify him."

Camville nodded. "If there is the slightest chance of finding a witness, we must pursue it. Go and speak to Alexander, the master builder at the cathedral. He is in overall charge of all the stone workers, both in the church and the quarry. He will know if any of his men were in the workshop at that time."

As the two men turned to leave the room, Bascot asked the sheriff's intentions with regard to the silver-smith. "I think, lord, Tasser has now told us all he knows. Do you wish to order his release?"

Camville had no need to ponder the question. "No," he replied decisively. "Coroner Pinchbeck has returned to Lincoln and is among the guests in the hall. He heard about the murders and, earlier this evening, asked how my investigation was faring. I told him I believe the silversmith is responsible but that, as yet, I am still collecting evidence to substantiate the charge. Pinchbeck seemed satisfied to leave it at that for the moment but, if I release Tasser, he will ask why and I have no desire to enlighten him. The silversmith should have told us earlier about Fardein's involvement with Brand. Since he did not, he has only himself to blame for the discomfort he is suffering."

Twenty-four
---✛---

THE NEXT MORNING, AFTER GIANNI HAD GONE TO the scriptorium, Bascot ordered a mount saddled and rode to the cathedral. He felt cleansed of the anger that had engulfed him the day before, having knelt by the pallet in his bedchamber once Gianni was asleep and begged God's forgiveness for his transgression, silently repeating the Confiteor in admission of his fault. Now, as he rode, he implored heaven to look favourably on his quest for a witness.

When he reached the church, he dismounted and walked up to the entrance. As he went through the huge portal, the soaring nave lay in front of him, and he genuflected at the marble font just inside the door. A stream of penitents was making its way to the chapel of St. John the Evangelist at the south end of the transept, where the body of Bishop Hugh of Lincoln had been interred in November of the year 1200. Many miracles had been reported by those who sought succour at the saintly bishop's tomb, and the number of hopeful supplicants increased daily.

As Bascot stood there, searching for a cleric who could help him locate Alexander, a secondary—one of the young men in training to become a priest—came bustling past. Accosting him, the Templar asked for Alexander. Although the secondary was obviously in a hurry, he nonetheless stopped and answered the enquiry courteously, pointing to a narrow set of stairs just off the entryway. The stairs led upwards and were almost hidden from view of anyone coming into the great church.

"The builder is usually at work in a chamber above," the young cleric replied. "If you go to the top of those stairs, you will find him in the room where plans of the cathedral are stored."

Mounting the small staircase, Bascot came out onto a tiny landing cluttered with tools, coils of rope and empty leather buckets and saw an open door leading into a low-ceilinged but capacious room. Voices came from inside, engaged in a discussion about the possibility that one of the gargoyles protecting the mouth of a waterspout at the western corner of the church was damaged.

"It may only be the trough that is blocked," an authoritative voice said, "but I noticed water spilling down the sides from above the opening. If the stone surround has cracked in the recent cold weather, it will need repairing. Go up and inspect it, and let me know what you find. In the meantime, I will have two men examine the interior portion of the wall. There is leakage on the inside as well; I noticed it yesterday after the midday service was over. Now that the holy days are passed and repair work will not disturb the services, the archdeacon has given me permission to do what is necessary."

Ducking through the low arch of the doorway, Bascot found two men inside, poring over a massive drawing on the floor. It was an extremely detailed outline of the cathedral walls, etched into a thin skin of lime plaster encased in a wooden frame and annotated with measurements of every elevation of the cathedral's structure as well as the differing sizes of stone blocks used in the walls and pillars.

One of the men leaning over the diagram was about forty years of age, sandy haired and wearing a serviceable tunic and hose of dark wool. From his age and confident bearing, Bascot surmised he must be Alexander, the master builder who had a vast array of workmen under his command—not only masons and stonecutters, but also roofers, scaffolders, mortar mixers, carters and general labourers.

The other man was much younger and clad in a leather apron similar to Cerlo's. As he listened to the orders Alexander was giving, he stood in an attitude of respectful attention, his leather cap clutched in hands that were rough and cracked.

They both looked up as Bascot entered the room and, after the Templar had identified himself and his purpose for being there, Alexander bid the young workman go about his allotted task. The builder then gave Bascot his full attention.

"I cannot recall for certain if any of my men were in the workshop four days before Christ's Mass, Sir Bascot," he responded politely to the Templar's question. "But if you will allow me a moment to consult my rota, I should be able to tell you if any were or not."

Alexander went to a large open-faced cupboard standing on one side of the room and extracted a roll of parchment. After studying it for a few moments, he said, "Two of the stonecutters were in the workshop on that day." The Templar felt his pulse quicken with hope as Alexander went on. "We are currently engaged in finishing the chapel of St. Mary Magdalene as well as commencing work on a great window that is destined to be sited in the north transept. Such inside work is usually done while the weather is bleak and, since two pieces of stone from the quarry had been taken to the workshop a week earlier, I sent the cutters there to shape them from a template. Once their work was finished—and it took a few days to complete—the stone pieces were brought to the cathedral and put in place by one of the masons."

"Cerlo told me that none of the church's employees were in the quarry on the day of the snowstorm. Would he not have been aware there were men in the workshop?"

"Not necessarily. Only the quarrymen were under Cerlo's supervision, not the stonecutters." Alexander replied. "Unless he saw the men on their way to the workshop or coming back to the cathedral, it is understandable he did not know they were on the site."

The builder's face looked sympathetic as he mentioned Cerlo's name and Bascot said he had been told of the mason's failing eyesight.

"Yes," Alexander replied. "His is a sad case. He has worked here in the cathedral for quite a few years, since just after the earthquake in 1185, when he was one of those sent to Lincoln by the mason's guild to repair the damage caused by the tremors. Bishop

Hugh, who was alive then and oversaw the restorations after his appointment as bishop in the year following the earthquake, was so impressed with Cerlo's work that he gave him a permanent post and allotted him one of the houses in Masons Row to use as a domicile. Now, after so many years of excellent craftsmanship, it seems tragic that Cerlo will be forced to leave."

Alexander's hazel eyes were full of compassion. "It is a fate that can come to any of us. I have kept him on long past the time I should have done, for his vision started to deteriorate some months ago; first the sight in one eye began to fail and then, a few weeks later, the other. He even spent a night in vigil, praying at Bishop Hugh's tomb, hoping the saintly man would favour him with one of the miracles he has extended to so many others but, sadly, Cerlo's plea went unheard. His guild will help him, of course, but he and his wife are not young and the combined loss of income and their home will be difficult to cope with. I have allowed him to carry out some simple commissions throughout the town—quite apart from his duties here—so he can store up a little money against the days of his leaving but, even so, I fear it will not be long before he and his wife are forced to live in a state close to destitution."

"Do they not have any children to help them?" Bascot asked.

"They have a daughter, who is married and lives with her husband in a village not far from town," Alexander said, "but, unfortunately, the daughter's husband, an osier weaver, does not earn much for his labour and they have a large brood of children. I fear any money Cerlo might have been able to save has been given to the daughter, to assist her with the purchase of food and clothing for his grandchildren. As I said, it is a sad situation for all of them."

Bascot added his commiserations to Alexander's and asked where he could find the stonecutters that had been in the quarry on the day of the snowstorm. The builder told him they were again at labour in the workshop on Masons Row, preparing blocks of stone for the extension of an interior staircase. Bascot, after thanking Alexander for his time, left the cathedral, mounted his horse and rode across the Minster.

As he urged his mount into a canter down Masons Row, he reflected on what Cerlo had told him about finding Peter Brand's body and wondered if it was the exact truth. If the motive for the clerk's murder had not been robbery, Brand's scrip may still have been attached to his belt when the mason found him. Had Cerlo's desperate need for money driven him, perhaps in collusion with the quarryman who had accompanied him that morning, to rob Brand before reporting the death? If so, had the pouch, as Gerard Camville suspected, contained more that just the one silver penny Gianni had found? And if it had, where were the coins now?

Twenty-five

❖—✠—❖

As Bascot was leaving the Minster and on his way to Masons Row, Gianni was running down the stairs of the north tower, sent by Master Blund to bring a fresh supply of quill-wiping cloths from the castle laundress. As he neared the bottom of the staircase, he saw that the door into the hall was open and the voices of Miles de Laxton and Stephen's father, Ralph of Turville, could be heard in conversation. He slowed his steps, not wishing to interrupt them.

"Do you fancy another few hours in the wine shop, Ralph?" Miles was asking. "Your fortune was good the other night, it may be so again."

There was hesitation in Ralph's voice as he answered. "Much as I would like to, Miles, I cannot, for I promised to escort my wife into town this afternoon to look for new bed linen. Besides, I doubt whether I would again find such an easy opponent as I had the other night. They do not often come across my path."

"Legerton, you mean?"

At mention of the exchanger, Gianni paused in his descent and listened.

"I did not know his name," Ralph replied, "but he seemed sore upset at his losses."

Miles chuckled. "He has plenty of money to lose. He is exchanger at the mint and receives a handsome stipend for the post."

"I thought he was a merchant, but, nonetheless, he was very distressed."

"Yes, I noticed he seemed downcast as we were leaving," Miles said and then added thoughtfully, "I wonder if the rumours I heard could be true? I have been told Legerton is indebted to a couple of other players and is being very tardy in redeeming the notes of promise he gave them."

Ralph gave a snort. "'Tis just as well, then, that I did not take his pledge when he offered it to me."

As Miles began to speak of other matters, Gianni continued down the staircase, squeezing by the two knights with a polite nod as he did so. Walter Legerton was one of the men his master had questioned about the death of Peter Brand on the day Bascot and Gianni had gone to the manor house at Canwick. His home had been a fine one and handsomely appointed. It was difficult to believe he had not repaid money he owed. While Gianni could not see how Legerton's insolvency could have any connection with the death of the clerk, Gianni thought it might still be of interest to the Templar and resolved to tell his master what he had overheard as soon as he could. As he collected the wiping cloths, another, and quite separate, reflection about the ramifications of Legerton's debts came to Gianni's mind and he decided it might be worthwhile mentioning that to his master as well.

* * *

BASCOT RODE HIS HORSE DOWN TO THE END OF
Masons Row and stopped in front of the workshop, a
wooden structure with large casements punctuating
each wall. The building was in one corner of a large
yard where stone blocks of various shapes and sizes
were piled alongside a couple of sturdy handcarts.
Hitching his horse to a ring beside a small door, which
was locked, Bascot walked around the side of the
building and found the main entrance. As he walked up
to the two large doors covering the opening, he could
hear a distant braying from the nearby stables.

One of the doors into the workshop was ajar and the
ticks and thumps of hammers came from inside. Bascot
pushed the door completely open and stepped through.

Two workbenches comprised of huge slabs of
wood ran down the middle of the room, and smaller
benches lined the walls. The surfaces of the narrower
benches were littered with a variety of tools including
dividers, set squares and touchstones. There were also
pulleys, grindstones, rope, pieces of leather and rough
sacking and, in a far corner, a cask of ale and a half
dozen wooden cups. The air was cloudy with stone
dust, and chips of limestone littered the floor.

Two men were at work on the central benches, a
horn lantern with a thick tallow candle set alongside to
bolster the daylight coming through the casements.
Both men were about the same age, some thirty-five to
forty years, and clad in heavy leather aprons and caps.
One of them was tapping a mallet made of hickory
onto the end of a straight chisel as he put the finishing
touches to an oblong piece of stone about five feet

long, glancing at a wooden template lying on the bench as he did so. On the end of the stone facing Bascot, the stonecutter had engraved his personal mark. This would identify him as the worker who had dressed the stone and, once the piece had been assessed and deemed acceptable, entitle the cutter to payment for his labour. The details of the work were exacting and the hewer was using a pair of dividers to check the measurements of the stone against the template. It was obvious that excellent eyesight would be one of the prerequisites for those who laboured with the unyielding blocks and so it was not to be wondered at that Cerlo's diminishing vision would cause loss of his employment.

The other man was working on a larger stone block of approximately the same size and shape, but the surface of this one was still rough. The cutter was using a lump hammer—a heavy round piece of dense wood capped on one end with a thick sheet of iron—to drive the broad base of a tool called a pitcher over the stone and bring it to smoothness.

As Bascot walked in, the cutter smoothing the unfinished block cursed as his tool slipped and made a deep gouge. "If I find the cowson that took my hammer," he said, "I'll swing for him. I swear I will." He threw down the hammer he was using and, picking up one of the lanterns, strode over to the bench and began to root among the tools.

"There's no one would take it, you fool," the other cutter said. "Why would they? There's plenty more in that there pile."

"I've had that same hammer since I was an apprentice," returned the other in an aggrieved tone. "My old da gave it to me and 'tis the only one that feels right in my hand. Everyone knows it's mine for my mark is on the handle, but someone has borrowed it anyway and not returned it. . . ."

His voice trailed off as he found the elusive hammer and pulled it from the heap. As he turned back to his work, he saw Bascot standing at the door. The other cutter noticed the knight at the same time and both men pulled off the leather caps they were wearing and touched a finger to their brows.

Bascot told them why he had come. "Master Alexander tells me both of you were at work here on the fourth day before Christ's Mass. It is almost certain that Peter Brand, the clerk found dead in the quarry, was murdered on that day. I have come to ask if either of you saw anyone in the precincts of the quarry at that time, or perhaps on the road that leads to the Minster, someone you might not have expected to be here."

The men looked at each other, puzzlement warring with excited interest as they pondered the question. Finally, the one who had been looking for his hammer said, "I don't recall anyone, lord." The other cutter shook his head in agreement. "The sky was overcast that day—heavy with the snow that fell later—and the light was so bad we left early and went back to our lodgings in the town."

Bascot nodded, but repeated his question to ensure they had given it enough thought. "You are quite certain you saw no one, not even someone you knew?"

Both men again shook their heads. "No, lord. But 'twas hardly surprising since anyone with any sense would have done the same as we did, sought out a place where it was warm and stayed there. You could smell there was snow in the air. 'Twas not a night for any 'cept homeless beggars to be out, lord."

A rational statement, Bascot thought, but also one that dashed any hope of helpful information from the two men.

Thanking the men for taking time from their work to answer his questions, the Templar left the workshop and rode back along Masons Row. As he neared the small row of houses, Cerlo came out of his home. Mindful of his thought that the mason may have robbed Brand of his scrip, Bascot reined in his horse.

"I wanted to speak to you again, Cerlo. We now know for a certainty that Brand was killed on the day of the snowstorm, and must have arrived in the quarry just as dusk was falling. Are you quite certain you were not abroad in the pit at that time?"

Cerlo shook his head but, still holding his head in a cocked manner to compensate for his failing vision, moved his eyes slightly sideways as he mumbled an assurance he had remained in his house all day. It could be a sign he was lying, Bascot thought, or at least not telling a complete truth.

"Your answer seems evasive, Cerlo," he said. "I want to know why."

Cerlo looked down, his weathered face hidden from view as he said, "'Tis only that I should have gone down into the pit that evening, lord, and I didn't. While I was acting for the quarry master, one of my duties was to ensure the covers on the equipment were secure at night. But, just as I was on my way out the door to check all was in order, my wife spilled a cauldron of hot pottage over herself, all down her arm and hand and even some on her foot. She was near to faintin' and I had to help her, but by

the time I'd got her seen to, it was dark and the snow had
started to fall, so I left my task in the pit undone. That's
why I went out so early on the day of Christ's Mass, lord.
I was worried the sledges would be damaged and I would
lose my post for dereliction."

Even though Bascot remembered seeing a bandage
on the hand and arm of Cerlo's wife on the morning he
had gone to their home, the mason's words had a false
ring to them, as though he was using the incident to
cover an omission in his tale. The mason's next statement, however, rang as true as one of the bells in the
cathedral tower. It quickly disabused the Templar of
the notion that Cerlo had robbed the dead clerk of his
scrip. The mason lifted his head and, turning his
dimmed eyes in the direction of the cliff top, said with
heartfelt emotion, "If I had of gone out that night like I
should of done, then perhaps I could have prevented
that thievin' bastard from murdering young Master
Brand."

Twenty-six

❖━❖

Bascot's mood as he rode back down Masons Row was one of disappointment. His questioning of the stonecutters had not gained any information, and Cerlo's passionate words made it seem unlikely the mason had robbed the clerk's corpse. He felt frustrated. It was as though the elusive facts he sought had been buried with Brand and Fardein's bodies underneath a screen of swirling snowflakes.

He slowed his horse, an even-tempered grey, as he approached the gate, trying to place the little he knew of the sequence of events on the night of December twenty-first in some sort of order. As he did so, a pile of refuse caught his attention. Comprised of pieces of broken stone, old shards of timber and leafless branches of dead trees, it was about thirty feet from the gate into the Minster and heaped against the high stone wall that encircled the cathedral ground. As Bascot looked at it, he could have sworn he saw one of the branches move. The quarryman's remark about only homeless beggars being out on a night of such terrible weather as the one when Brand was murdered came into his mind and he guided the grey towards the pile. As he approached it, the horse tossed its head slightly and gave a soft whicker.

Bringing the grey to a halt, Bascot sat regarding the pile and, after a moment or two, thought he could see an eye watching from the depths of the debris. Dismounting, he walked towards the heap. He felt, rather than saw, the presence of something living within it. It was probably only an animal—a feral cat or even a rat—but he decided it was worth investigating and, as he drew close enough for his feet to almost touch the edge of the discarded material, he caught sight of a fringe of dirty blond hair above an eye that could only be human.

"Come out," he called softly. "I mean you no harm."

There was no response. He hunkered down so as to be on the same level as the person who was hiding, putting his weight on his right foot to take the strain from the old injury in his left ankle. Reaching into the scrip at his belt, he extracted a silver penny and held it up in plain view. "If you show yourself," he said quietly, "you may have this."

Slowly the screen of dead tree limbs parted and a head came into sight. It was a young girl, her hair a dirty blond mat above an equally filthy face. She looked to be no more than six or seven years of age, and her fear was palpable, only overcome by the lure of the shining coin Bascot held in his hand.

Reaching towards her, the Templar held out the penny. The child's hand, the fingernails torn and ragged, darted out and snatched it from his grasp. Before she could retreat into her hiding place, Bascot took another coin from his purse. "You may have this penny as well if you will talk to me. I promise I will not hurt you."

Slowly the child pushed her head and shoulders into view. She was pitifully thin and reminded the Templar of the time he had first seen Gianni. Like the boy, this little girl had sores on her face and her eyes were devoid of hope. Compassion flooded through Bascot. There were many such children in every town in England and, indeed, all over the world, but their desolation never failed to instil a deep pity in him.

"What is your name?" he asked.

"Whatcher want to know fer?" the child said, her eyes suspicious.

"So I may call you by it," Bascot replied. "But if you do not want to tell me, it doesn't matter."

"Me name's Mary," the child said grudgingly, her eyes still on the penny the one-eyed knight was holding.

"Do you live here all on your own, Mary?" Bascot asked.

The girl's eyes grew hard. "No, I doesn't. My bruvver lives here, too. He'll be back any minute. And he's bigger than me, much bigger." Her voice faltered as she took in the solid muscular build of the man in front of her and the sword that hung from his belt. No matter how much larger her brother, he would be no match for the strength of a grown man trained to arms. Bascot had thrown back his cloak as he crouched down and the child's gaze slid to the Templar badge on his tunic. It seemed to reassure her a little, but not much.

Not wanting to alarm her further, Bascot edged back a space. "If your brother returns while I am here, there will be a penny for him, too," he said. "I only want to speak to you, Mary, nothing else."

The small face relaxed slightly, but her eyes remained wary. "Whatcher want to talk about?" she asked.

"I want to know if you and your brother sleep here at night."

Mary gave a slight shrug of her shoulders. "Most times we do. We ain't breakin' no law when we does," she added defiantly. "The guards only chase us away if we stays inside the wall, not outside."

Regrettably, what she said was all too true. There was a fair number of beggars in Lincoln, just as in most towns, but unless they could find a sheltered spot within the city walls where they would be safe from discovery by the town guards, they were forced to go outside.

"I know you are permitted to stay here," Bascot said. "That is not why I wish to speak to you. I want to ask if you, or your brother, were here on the night of the snowstorm, just a few days before Christ's Mass."

"What if we were?" Mary retorted.

"Then I would like to know if you saw anybody down there, on the track by the shed." As he spoke the Templar gestured behind him, toward the path that veered off Masons Row. From this vantage point, the top of the cliff face above the quarry could just be seen, as could the shack that sat atop it.

"We might o' done," Mary said, her confidence growing and her eyes still fixed on the penny.

The Templar extracted another coin from his scrip. "I do not want any lies, Mary. If you do not tell me the truth, then the pennies will go back in my purse and not into your hand. If you did not see anybody, then say so, and the pennies will still be yours."

The child gave him a measuring look and, after a few moments she nodded. "We did see some men," she said slowly. "The first one came just before it got dark. I was by myself then, my bruvver didn't come back 'til later, just after the second man come."

"What did he look like, the first man?" Bascot asked, holding his breath as he waited for her reply.

"He were as tall as you," Mary said, "and wore a brown cloak. It were a good one," she added wistfully. "He weren't riding a horse, nor was the man who came after. The first man walked down the track to the cliff top and just stood there, like he was waitin' for someone."

That must have been Peter Brand, Bascot surmised. "And the second man; was it light enough for you to see what he looked like?"

"Not much," Mary said. "There were a little bit of moon, but all I could see was it gleamin' on his shoulders. Looked like he didn't have as fine a cloak as the first man what come."

Roger Fardein, Bascot thought. Tasser had been correct in his assumption that his apprentice had been following the clerk. "And the second man, did he go and speak to the other man?"

Mary shook her head vehemently. "No. He hid, crept up behind the shack that's down there when the other man wasn't lookin'. That's when my bruvver come. We stayed in here close and tight, in case one of them saw us, and watched."

"Were both of them there a long time?" Bascot asked.

Mary nodded. "The wind came up and we couldn't see right well, but we was scared to go to sleep for fear one of them might find us. The first man kept pacin' up and down for a bit and then he walked towards the shack."

"And what happened then?"

"I dunno," Mary replied with a shrug of her thin shoulders. "We couldn't see good enough. But they was both there for a little while before the other man came."

This must have been the one who murdered the clerk, Bascot thought. At last he had found a witness. "Did you get a look at the face of the other man as he came through the gate, Mary?" he asked.

"He didn't come from the Minster, he come from down there," Mary replied, having gained enough confidence to extract her hand from the pile of rubbish and point in the direction of Masons Row. Bascot saw that her arm, bare except for a torn fold of some ragged material, was as thin as one of the sticks of her makeshift nest. The skin was ingrained with dirt.

"Did you recognise him?" Bascot asked.

Mary looked at Bascot as though he were an idiot. "'Course not. It were too dark by then. He was carrying a horn lantern, but it was hooded and he held it down low so as to cast a glim where he trod."

Suppressing a smile at her insolence, Bascot realised the other man must have been Cerlo. He had lied when he said he had not come to the quarry that night. Had it been he, after all, who killed Peter Brand?

"Did the man with the lantern speak to either of the first two men?" he asked.

"I don't think so, 'cause we didn't hear no voices. He just walked up to where the first man had been afore he went over to the shack, on top of that bit where the ground drops down, and stayed there for a bit. We could see the light from the lantern alongside o' him and it never moved. Then he went back down the road."

"And he didn't come back again?"

Mary gave a negative shake of her head.

"And the first two men—did you see either of them again?"

"Only one of them. It was a little while after the man with the lantern had gone. He passed us as he went out through the gate. I don't know which one it was 'cause it was too dark to see more than his shape. We never saw the other man again, even though we stayed awake for a long time in case he come by. Then my bruvver said he must have gone to sleep in the shack and so we didn't watch no more."

The man who had not reappeared must have been Peter Brand. Mary's brother had been right about him sleeping, but it had been the long sleep of death, not the natural one of slumber.

"The man with the lantern—are you sure he didn't walk over to the shack where the first two men went; or speak to one of them?"

Mary was positive in her denial. "No."

"Did either you or your brother hear any sounds of an argument while the men were there? Voices raised in anger, or perhaps the noise of a fight?"

Again, the child was positive in her response. "'Tweren't no sounds at all, not voices nor nuthin' else."

"And you saw only those three men; no one else came through the gate or up the road to the quarry?"

Again, the beggar child gave a definite "no" to his question.

Bascot felt his mind whirl. As he had thought, there had been a third man in the quarry that night and it had been Cerlo. But if the child's tale was to be believed—and he thought it was—the mason could not have killed Brand for, according to Mary, he did not appear to have spoken to the clerk, or even been aware of his presence by the shack. That left only Fardein. He had already been behind the shed when Brand walked over there and, since the clerk never appeared again, it must have been the apprentice who killed him. Instead of being a witness to the crime, as the Templar had thought, Fardein had committed it.

Whether his motive had been fear of discovery or greed, Fardein had used the cudgel found amongst his belongings to hit the clerk over the head and then used his knife to administer the deathblow. Once Brand was dead, it would be the work of a moment to remove the clerk's scrip and push his lifeless body over the edge of the cliff face. Had that been when Cerlo appeared?

It must have been the mason that Brand had come to meet, but Cerlo had been delayed by the need to attend to the burns on his wife's hand and arm. When he finally arrived, he had waited atop the cliff face in vain, for by that time the clerk was either unconscious or dead. But what had been the purpose of their assignation? The two were unlikely associates—one an educated clerk and the other a man who laboured with his hands. Did their connection with each other involve, as the sheriff believed, the discovery of a trove?

And who, in turn, had murdered Fardein? Had it been Cerlo, or was there yet someone else involved, someone who had not come to the quarry but had known the secret the mason and the clerk shared; someone such as Tasser?

The myriad of unanswered questions chased one after another in the Templar's mind until he realised that Mary was watching him with anxious eyes, fearful that the tale she had told was not enough to merit the two pennies the knight had promised.

Bascot gave the destitute child, who was shivering with cold, a reassuring nod and handed her the coins. "Your words have helped me greatly, Mary," he said. "So much so that you deserve a greater reward." Pulling off his cloak, he bundled it up and handed it to her. "That should keep you and your brother warm at night until the milder days of spring arrive," he said gently.

Mary's eyes grew round with wonder as her fingers touched the heavy material. Lovingly she stroked it with her thin hand as though she could not believe it was real. She did not say a word of thanks, but Bascot did not need any. The look of joy that flooded her face was reward enough.

Twenty-seven

❖

BASCOT RESISTED THE TEMPTATION TO RETURN TO THE quarry and confront Cerlo. Before he did that, he needed to think through what he had learned. Reining his mount to slowness, he rode back through the gate in the city wall and entered the grounds of the Minster.

There were more people about now than there had been earlier. A queue of people was seeking admittance to the Priory of All Saints to obtain remedies from the monks in the infirmary for a variety of winter ailments. And, around the perimeter of the grounds, customers patronised stalls selling hot roasted chestnuts and thin wine. Among the throng were quite a few clerics, a complex mixture of priests, monks, vicars and secondaries, all hastening in and out of the cathedral as they carried out the duties entailed in their service to God.

At a corner on the western front of the church, some sixty or seventy feet above the ground, ladders had been set up and two workmen were atop them inspecting the spot where the water troughs along

the eaves debouched into the garish face of a gargoyle. One of the workers was pushing a metal pole
into the mouth of the carved-stone face, trying to
dislodge debris that was blocking the gutter. Even
though the ladders were sturdy—short lengths securely tied, one to another, and supported in the
middle by scaffolding—it was not a task for the
fainthearted. The Templar admired the seeming non-
chalance of the men perched on the roof, both of
them standing easily atop the great height as they
went about their task.

As Bascot rode along a path in front of the
church, he tried to sort the known facts into a logical
order, using reasonable supposition as a guide.
Brand had taken expensive old-fashioned jewellery
to Tasser and sold it to the silversmith. Fardein had
known of the sale and followed the clerk, probably
hoping to learn if Brand was in possession of more
valuables. In the course of doing so, the apprentice
had followed the clerk to the quarry and subsequently killed him. It might have been to prevent
Brand from finding him lurking nearby, but it could
just as easily have been for the contents of the
clerk's pouch. If Brand's scrip had contained silver
pennies from King Stephen's reign identical to the
one Gianni had found, it would have been reasonable for Fardein to guess the coins were part of a
trove. But, once Brand was dead, the apprentice had
no way to determine the cache's whereabouts. His
only recourse was to try to gain that information
from whomever the clerk was meeting.

According to the tale Mary had told, Fardein
stayed by the shack as Cerlo—if it was he—had

come to keep his appointment with Brand. As the apprentice had been much nearer to the mason than the beggar child, Fardein had likely been able to identify him. Had Fardein's suspicion of an unreported trove prompted him to confront the mason and try to coerce Cerlo into parting with some of the hidden wealth? If so, had Cerlo then killed Fardein to keep the secret safe?

Bascot recalled the lump hammer the stonecutter in the workshop had been using. There had been an iron cap fitted over one end and, as the image of it flashed across the Templar's mind, he realised that the hammer, used as a weapon, could easily have caused the indentation he had found on the back of Fardein's head. And the ragged wound left by the implement that had stabbed the apprentice in the heart—it, too, could have been made by one of the implements that were part of a stone worker's trade, such as a punch or straight chisel. Both would be clumsier to use than the knife found among Fardein's belongings, but just as effective, for the ends of a mason's chisel became razor sharp from constant contact with stone surfaces. In the hands of a man accustomed to work with such tools, they could be wielded with deadly efficiency.

Bascot recalled Cerlo's emotional outrage at being unable to prevent Brand's death. If the mason had discovered it was Fardein who murdered the clerk, it was quite possible he had meted out what seemed to him a justifiable retribution. Killing the apprentice in the same manner as Brand—by a blow to the head and a fatal thrust to the heart—would have achieved his revenge. But if all of this was so,

the root cause had been Cerlo's collusion with
Brand in the discovery of a trove. Where had they
found it?

Bascot remembered the master builder, Alexander,
saying he had given Cerlo permission to carry out
small jobs around the town to earn extra money. Then
the Templar recalled de Stow mentioning how the mint
had needed repairs to one of the outside walls. Had
Cerlo done the work? Had the mason, while carrying
out the repair, discovered a cache hidden there by a
moneyer during the turbulent times of King Stephen's
reign? And had Cerlo then confided in Brand, perhaps
prompted by hearing the employees at the mint mention the clerk was desperate for money to wed his
sweetheart? Did the two of them subsequently conspire
to keep the contents of the cache for their own gain? It
would explain the excitement the guard had noticed in
Brand's behaviour in the days before his death and also
the unlikely acquaintanceship between the clerk and
Cerlo. The reason Brand had gone to the quarry that
night could have been to give the mason his share of
the treasure.

Bascot reined in the grey. The scenario seemed a
reasonable one—Fardein had killed Brand and Cerlo,
in turn, had killed Fardein—and both murders had
been committed because of the need to conceal the
discovery of a trove. But unless he found some evidence, there was no way to prove the mason's complicity, or discover the whereabouts of the treasure.

The Templar got down from his mount and tied
the horse to an iron hitching ring near the cathedral
entrance. Before he gave any credence to his theory
he must find out if Cerlo had ever done any work at

the mint. It might be that Alexander would have the information in his records.

The Templar found the builder in the same room as on his previous visit, poring over a list of supplies. When Bascot asked him if he had a record of the jobs Cerlo had been allowed to do outside of the cathedral, Alexander looked surprised at the question but nodded in reply.

"He used materials from the cathedral store, as well as church transport to carry them, so I kept a record in order to dock his wages for the cost." The builder went over to the shelves where he kept his records and extracted a small piece of parchment. "Cerlo's eyes began to fail last summer, so it was only after that time I allowed him to accept commissions for outside work," he said. "The first, I believe, was about the beginning of September and should be detailed on this list, which is a record of outside expenses for the last six months."

Unrolling the parchment, he scanned the contents and then said, "I was right. Cerlo fixed a loose stone in the oven of a baker on the fifth day of September." He paused and looked up at Bascot. "Do you wish the baker's name?"

When Bascot told him he did not, Alexander went on. "Then, in October, he repaired some steps on the guild hall. He did not do any more work until November, when he did some renovation work on a wall at the rear of the mint. Shortly after that he did a job in a suburb just south of Lincoln. . . ."

Bascot checked Alexander's precise tones. "Did you say Cerlo repaired a wall in the mint?"

Alexander looked mildly affronted at being

stopped in the midst of his recitation, but answered
the question all the same. "Yes. It was the rear wall,
the one that surrounds the moneyer's forge. I do
not know the precise nature of the repair, but I
have a list of the materials Cerlo used, if you wish
them. . . ."

Bascot cut the builder short as he began to read
out the amount of sand and lime the mason had used
to make mortar and the length of time it had taken
for the mule and cart to haul the supplies, gave
Alexander his thanks and hurriedly took his leave.
As the builder watched him go with a puzzled expression on his face, Bascot sent up a prayer of
thanks to God for giving Alexander the gift of me-
ticulous record keeping. Leaving the cathedral, he
untied the grey from the hitching post and got into
the saddle. He now had enough evidence for the
sheriff to order Cerlo's arrest. Once he had Camville's warrant, he would bring the mason to the castle gaol for questioning.

THE TEMPLAR FOUND GERARD CAMVILLE IN THE
mews, a large building situated next to the castle
herb garden. It was fitted with several shallow casements to give the birds a comfortable amount of
light. Nicolaa de la Haye and Gilbert Bassett were
with the sheriff, engaged in conversation with the
head falconer about which birds to take on a large
hawking party planned for the last day of the baron's
visit. The air in the chamber was redolent of drop-
pings and the air slightly dusty with floating feathers. There were about twenty birds tethered to

perches along a central aisle and, as the two barons and Nicolaa walked along the open space behind the falconer, the raptors stirred restlessly and swivelled their heads from side to side, regarding the humans curiously with their bright, aggressive eyes.

When Bascot entered the mews all the heads, both human and avian, turned in his direction. Gerard Camville noted the look of urgency on Bascot's face and dismissed the falconer, telling him to take himself outside and wait there until he was recalled.

Once the falconer left, Bascot told the sheriff of the three men the young beggar child had seen, and their movements.

"I believe it was Cerlo that Peter Brand went to meet in the quarry that night and Fardein followed him there. The mason was delayed in keeping his appointment with the clerk and, while Brand was waiting, Fardein killed and robbed him. When Cerlo came, Fardein must still have been lurking behind the shed and the mason didn't see him, or Brand's body, which could have been on the quarry floor by that time. The beggar child said the man with the lantern just stood atop the cliff face—presumably waiting for Brand—and then left. Fardein must have seen, and recognised, the mason, from his hiding place.

"I think it more than likely that Brand's purse contained money from King Stephen's reign and when Fardein—knowledgeable about coins from his work in Tasser's manufactory—later examined the contents of the purse he realised, just as you did, Sir Gerard, that they must have come from a treasure trove. This notion would have been reinforced by the age of the jewellery Brand took to Tasser to sell. Since Fardein had already killed for profit, it indicates he was a greedy and unscrupulous man. I think he surmised there might be more coins or valuables to be had and approached Cerlo and demanded a share, perhaps threatening to reveal what he knew if Cerlo refused to comply.

"That was a fatal mistake. The mason not only seems to have been truly outraged by Brand's death, he also had to ensure his complicity in not reporting the trove was protected. After Fardein approached the mason, Cerlo killed him."

"The mason was foolish to kill the apprentice in the same manner as the clerk," Bassett said. "It made it obvious there was a link between the two crimes."

"I think Cerlo saw it as fair reprisal for Brand's death. The mason is not, I believe, dishonest by nature, nor the type that would willingly take another man's life. I think it is his desperate circumstances—his failing eyesight and the imminent loss of his livelihood—that led him to conspire with Brand. He could not foresee their actions would lead to murder."

"But all this is conjecture, de Marins," Nicolaa said. "What makes you believe the mason and the clerk were even acquainted with each other, let alone had common knowledge of a treasure trove?"

"That puzzled me, too, lady," Bascot replied, "until I remembered that de Stow told me he had arranged for remedial work to be done on the mint and that Alexander, the master builder at the cathedral, mentioned he had given Cerlo leave to do private work around the town. I have just spoken to Alexander. One of the jobs that Cerlo did was a repair on the wall surrounding the moneyer's forge."

"And the mint is the very place where Brand was employed," Gerard growled. "It all fits, just as you say, de Marins. The mason discovers a cache of coin and jewellery, hidden there perhaps by a moneyer during the battle between King Stephen and Matilda's forces here in Lincoln. Either the mason tells the clerk, or the clerk is present when the treasure is uncovered, and they decide to keep it for themselves. Brand would know it would not be an easy task to exchange such old coins for new, but the jewellery would not be so closely scrutinised, so he takes it to Tasser, spinning him some tale about it being part of an inheritance. Then he and the mason split the proceeds."

Gerard began to pace up and down the aisle between the perches. His sudden movement disturbed the hawks and they grew restless, flapping their wings and bobbing up and down in agitation. "Because the coins could not be so easily disposed of, the pair must have decided to wait until they could find a way to do so safely. Peter Brand was going to Grantham, to visit his mother. It is possible he was taking the coins to Cerlo, so the mason could keep them safe while the clerk was away from his lodgings in de Stow's house." The sheriff's brow furrowed in concentration as he thought the probable sequence of events through.

Finally, he came to a standstill, hands clenched together in a fist behind his back. "But where are the coins now? They were not among Fardein's belongings; he must have hidden them elsewhere. May Christ's angels weep," Camville swore angrily, "they could be anywhere. This coil has more twists and turns than the course of a startled hare."

"It could be that Cerlo retrieved the coins when he killed Fardein," Bascot said. "If you will give me your warrant, I will arrest the mason and search his house. It is a small dwelling; there are not many places he could hide them."

"You shall gladly have my warrant, de Marins," Camville replied. "And let us hope your search will finally reveal the truth of this matter."

Twenty-eight

✦

WHILE BASCOT WAITED FOR A GROOM TO SADDLE mounts for the two men-at-arms that were to accompany him to arrest Cerlo, the bells of the cathedral tolled the hour of Sext and the Templar realised it was time for the midday meal. As outside servants began to make their way towards the hall, Gianni descended the steps of the forebuilding and ran across the bail towards him.

When Gianni reached his master, the boy quickly made the sign they used to communicate a desire for private speech—Gianni pointed at Bascot, then at his own mouth, and meshed the fingers of both his hands together. The Templar glanced towards the stable door and saw the grooms were still inside; it would be a few minutes yet before they appeared with mounts for the waiting soldiers. He asked Gianni if his message was urgent and the boy seesawed one of his hands back and forth—it might be. Bascot motioned for him to move a little to one side and asked what he had to tell.

Gianni pulled his wax tablet and stylus loose of the strap that held them to his belt and, with a combination of gestures and written words, conveyed the essence of the conversation he had overheard between Miles de Laxton and Ralph of Turville and how they had spoken of the exchanger, Walter Legerton, being in debt due to gaming losses. The boy then added a supposition of his own, recalling the list that he and his master had found among Tasser's records, the page where the silversmith had appended four single letters with substantial sums written beside each one. One of these, Gianni recalled, had been the letter *L*. Could it be that the exchanger was in debt to the silversmith?

Bascot considered the question. Usury was considered a grave sin if the person who loaned the money was a Christian; most moneylenders were of the Jewish faith. But that did not mean wealthy members of the Christian populace did not engage in the practice; they merely increased the actual sum of money loaned to include an amount of interest and any agreements that were drawn up, whether verbal or written, stipulated the higher sum as the amount that had been borrowed. Still, such practise was frowned upon and most men of means would not be tempted to engage in it. Tasser, however, had no such scruples. It was quite likely he indulged in usury and Bascot imagined his rate of interest would be a high one.

"You are probably correct, Gianni," Bascot said to the boy. "But even if you are, I do not think it has any bearing on the murders. I am on my way now to arrest Cerlo, the mason. It was he, I think, who found the hidden cache of valuables and was involved in the slayings of both men."

Bascot looked up and saw the soldiers were waiting for him, standing beside the saddled horses. Gianni nodded his understanding with a dejected look as he wiped the surface of the wax tablet clean and replaced it on his belt.

"Your information will still be of interest to Sheriff Camville," Bascot said consolingly. "If Tasser is practicing usury, the evidence you have uncovered will strengthen the charges against him. Sir Gerard will be pleased with your information."

Somewhat comforted, Gianni watched the Templar mount his horse and then, as he had been told to do, went to the barracks to await his master's return.

When Bascot and the two men-at-arms entered the Minster grounds, it was just as crowded as it had been earlier that morning. As they approached the front of the cathedral, Bascot saw Cerlo standing just outside the entrance in conversation with Alexander. The mason was facing the route along which the Templar and two men-at-arms were riding and, as they neared, Bascot saw him screw up his eyes and stare over Alexander's shoulder in their direction. The builder turned to see what had attracted his companion's attention and, as he did so, Cerlo turned away and broke into a run, heading for the corner of the church. Bascot knew that if he disappeared out of sight around the side of the building, he would have a good chance of being lost in the crowd. He called to one of the men-at-arms to head Cerlo off.

The soldier dug his heels into his mount and quickly barred the mason's path. Cerlo turned, saw any other escape route was blocked, and began to scramble up one of the ladders the workmen had been using earlier to investigate the cause of the leaking gutter. The Templar slid his horse to a halt.

The mason climbed like a monkey, his long years of working atop ladders giving him an agility most men did not possess. On the ground, passersby stopped to stare at the knight and two soldiers, and then gazed upwards at the climbing figure. Alexander also watched, mouth agape, as did a couple of canons who had been on the point of entering the cathedral.

"I can get an archer from the castle, Sir Bascot," one of the men-at-arms offered. "He can try to bring the mason down with an arrow shot."

"No," Bascot said as one of the clerics overheard the soldier's suggestion and began to protest vociferously, saying they were in the precincts of a house of God and it would be sacrilege to commit such violence. "Wait here. I'll go up."

"You can't." The words burst from the other man-at-arms, the soldier forgetting Bascot's rank at the danger in the Templar's proposal. Belatedly he remembered himself and, a dark flush rising on his cheeks, added, "Sir Bascot, all the mason has to do is wait until you're halfway up and push the ladder away. It will be certain injury or death to try."

The Templar gave the man-at-arms a wry smile. "I am well aware of that, but I do not think he will try to cause me harm. Wait here and keep the crowd back."

The two soldiers nodded, their faces plainly showing their doubt of Bascot's opinion, but they did as he ordered and cleared the area around the base of the ladder as the Templar put his foot on the bottom rung.

Bascot went up slowly. Having taken part in many assaults on the walls of enemy castles during his youth, and later in the Holy Land, he had no fear of heights, but the loss of half his vision always caused a momentary dizziness whenever he was up high. He took the first dozen rungs at an easy pace until his eye adjusted to the changed perspective and then began to climb more rapidly.

Looking up, he could see Cerlo above him, kneeling behind the low stone curb that ran along the edge of the roof and perhaps twenty feet from the top of the ladder at the corner of the building. Behind the mason the roof rose steeply, culminating in one of the bell towers. The sky above was as murkily grey as the sheets of lead that covered the roof. As Bascot ascended, the breeze that had been blowing gently at ground level increased in intensity and stung his eye, making it water for a moment. Above him, Cerlo's head was turned slightly to one side as he peered at the Templar through his distorted vision, but he made no move towards the top of the ladder and Bascot began to breathe more easily. He had been right in his assumption that violence did not come naturally to Cerlo. The mason had no wish to attack the men who had come to arrest him, just to escape them.

The distance from the ground to the edge of the roof was perhaps sixty-five feet and, as the Templar climbed, he passed the top of a smaller door set beside the main entrance, then a frieze supporting a row of decorative pillars, and finally a ledge on which rested larger columns topped with small curved arches of stone. When he reached the lip of the roof he came to a halt alongside the stone gargoyle that Alexander suspected of being damaged. The gargoyle was a hideous creature, half man and half bat, with distended wings and a face of extreme ugliness. It leered at Bascot with its bulbous eyes, the contemptuous curl of its overlarge mouth set in a mocking grimace. From between the gargoyle's lips a tongue protruded. It was almost the length of a man's arm and formed the spout over which water from the eaves would gush. For all its grotesqueness, the stone face was wonderfully carved, with a delicacy that made it seem as though it would spring to life at any moment.

"Don't come any nearer, Sir Bascot," Cerlo shouted, pulling a lump hammer from a loop on his belt and raising it threateningly.

Bascot spoke to the mason in even tones. "Come down, Cerlo. You cannot escape."

"What, come down so's the sheriff can hang me from a noose?" Cerlo retorted. "I'd rather die here where I spent most of my life working." He pointed to the gargoyle. "See that, I made that, I did, for Bishop Hugh. He said I was one of the finest masons he'd ever seen. And I'd still be one if this accursed blight had not struck my eyes."

The mason peered down at Bascot. "I knew you'd figure it out, right from that first day in the quarry. All the folk in town say how clever you are, and they're right. I thought that little beggar girl at the gate might have seen me on the night Brand was killed and when one of the stonecutters said he'd seen you talkin' to her, I knew it wouldn't be long before you come after me. And then Master Alexander said you'd been askin' about where I worked. . . ."

"I know you didn't kill Peter Brand—"

The mason cut Bascot words short. "No, but you knows I killed that murderin' bastard of an apprentice. And you knows about the treasure we found, don't you?"

Bascot made no reply and the mason nodded his head as he saw his conjecture was correct. "Fardein figured it out about the cache, too," Cerlo said, "and he was so greedy to get more that he swallowed my promise to change the money he'd taken from Peter into new coin and give him another full pouch besides. He thought I was just a thick-witted dolt. Followed right willingly outside the city walls, he did, and gave me the silver without a qualm, then held out his hand for his bloodstained booty." The mason gave a short bark of bitter laughter. "The rotten sod never dreamed for one moment as how he'd soon be just as dead as the lad. I took no pleasure in killin' him, but it was a just reward for his murdering Brand. We wouldn't have involved the boy if we'd known he'd come to harm."

Bascot kept silent. Cerlo's use of the plural "we" was puzzling. It implied that yet another person was involved in discovering the trove apart from Brand.

The mason was almost sobbing with anger as he went on. "I didn't know Brand was dead until I found his body on the morning of Christ's Mass. Young Peter didn't deserve to die. He was nobbut a lad wantin' to earn a few pennies so he could wed the girl he loved. He had nothin' to do with any of the other, nothin' at all."

"Do you mean Brand didn't know anything about the trove you found at the mint?"

Bascot's question jolted the mason and his face took on a look of surprise, which was quickly replaced by an expression of grim humour.

"At the mint?" he said disbelievingly. "Mebbe you ain't as clever as I reckoned, Sir Bascot. 'Twasn't at the mint we found all that silver and gold."

"Then where was it? And who was with you if it wasn't Brand?" Bascot asked.

Cerlo shook his head, almost sadly. "I'll not tell you," he said. "If the only ones you knows about is me and the clerk, then I'll not betray someone as has never done me any harm. And I'll not see him, nor me, swing from the sheriff's noose, neither."

The mason rose from his crouching position and, dropping the hammer onto the slope of the roof, stepped up onto the low curb in front of him. Bascot drew in his breath sharply as he realised Cerlo's intent.

Pushing aside the questions burning in his mind, the Templar attempted to dissuade the mason from his deadly purpose. "Cerlo, to kill yourself is a mortal sin. You will burn in the flames of hell."

"Reckon I'm already bound there, Sir Bascot, for killing Fardein."

"You can confess to a priest, obtain absolution," Bascot said desperately.

Cerlo laughed. "God might pardon me, but the sheriff won't. I'll still hang."

"What about your wife, your daughter and grandchildren?" Bascot said harshly, gauging his chances of preventing the mason from jumping. He knew it was hopeless; he was too far away to grab hold of the man and, even if he were closer, his precarious position on top of ladder would most likely send him to his death as well if he made the attempt. "You will deny yourself the right to a life in heaven. Is it fair to refuse your family the hope of joining you there?"

"I reckon as how they'd a been better off without me in this earthly life," Cerlo replied. "'Twill most like be the same in the hereafter."

So saying, and with one final look at the gargoyle, he stepped off the roof and out into open space. He did not scream, and the only noise that could be heard was a collective gasp from the spectators below and the dull thud of his body hitting the ground.

By the time Bascot descended the ladder, a crowd had gathered around Cerlo's corpse. Most were standing a little back from the body, looking in horror at the blood trickling from the mason's nose and the terrible way his legs were crumpled beneath him. Cerlo's eyes were open, but a canon dropped to his knees beside the dead man and gently closed them as Bascot pushed his way through the crowd. The priest looked up at the Templar with a sorrowful face and said, "We are all witness that he died of his own volition. I wish I could give his soul ease, but I cannot."

Bascot nodded. Absolution and Extreme Unction could not be administered to a suicide. The mason would go to meet his Maker unshriven and be buried in unconsecrated ground. The Templar felt a deep sorrow for the unfortunate man.

As Alexander ordered two of his workmen to bring some means of conveying Cerlo's body to the death house at the Priory of All Saints, and the canon ordered a secondary to disperse the crowd, Bascot considered what the mason had said in the moments before he stepped off the roof. It was not likely that Cerlo, about to take his own life, had lied. From the few words he had spoken it would appear that Bascot's conjecture about the murders had been correct—Fardein had killed Brand and Cerlo had subsequently murdered Fardein—but his supposition that the trove had been buried in the mint was completely erroneous. The mason had also said that another person was involved, someone he would not name. The Templar again went

through the steps that had led him to conclude that
Cerlo had been involved in the murders—his questioning of the mason and his uneasy answers, how the beggar child told of seeing three men in the quarry, how
Alexander had said Cerlo had done some renovation
work on a wall in the mint. . . . There he stopped. He
had not let Alexander name all the places where Cerlo
had carried out his extraneous work. Once Bascot
heard mention of the mint, he had not waited to hear
the other sites on the list. Castigating himself for being
precipitous, he walked over to where the master builder
was sombrely watching Cerlo's body being laid on a
makeshift bier.

"I must ask you to consult your records once again,
Master Alexander," he said. "And urgently."

Twenty-nine

❖–I–❖

WELL OVER AN HOUR HAD PASSED BY THE TIME
Bascot returned to the castle. During that time, he had
sent the two men-at-arms to report the mason's death
to Gerard Camville and reviewed the list of additional
work Cerlo had carried out with Alexander. Once he
finished speaking to the builder, he went to see the
mason's widow.

Afterwards, as he left Cerlo's house in Masons Row
and rode back through the Minster to the castle ward,
the sky fulfilled its promise of threatened rain and large
drops of moisture began to fall. Hastening into the
keep, he went immediately to the sheriff's chamber
and found Camville impatiently awaiting his arrival.
With the sheriff were Nicolaa and their son, Richard.

Camville greeted Bascot testily, but his choler was
mollified when the Templar dropped a large leather
purse onto the sheriff's wine table. Loosening the neck
of the scrip, Bascot spilled out the contents. A stream
of silver pennies burst forth, all newly bright and

stamped with the image of King Stephen. In the glow from the fire and the candles set around the room, they had an almost lascivious gleam.

"So there *was* a trove," Camville said with satisfaction, picking up one of the coins. "And you were correct, de Marins, about the mason being the one who found it."

"Yes, lord, but I was in error about where it was discovered. And also in thinking that the clerk was closely involved," Bascot replied. He paused and then added, "I have just been speaking to Cerlo's wife. From what she told me I believe these coins and the jewellery comprise only a small part of the cache. I am certain there is more."

Camville swore and let out a grunt of dismay. Nicolaa and her son exchanged a worried glance as Bascot went on to relate what Cerlo had said to him before he leapt to his death.

"It was Fardein who killed Brand and was in turn murdered by Cerlo," Bascot said, "but from what the mason said to me, it is clear that it was someone other than the clerk who was party to the trove's discovery. And the cache was not, as I thought, secreted in the mint."

"Are you sure the mason was telling the truth?" Camville asked sceptically.

"He was about to take his own life, lord. I do not think he would lie," Bascot replied.

The sheriff nodded and Bascot continued. "After Cerlo killed himself, I realised I had not waited for Alexander to give me a complete list of places where the mason had done extra work. I asked Alexander to again consult his list and tell me the sites I had not given him a chance to mention. There were six in all, four of which were only minor repairs to outside steps or the like and so not pertinent. One of the other two was the mint, but the sixth place is where I now believe Cerlo must have uncovered the treasure."

"And where was it?" Nicolaa asked.

"The exchanger's manor house at Canwick," Bascot replied. There was surprise on the faces of all who were listening as he continued. "Cerlo repaired the floor in one of the smaller rooms of the house. The stone flags in one corner were sinking and needed removing so the ground could be shored up and the flags relaid. Considering the age of the manor house, it is quite conceivable this portion of floor was part of the original building and, if I remember correctly, lady, I believe you said it was erected in the early part of King Stephen's reign, about sixty years ago."

As Nicolaa nodded her confirmation, Bascot went on. "So it is conceivable that the coins and jewellery could have been buried by whoever was in the possession of the manor house at that time. If that person died without revealing the secret of his hiding place, the valuables would have lain undiscovered until the mason found them when he repaired the floor."

"Why do you think there is more treasure?" Richard Camville asked.

"Because of what Cerlo's wife told me," Bascot explained. "It was she who gave me the sack. She claimed—and I believe her—that the mason never revealed to her where they came from, only that they were token of a larger fortune to come. She gave them to me willingly and told me the little she knew without hesitation."

As Bascot related what Cerlo's widow had said to him,

her face came into his mind's eye. She had already known of her husband's death by the time he had ridden to Masons Row and stopped in front of the small house she and Cerlo had shared for so many years. One of the quarrymen had been in the Minster grounds when the mason leapt to his death and hastened to tell her. When Bascot arrived, she was resigned rather than distraught, almost as though Cerlo's demise had not been a surprise. She immediately handed the sack of coins to Bascot.

"Cerlo told me I was to keep these by me if aught should happen to him," she said. "And that I was to rub them with sand to age them and change them slowly, just one at a time so it would not be noticed how old they were. But I do not want them, lord. They are cursed. Because of them three men are dead, and one of them my husband." Her face, although unstained by tears, showed a deep weariness.

Bascot told Camville and the others what Cerlo's wife had then related. "She said that Cerlo had been morose about his failing eyesight up until a few weeks ago which, according to Alexander's records, was when the mason worked on the floor at Legerton's manor house. About that time, he came home one night and told her they no longer had to worry about their future because he would soon have enough money to buy a little house of their own. There would also be enough silver, he said, to see them through the years they had left and to give their daughter assistance as well. She pressed him to tell her how this could be so, but Cerlo would not, telling her it was not safe for her to know where the funds were coming from.

"She then told me that on the night Brand died, she had burned herself with hot pottage, just as Cerlo claimed, but the mason had lied when he assured me he had not gone to the quarry after tending her injury. His wife said that as soon as she was resting comfortably, Cerlo grabbed a lantern and rushed outside. He did not return until more than an hour had passed. When he finally came back, he was shaking his head with anxiety and continued in that worrisome state until the morning of Christ's Mass when he found the clerk's body.

"After that, according to his widow, Cerlo's mood changed. His former attitude of hopeful expectancy became one of anger and despair. Only a day or two later he gave his wife the coins and told her they were to be used for her security if he should no longer be able to provide for her."

Bascot looked at his listeners. "I think that must have been about the time when Fardein, having realised from the contents of Brand's scrip that a trove had been discovered, approached Cerlo and demanded a share. Cerlo, driven by the desperate need to keep the horde a secret and enraged by Brand's death, killed Fardein. When the mason was told I had been seen speaking to the beggar girl, and Alexander subsequently mentioned that I had been asking about the places he had worked, Cerlo realised his involvement in the murders and the hiding of the trove was uncovered. Rather than be hung for his crimes, he decided to end his life in a manner of his own choosing. But before he died, he unintentionally let slip that it was not Brand who was his accomplice, but some other person he refused to name."

Bascot pointed to the pile of silver coins. "There is five pounds there, all but one penny. The missing coin is the one my servant found on the cliff face. Cerlo's wife did not know why the clerk intended to give them to her husband on the night Brand was killed, but now we know another person is involved, I would guess the coins were security against a forthcoming share of the profits. There were no other coins or valuables in Cerlo's house, so the rest of the cache must have been retained by his accomplice."

Richard Camville looked at the coins with distaste. "Five pounds would be a fortune to a mason, whose wage is only three pence a day. It would constitute more than one year's pay. Yet it is a paltry sum when balanced against the lives of three men."

"If the trove was found at the Canwick manor house, then it must be Legerton who conspired with the mason," Camville said.

As Bascot nodded in agreement, Nicolaa made an objection to their surmise. "But surely, no matter how large the cache, Legerton would not take such a risk," she said. "The betrayal of his oath of office will carry a heavy punishment, perhaps castration or blinding. No amount of treasure is worth such a gamble."

"I think it is his nature to take risks, lady," Bascot countered. "I have recently learned that Legerton is an inveterate chance-taker, although he is, unfortunately, an unsuccessful one. His passion for the gaming tables has led him deeply into debt. If the value of the horde is considerable, I am sure he would have been unable to resist making use of it as a way to solve his financial difficulties."

Bascot related the conversation Gianni had overheard about Legerton's gambling debts and of the list of initials among Tasser's records. "I have yet to ask the silversmith if the initials are his cryptic way of recording the names of those that borrow money from him, but I think it is likely, and if so, then it is also probable Legerton is one of them. The sum was quite substantial—almost one hundred pounds."

Camville nodded. "Add that debt to the money he owes for his gambling losses and the amount is more than enough to tempt a man to betray his oath of office, and his king."

"But how did he intend to realise any wealth from the cache?" Richard wondered. "Even though he was able—by sending Brand to Tasser—to gain a few pounds for the jewellery, the coins would be much harder to dispose of."

"It is possible he intended to take the coins to London or some other large town outside of Lincoln and exchange or sell them to a man of Tasser's ilk," Bascot suggested. "If the horde is large enough, it might even be worthwhile to take them abroad—to Brittany or Ireland. Their provenance and age would be of no concern in a foreign country. If he did that, he would gain the full value of the silver."

"If he was devious enough to hide the discovery of the trove, he is cunning enough to formulate a scheme to benefit from it," Camville said. "I am convinced Legerton is the one we seek. It only remains to snare the bastard."

The sheriff placed his wine cup on the table, his brow furrowed in concentration. "These coins and the jewellery constitute solid evidence that a trove had been found and not reported. The testimony of Alexander's records and the mason's wife point to it having been secreted on Legerton's property. Whether or not the exchanger was actively involved in the trove's discovery is immaterial. Legerton still bears responsibility for crimes that take place on his land."

"Are you going to issue a warrant for his arrest, Father?" Richard asked.

"I am," Camville said. "It is time this matter was brought out into the open. It is the only way I can ensure the taint of complicity does not sully my reputation." He addressed the Templar. "Are you willing to serve the warrant, de Marins?"

"I am, lord," Bascot replied.

"Then do so, and with all haste. It is likely the cache is still at Canwick; it would be difficult to transport it elsewhere in complete secrecy. Nevertheless, once news of Cerlo's suicide spreads, Legerton may fear the mason named his accomplice before he died and try to move the rest of the trove to a more secure hiding place. His manor house must be searched before he has a chance to do that."

"Unless Legerton is gaming, he will be at Canwick, since the exchange is not open today," Nicolaa said.

"Are you sure, Wife?" Camville asked her.

Nicolaa nodded. "He is not due into his office until tomorrow," she said. "And, unlike de Stow, Legerton is not an industrious man. Even when he is abroad in Lincoln, he never goes into the exchange unless it is one of the scheduled opening days, insisting any who wish to see him make an appointment."

"Then go to Canwick now, de Marins, before he is forewarned by the mason's suicide. Take de Laxton with you and an escort of men-at-arms from the barracks. Search Legerton's manor house and, if he is there, arrest him. If fortune is with us, you will find the trove."

Thirty

◆I◆

As BASCOT AND THE MEN OF THE ESCORT LEFT THE bail, Walter Legerton was sitting on the dais in the hall of his manor house. He was in a foul temper and roundly cursed a servant who brought him a cup of wine for spilling some as it was placed on the table.

Morosely the exchanger surveyed the trappings of his hall—the exquisitely stitched tapestries on the walls, the fine pewter candlestick holders and the expensive silver cup out of which he was drinking—and realised that none of these acquisitions had made him a happy man. The manor house had cost far more to renovate than he had calculated and the wealth he had acquired from the sale of his father's silver manufactory had been gone almost before he had time to count it. He should have listened to his sister when she cautioned him against buying it; Silvana had inherited their father's canniness with money and her advice had been sound. He prayed she would never discover how deeply in debt he truly was, nor the means by which he had tried to recoup his losses.

His gaze wandered over the people gathered in the hall. All the guests he had entertained at the season of Christ's Mass had gone home, thank God, but there was still a sizeable number of servants in attendance, far more than necessary for a manor house the size of this one. He would be forced to dismiss many of them if his schemes came to naught.

He saw Simon Partager enter the hall, a sheaf of documents in his hand, and the sour bile of anger rose in his throat. Yesterday the assayer had come to him and given notice of his intent to leave Legerton's employ, saying he had been offered a position as assayer in a silver mine in the far north of England and had accepted it. Since the salary for the new post would be far less than Simon earned at the exchange, Legerton supposed his affair with Iseult might have influenced the assayer's decision to leave Lincoln. If so, the resentment was misplaced. If he had not bedded the beautiful, but empty-headed, wife of his assayer, she would not have been slow to find another paramour. She was as lascivious as she was greedy, and would bed any man who took her fancy, especially if a prospective lover promised to shower her with gifts. Partager would be hard pressed to keep Iseult satisfied on the pittance he would receive at the mine. Walter had no doubt she would soon find a new lover wherever her husband took her, even if it was to the desolation of the Northumbria moors.

His recollection of the incident prompted him to remember another event of the previous day, when Helias de Stow had come to his office to discuss the arrest of

Tasser. De Stow was full of worry about the money he, at Legerton's urging, had borrowed from the silversmith, fearing his indebtedness would be revealed during the course of the sheriff's investigation into the recent murders. If it became known that he had dealings with such an unscrupulous man as Tasser, Helias said fearfully, he would be in jeopardy of losing his post, since it would not be considered appropriate for a man who had charge of money belonging to the king's treasury to have traffic with a person of such ill repute. Legerton forced from his mind the guilty knowledge that de Stow would not have needed to borrow money if he had been given the funds the Exchange in London had sent to cover the cost of replacing equipment in the mint. He had not really meant to appropriate it, only borrow it for a few days, but he had lost it all in one night at the gaming tables and did not have the funds to replace it.

Legerton had tried to reassure de Stow, telling the moneyer it was unlikely his indebtedness to Tasser would be revealed, but he had done it halfheartedly. De Stow's concerns seemed small in comparison with his own.

The exchanger banged his cup on the table as a signal for it to be refilled. As a manservant hurried forward with a jug of wine, Partager approached the dais, the parcel of papers still clutched in his hand and a look of self-righteous determination on his face. Legerton groaned. Was he about to be given more distressing news?

ISEULT PARTAGER ALSO WATCHED HER HUSBAND advance up the hall with a flicker of unease. Simon had told her earlier that day to pack up her clothing and any other possessions she wished to take with her and be ready to leave for Northumbria in the morning. Iseult had made a determined protest, but it had fallen on deaf ears. Simon had been adamant they were leaving; she had even tried to detract him from his plan with a bold invitation to lovemaking, but he had roughly thrust her aside, saying he had no time for such games. Never before had she seen Simon in such an inflexible mood, and it frightened her.

Although her husband had not mentioned Legerton's name, she thought it must be something to do with the exchanger that was at the root of Simon's purpose in leaving. Since he had never given any sign that he knew of her liaison with his employer, she doubted it could be that, but something he said had struck a chord of disquietude within her. It had been when he was telling her to pack up her clothing and had noticed, laying on a table in their chamber, the tawdry cloak clasp that Legerton had given her on the first day of the New Year.

Picking the brooch up, Simon had thrown it on the floor and ground it under the heel of his boot, saying Legerton would have been better advised to have kept the money he spent on the gift in his scrip for, when it became known he fraternized with people of unsavoury reputation, he would lose his post and need every penny he could find.

Iseult was not sure what he meant, but she knew Legerton loved to gamble and often lost money at the gaming tables. Simon was the exchanger's clerk as well as his assayer and therefore privy to Legerton's personal accounts. Had her lover become indebted to men of bad character, ones who had no qualms about making his losses publically known, thereby damaging his reputation so badly the officials in London would deem him untrustworthy? Or was it something to do with Tasser, the silversmith who had been arrested and, it was said, would soon be charged with murdering his apprentice? Surely Legerton could not be involved in that affair? Or could he?

SILVANA, TOO, WAS IN A STATE OF WORRY. AS SHE shepherded her two young nephews—boys of eight and ten years—into the hall to take their seats for the evening meal, she looked to where her brother sat and saw the deep worry lines creasing his face. Even though he thought her unaware of his penchant for games of chance, she knew of it, and that he sadly lacked the skill to win. He had always been impulsive and far too optimistic for his own good. She loved him dearly, but her affection did not make her blind to his faults. Recently she had come to suspect he was in far deeper debt than he admitted and had taken drastic measures to try to remedy the situation, such as borrowing money to stake at the gaming tables in a desperate bid to recoup his losses. If this was what he had done, and it became known, it was more than likely he would be dismissed from his post. If that happened, Walter would be forced to sell the manor house and buy a home of much humbler proportions; perhaps even go to work for an employer in a gold or silver manufactory.

For herself, Silvana had no fear of poverty; her requirements were small and she would stand by her

brother and his sons however low in station they became. But she worried about the effect of such an outcome on her brother. The loss of the manor house
would be a devastating blow to his pride and she could
well imagine that many of those who had curried his
favour while he appeared to be rich would quickly turn
aside when it became known he was not. The verse in
the Bible, in Proverbs, warning of pride coming before
destruction and a haughty spirit before a fall would
most certainly prove to be true in her brother's case.
She hoped he would not have to learn such a lesson
but, if he did, perhaps it might teach him a modicum of
humility.

WHILE BASCOT WAITED FOR DE LAXTON AND THE
castle men-at-arms to assemble, he paid a short visit
to the cell where Warner Tasser was incarcerated. The
silversmith, weary of his confinement, willingly confirmed Gianni's suspicion that the list he and his master had found was a list of debtors, and that the *L*
identified Legerton. When asked about the other cryp-
tically notated initials, the Templar was surprised to
learn one of them was Helias de Stow. Bascot was
sure King John would not be pleased to learn that the
integrity of two men entrusted to oversee the purity
of his coinage was fallible. Gerard Camville, on the
other hand, would derive great pleasure from the information.

By the time the Templar had finished questioning
Tasser, Miles de Laxton had assembled a half dozen
men-at-arms in front of the stables, and the small cavalcade set off for Canwick. The short winter day had

begun to darken with the approach of evening by the time they reached the bridge that spanned the river Witham and they called a halt while one of the soldiers used flint and tinder to light a torch. As the man-at-arms held the flaming brand aloft, the rain that had been spattering all day began to fall in earnest. Their cloaks were soon soaked with moisture.

As they rode towards Canwick, Bascot explained to de Laxton the purpose of their journey. Now the sheriff had decided to charge Legerton with concealment of hidden treasure, it would be only a short time before the whole of Lincoln knew of it and Miles needed to be aware of the nature of their duty.

De Laxton had listened openmouthed as Bascot explained how the coin found on the cliff top had led the sheriff to suspect a hidden cache of valuables from King Stephen's reign was involved in the murder of Peter Brand. He then briefly recounted the torturous route that led to knowledge of the involvement of Cerlo and eventually to Legerton's manor house.

"I wonder the exchanger did not use some of the treasure to pay off his debts. There are a couple of men of my acquaintance that would be more than pleased to receive the sum he owes them," de Laxton said when Bascot finished.

"Legerton could not pay them in old coin without it being remarked upon. Only the jewellery could be turned into current coinage by selling it to someone such as Tasser. Legerton could not take it to the silversmith himself without Tasser becoming suspicious as to why the exchanger needed to borrow money when he had such valuables to sell, and if Cerlo, a lowly mason, had taken it, the silversmith would have immediately become suspicious of the jewellery's provenance. I think the pair, knowing how desperate Brand was to save enough money to wed a girl in Grantham, paid the clerk to take it to Tasser. He was an educated lad and not from Lincoln, his story of the jewellery being part of an inheritance would seem plausible."

"But how did they intend to realise any profit from the cache if it could not be exchanged anywhere?" de Laxton asked.

"I think Legerton intended to wait until he could travel outside of Lincoln," Bascot replied, "or even outside the realm, perhaps, and arrange for it to be exchanged or sold. And such a scheme would have worked if Brand had not been murdered by Fardein. Cerlo, I think, would have been content to wait for his share until Legerton had made such a trip, Brand was happy with the payment he received for his involvement, and Legerton looked forward to having enough money to pay off his debts and resume his extravagant lifestyle. It was a well-laid plan, and only foiled by the greed of Tasser's apprentice."

"And the coins Brand was taking to the mason must have been Legerton's surety he would fulfill his part of the bargain with Cerlo," de Laxton said. "If the exchanger had betrayed the agreement, the mason had evidence of an unreported cache. That would be enough to ensure Legerton turned over his share."

"I think so," Bascot replied. "I am not certain why the mason did not take some of the coins at the time the trove was found, but it could be they did not come to any arrangement until later."

"And you believe the trove is still on the exchanger's property?" de Laxton asked.

"It would be difficult to move sacks of coin and valuables to another location without someone in Legerton's household taking notice. The sheriff thinks it likely it has been kept in the place it was found," Bascot replied and, as the gates of the manor house came into view added, "We will soon find out if he is right."

Thirty-one

✦┼✦

THE GATE IN THE PALISADE ENCIRCLING THE PROPERTY was open when Bascot and de Laxton arrived. Ignoring the shout of the gateward, they swept through the portal, the mounted soldiers close behind. As they dismounted in front of the manor house, a manservant came running out, alarmed by shouts of warning from the guard on the gate. Bascot pushed the manservant aside and strode into the hall.

When they entered, Legerton was sitting at the table on the dais in conversation with Simon Partager, who was standing beside the exchanger's chair. Both men looked up in surprise, as did Legerton's sister, Silvana, who was directing servants in erecting trestle tables for the evening meal, as the two knights and troop of soldiers burst into the room. Sitting at one of the tables was Iseult Partager, and her huge blue eyes grew round with astonishment at sight of the armed contingent.

"Sir Bascot," Legerton exclaimed, "what is the meaning—"

The Templar cut him short. "I am here to arrest you, Master Legerton, on a charge of complicity in concealment of a treasure trove. You are to be taken to the castle for questioning and your property searched."

As he spoke, Bascot pulled the warrant Camville had given him before he left the castle from the inside of his tunic. The sheriff's seal dangled from the parchment. Legerton gaped at it in astonishment.

"Treasure trove?" he gasped. "I know nothing of any trove."

"Do you deny that you employed a stonemason named Cerlo to carry out repairs to your property and that, while he did so, he found a hidden cache of valuables? Or that you agreed with him to suppress the discovery?"

All of Legerton's bombastic self-assurance drained from him. In a bewildered fashion, he repeated his denial. "I know nothing of this matter, nothing at all."

"Your accomplice, the mason, is dead, Legerton." Beside the exchanger, Partager took a step backwards, his face ashen as Bascot went on. "But before he died he revealed the secret you shared. You will remain under guard while we search your home."

Signalling to two of the men-at-arms, he ordered them to take the exchanger prisoner. As they started for the dais Silvana stepped in front of the soldiers and blocked their passage. "It was not my brother who hired the mason, Sir Bascot," she declared defiantly. "It was me. Walter was not even here when Cerlo carried out the work. He was in London, attending a meeting of exchangers at the treasury. It was because of Walter being away that I arranged for the work to be done, so he would not be disturbed by the upheaval."

The Templar regarded her for a long moment. She
seemed composed, but he could see that her hands
were shaking and she quickly hid them from sight in
the folds of her gown. Was her claim a desperate attempt to shield her brother, Bascot wondered, or was it
the truth?

"Then, mistress, it seems it is you I must take into
custody."

"If you will," Silvana replied quietly. "But I, like my
brother, know nothing of the mason discovering a
treasure trove while he was at work here."

"So you say. But since I know he did, how do you
explain your ignorance of its existence? If the excellent
condition of this manor house is used as a rule by
which to judge your competence, I do not believe you
would leave a workman completely unsupervised. Did
you not inspect his work while it was in progress?"

"No," Silvana said, "I did not." Her tone faltered for a
moment and under the chilly gaze of Bascot's blue eye,
she looked desperately towards where her brother sat,
Simon Partager still standing by his side. All those in the
hall, the servants, de Laxton and the men-at-arms had
fallen silent at her intervention and there was a hush as
they listened to the exchange between her and the Templar.

Bascot did not give Silvana time to concoct an excuse. "I am waiting, mistress, for an explanation of
your statement," he said abruptly. "I know that Cerlo
shared his discovery of the trove with another person at
this manor. If it was not you, and you claim it was not
your brother, who was it?"

Silvana took a deep breath and steadied herself. "I
can judge the skill of a cook or a sempstress," she said,
"but to assess the competence of a mason is more the

province of a man than a woman. I asked one of my husband's employees to oversee Cerlo's work."

"And his name?" Bascot said impatiently, still not sure whether Silvana was prevaricating or simply trying to delay her brother's arrest.

"It was—"

Silvana's reply was curtailed by a cry from her brother and a shout from Simon Partager. Everyone jumped with alarm as the assayer grasped Legerton around the neck and pulled the dagger he wore from his belt. He pressed the point of the blade to the exchanger's throat.

"It was me," Partager said as he wrested Legerton to his feet and held him fast. "And I will kill this fornicating bastard if you do not let me leave here unharmed."

Iseult gave a cry of alarm at her husband's admission. The sound brought a bitter peal of laughter from Simon. "I did it for you, you bitch," he cried. "So I could have enough money to buy the baubles that entice you to other men's beds. You are nothing but a trollop, but I love you. . . ."

His words ended on a sob and Bascot, seeing Iseult's outcry had distracted her husband for a moment, took a step forward, his hand on his sword, but Simon noticed the movement and pushed the dagger deeper into Legerton's neck. A thin stream of blood began to trickle from the wound.

"Stay where you are, Templar, else I will kill him," Simon warned. "And tell that other knight and your men to keep back. It is not my intent to die, but if I must, I will take this whoreson with me."

"For the love of God," Legerton cried in a strangled tone, "do as he says, I beg of you."

Bascot motioned to de Laxton and the men-at-arms to move back a pace. Partager was wound up as tight as a crossbow ready to release its bolt. The Templar rapidly assessed the implications of the assayer's statement. It would seem Partager's wife had been playing the trollop with her husband's employer and it had been the assayer, not Legerton, who had conspired with Cerlo to conceal the discovery of the trove, hoping to buy back his wife's love with the proceeds. Now that the plan had gone awry, his jealousy and hatred of Legerton was gushing forth in full spate. He desperately wanted to kill the man who had made him a cuckold; only the fact it would require forfeit of his own life was keeping that primal urge at bay. If any of them made a move towards him, Bascot knew Partager would slice Legerton's throat open without hesitation.

Once he saw that de Laxton and the men-at-arms had obeyed the Templar's command, Partager roughly pushed the exchanger down the two shallow steps of the dais and onto the floor of the hall. Keeping a wary eye on the knights and soldiers, the assayer then dragged Legerton in the direction of the door, the knife still at his captive's throat.

"If you value this miserable cur's life, Templar, you and your men will stay here until I am well away from this accursed house. Once I am safe, I will release him."

As Partager uttered his threat, Bascot caught a flash of movement among the crowd of servants and women cowering behind one of the trestle tables. It was Silvana. While the assayer's attention was concentrated on the armed men in front of him, she darted forward and grabbed one of the heavy pewter salvers that lay on the table. Without a pause, and in one smooth motion, she swung it up in her arms and brought it crashing down on the back of his head.

Partager fell almost instantly, his eyes glazing over as he dropped to the floor. Legerton tumbled free and picked himself up, his hands clutching at the wound on his neck. Bascot quickly retrieved the knife and motioned for two of the men-at-arms to take hold of the assayer.

As they hauled the half-unconscious man to his feet, the Templar picked up the salver and handed it to Silvana.

"You may not believe you are competent to do a man's work, mistress," he said with a small smile, "but I think you are mistaken. You wielded that tray with the skill of a seasoned man-at-arms and with just as much courage. Your brother is a fortunate man to have a woman such as you for a sister."

Thirty-two

❖

IT WAS LATE IN THE EVENING BY THE TIME BASCOT and de Laxton returned to the castle with their prisoner. One of the soldiers in the escort was leading a palfrey laden with sacks containing a large quantity of coin and jewellery. When they arrived at Lincoln castle, Gerard Camville and Gilbert Bassett were waiting for them in the hall.

Once Simon Partager had been secured in a holding cell, the sheriff directed two men-at-arms to carry the sacks up to his chamber, and the barons, along with Bascot and de Laxton, followed them up the stairs. After the soldiers had completed their chore, Camville dismissed them and de Laxton opened one of the bags. It was packed with a quantity of smaller pouches, ten in all.

"We counted the coins in one of these," he said to the sheriff, lifting out a bag and hefting it. "It contains five pounds and, judging by the weight, so do all the others. That means there is fifty pounds in each of the larger sacks, of which there are four—a sum of two hundred pounds in all—as well as a pouch containing various items of jewellery. Even if the coins do not each contain a full pennyweight of silver, this is a sizeable treasure trove, to be sure."

As de Laxton removed the jewellery and laid it on a table, Bassett expelled his breath in amazement. There were at least five necklaces—comprised of heavy links of gold chain—and a half dozen brooches and cloak clasps of the same material, all encrusted with precious stones. Among them were also a number of silver thumb rings and a torque that looked to be of Celtic workmanship, with strands of silver woven in the interlocking design much favoured by that race.

Camville picked up the torque. "This will fetch a pretty price," he said, "as will the rest of it."

He and Bassett listened attentively as Bascot explained how it had not been Legerton that the mason had taken into his confidence, but the assayer, Simon Partager. After Partager had been taken prisoner, and realised there could be no escape, he revealed how the trove had been uncovered and the plans he and Cerlo had made for its disposal.

"Apparently Partager came into the chamber where Cerlo was working just as the mason had removed the tiles that covered the floor. The sacks lay just below. When the pair saw the size of the cache, it did not take long for them to come to an agreement to keep the contents. Cerlo was desperate for money to sustain himself and his wife, and Partager wanted funds to get his wife away from Lincoln and Legerton's bed. The trove seemed like a heaven-sent answer to both men's problems. They acted quickly, using the bag that contained Cerlo's work tools to carry the sacks to the assayer's room and hide them underneath some garments in his clothes chest. They had to make two or three trips over the course of the day to get it all safely stowed and be sure none of the servants noticed their comings and goings. Fortunately for them, Legerton's sister, Silvana, was keeping all the staff busy giving the house a thorough cleansing while her brother was away and Partager's wife, Iseult, had gone to Lincoln to visit her sister.

"After they had hidden the contents of the trove, Cerlo and Partager discussed how they could dispose of it. They knew the age of the coins would prevent them from being exchanged, so they decided to leave the silver, and the jewellery, in the chest while the assayer applied for a vacancy at a mine in Tynedale. Once there, under the guise of carrying out his duties, Partager had enough skill to use the mine's forge to melt the coins down slowly, just a few at a time, and fashion them into ingots. His actions would not be questioned—it is common for assayers to use a crucible for testing the purity of silver ore. Partager could then sell the ingots and the rest of the jewellery slowly, one piece at a time, to different gold- and silversmiths in one or more of the larger northern towns.

"Although it would have taken a long time to realise the full value of the trove, neither Partager nor Cerlo were in a hurry for their profit. Cerlo was content to receive a steady supply of small sums of money that Partager would bring to Lincoln once or twice a year, and the assayer simply wanted the wherewithal to keep his errant wife from straying. It might have taken them years to dispose of it all, but it would most certainly have provided an ample extra income for both men."

"Why did they decide to divulge the secret to the

clerk, Peter Brand?" Bassett asked. "Surely they were taking a grave risk by doing so."

"To secure the post at Tynedale Partager had to pay a fee of five pounds to the overseer of the mine; he would also need some silver to finance his and Iseult's journey north. He and Cerlo decided to sell a few of the smaller pieces of jewellery to cover the cost of the venture. They chose to approach Tasser because of his unsavoury reputation; even if he suspected the provenance of the items, they reckoned his greed would overcome any scruples he might have. But they were still wary—it would be best if neither of them was involved in the sale. Tasser knew Partager worked at the exchange, he would immediately wonder how the assayer had come by such sudden wealth and the same could be said of Cerlo, a lowly mason at the cathedral. If either of them attempted to carry out the transaction, they would be risking extortion by the silversmith. So they decided to use someone who was unknown to Tasser; a person who could spin the silversmith a tale about the origin of the jewellery and not be suspected of lying. Brand seemed the perfect choice—he had only lived in Lincoln for just over a year and was relatively unknown about the town. Partager had heard from other employees at the mint about the clerk's impatience to save enough money to wed a girl in Grantham and approached him. When he asked if Brand was willing to help them for a small consideration, the clerk readily agreed.

"Partager never told Brand the extent of the horde he and Cerlo had found or where they discovered it. The assayer merely said the mason had found a few bits of jewellery and one small bag of coins in the foundations of an old house near the quarry and had come to the assayer for advice on how to dispose of it.

It was Partager who fabricated the tale Brand told Tasser about inheriting the jewellery and, if Fardein had not been present when the clerk related the story, it might have worked. Tasser was suspicious, but not unduly so."

"And the coins that Brand had in his purse on the night he was murdered?" Camville asked. "Why was he taking them to the quarry?"

"Partager told Cerlo that as soon as he heard whether or not he had been awarded the position at the mine he would come to the cathedral for early-morning Mass—a service the mason always attended—and let his accomplice know the outcome. And, on the twentieth day of December, that is what the assayer did; he went to the cathedral, found Cerlo and told him the position was secured and he was expected to commence his new employment by the middle of January. He had formerly promised Cerlo, as evidence of good faith, that he would give the mason a bag of the old coins, but because he didn't want to give them to Cerlo in full view of the parishioners attending Mass in the cathedral, he said he would send Brand to the quarry with them the next day. They agreed that dusk would be the best time for the clerk to arrive; even though the quarry was shut down due to the winch being inoperative, there might be some of the quarrymen about the pit during the daylight hours. And that is why the clerk was there on the twenty-first day of December, and at that time."

"And because his wife's accident made the mason late for the appointment, Brand was killed by Fardein, who saw his chance to rob the clerk and took it," Bassett said.

"Which led the apprentice into demanding a share

MURDER FOR CHRIST'S MASS   281

in the trove from Cerlo," Bascot confirmed, "and to Fardein's death when the mason lured him outside the walls of Lincoln and killed him."

They looked at the riches contained in the sacks piled on the table. "It may be a valuable find," the Templar said, "but it has caused untold misery to many people."

"Whether it has or not, it can now be turned over to the Exchequer," Camville said with satisfaction. "I will leave it to one of their officials to try and discover if there is an heir that may have a legitimate claim to the trove, or whether they are all dead."

"I think we may have found the answer to that, Gerard," Nicolaa said from the doorway. She and Richard entered the room, the castellan holding a piece of parchment in her hand.

When both Nicolaa and her son were seated and had full cups of wine in their hands, Bascot repeated, at the castellan's request, the circumstances of how it had been discovered that it had not been Walter Legerton who had conspired with Cerlo but his assayer, Simon Partager. When he finished, the sheriff asked his wife what she had meant by her earlier statement that she knew who had secreted the cache.

"After de Marins and de Laxton left to arrest Legerton, Richard and I searched the castle archives—with John Blund's help—for records of who had owned the property at Canwick in the days of King Stephen. I remembered my father saying that my grandsire had granted the fee of a Haye property there in perpetuity to the church of St. Clement as a gesture of thanksgiving for the birth of his son. I thought that if I consulted the record of his gift, it might also give the name of the people who held other properties in the area."

This was a distinct possibility. Land was often delineated by naming those adjoining it and usually included the information of whether it was held in fee from a lord or the crown, and by whom.

Nicolaa took up the piece of parchment she had been holding. "John Blund found this. It is the record of my grandsire's donation to the abbey and mentions a property—one arpent in size—on the northern border of the Haye land. It was a small property and is recorded to have been held in fee from the see of Lincoln by one Otto, minter to the crown."

She looked up. "There were six mints in Lincoln in the days of King Stephen and Otto must have operated one of them. At that time the office of exchanger had not been instituted and moneyers not only produced the monarch's coins, they also fulfilled the office of exchanging them for new. Because of Stephen's tenuous hold on the throne and the unsettled state of the kingdom, the Exchequer was often unable to enforce the king's edicts and there was much scope for reaping illegal profits. Silver was debased with other, less precious metals and many of the coins were of short weight. Barring the few that were caught and punished for these criminal acts—and not many were charged during Stephen's reign—the rest became wealthy, mostly through embezzling royal funds. I think Otto must have been one of them. If he has any relatives still living, they would have a hard time proving he came by the contents of the trove legally."

She pointed at the sacks of silver coins. "It is quite likely all of this money should have originally been paid into the royal coffers. It seems only just that now, after so many years, it will find its way to its true destination." She glanced at her husband. "I think King John will be appreciative of your services in returning it, Gerard."

Camville gave a snort of disbelief. "It is more likely he will want proof I did not remove any of it before I despatched it to the Exchequer."

A flicker of annoyance for her husband's disparagement of the king crossed Nicolaa's face, but she did not voice her irritation, saying instead, "I cannot imagine that Legerton's part in all this will be lightly glossed over by the royal officials. Even if he is innocent of keeping the discovery of the horde secret, Simon Partager was his employee and as such, Legerton must bear some of the responsibility for his dishonesty. I have no doubt that, at the very least, he will be dismissed from his post as exchanger and ordered to pay a heavy fine."

Miles de Laxton gave a chuckle of amusement. "Legerton is deeply in debt already, lady. If he loses his post at the exchange and is fined as well, he will have no choice but to sell his manor house to settle his outstanding debts. That will force him to live in circumstances to which he is not accustomed."

"I cannot feel any empathy for him," Richard said. "He is an insufferably arrogant man. Perhaps this misfortune is God's way of punishing him for his pride."

"And for his infidelity," Nicolaa added. "If Legerton had not been bedding Partager's wife, the assayer would not have succumbed to the temptation of stealing the cache. I do not think either Partager or Cerlo were dishonest men at heart; it was desperation rather then avarice that drove them to commit their crimes."

Thirty-three

✦✦✦

THE NEXT MORNING DAWNED COLD BUT CLEAR. IT WAS
the last day Gilbert Bassett and his family—including
Ralph of Turville, his wife and son—would spend as
guests in Lincoln castle and the clement weather enabled Gerard Camville to hold the planned hawking
party before their leave-taking.

As soon as the morning meal had been served, the
hosts and their guests assembled in the bail and made
ready to depart. Even young Stephen of Turville had
been given leave to accompany the others, the only
proviso his mother attached to her reluctant permission being that he kept his ears well covered. Horses
were brought from the stables and a pack of rache and
bercelet hounds, much smaller than the large dogs
used to hunt boar or deer, came yapping and barking
from the kennels. Finally the falconer entered the
ward, his three assistants behind him, carrying the
hooded raptors on portable leather-covered perches
slung from their shoulders. The birds of prey were

hooded and sat quietly, only one or two ruffling their feathers as they were carried forward and transferred to the gauntleted wrists of the nobles.

As the cavalcade started off through the western gate, Bascot and Gianni came through the small postern door in the northern wall of the bail. They had just been attending the service of Prime in the church of St. Clement. As they crossed the empty expanse of the ward, Roget came in through the eastern gate of the castle and hailed them.

"*Hola*, de Marins," the captain called. "I have come to take Tasser back to the town gaol but, if you are agreeable, I have a wine of good vintage that I am willing to share before I do so." The former mercenary patted the wineskin that hung from his belt.

"The silversmith is to be released today?" Bascot asked.

Roget nodded. "Sir Gerard sent word to me last night that I should collect him this morning, but he is to stay in custody in the town gaol until he has paid a surety. He is to be charged with profiting from the commission of robberies."

Bascot agreed to drinking a cup of Roget's wine—the captain had an uncanny knack of being in possession of fine vintages, which, the Templar knew, were often given him by merchants about the town in gratitude for his vigilance—but first sent Gianni to report for duty in the scriptorium.

The boy raced off with the speed of an arrow shot and as Roget watched him go, amazed at the hastiness of his departure, the Templar explained the reason for Gianni's eagerness.

"He is anxious to help Lambert put the finishing touches on a manual of the gestures they have been teaching Ralph of Turville's son, Stephen. The book is to be presented to Master Stephen tonight, after the evening meal, and both Gianni and Blund's clerk are keen to have it as near to perfect as possible."

Roget gave a chuckle of amusement. "Only clerks can be that much in love with their duties," he said wryly. "If my men showed such devotion, I would think they were ailing with a sickness."

The pair walked over to the barracks; neither of them had yet broken their fast and Ernulf would have some food to accompany Roget's wine in his emergency rations.

They found the serjeant inside the long, low room that served as living quarters for the castle men-at-arms issuing orders to the soldiers that would be on guard duty on the castle walls that day. He welcomed Roget's offer to share his wine and the three men went into the cubicle. Chunks of smoked bacon and slices of cheese from Ernulf's store were laid out on a rough wooden trencher and Roget poured them all a cup of the wine he had brought. His boast of it being a good vintage had been a true one; it was full-bodied and smooth and, combined with the meat and cheese, made a good meal.

"That assayer's in a sorry state," Ernulf said to Bascot as Roget poured them each another cup of wine. "Hasn't spoken a word since de Laxton brought him in, just lies curled up in a ball in the corner of his cell. Won't even take any food or drink." He gave Bascot a speculative look. "The men that went with you to Canwick last night told me all about the treasure he stole." As Ernulf said this, Roget nodded his head. Apparently the story of Partager's arrest had spread not only through the castle, but also reached as far as the town gaol. "You going to tell us what made him steal it, or do we have to wait until we hear it at his trial? It'll be some time before the judges arrive, maybe not until after Eastertide. And the trial might not even be held in Lincoln; the king may decide to have the assayer sent to London."

Even though Partager's crime had not been one of murder, his offence of defrauding the crown was far too serious to be heard in the sheriff's court. Gerard Camville would advise the Exchequer of the crime when he despatched the contents of the trove to London, and then wait to see if the case was to be tried in Lincoln by the royal judges of the itinerant court or if he was to send Partager to London to stand trial there. The Templar was well aware of Ernulf and Roget's curiosity and felt he owed it to them both to satisfy it. In all the previous cases of murder the Templar had solved, both men had been involved in his investigations and had, in more than one instance, given their willing assistance to track down the culprits. Neither of them seemed to bear any resentment for being kept apart from the circumstances surrounding these latest murders, but the Templar felt that, because of their previous support, the request was a reasonable one.

As Bascot began to relate the tale of how he had come to discover the hiding place of the treasure and how it was that Cerlo, Fardein and Simon Partager were involved, both of his companions leaned forward and listened without interruption. The wine in Roget's flask had been drunk and all the bacon and cheese consumed by the time the Templar finished.

At the end of the recounting, both men shook their heads in wonder. "So a murderer was secretly slain by another killer who then took his own life," Ernulf said.

"Saves the sheriff the expense of a hangman's noose, but I reckon the assayer will wish he could meet such an easy end as Cerlo. King John is not known for his mercy. Partager will probably lose at least one of his hands and then be banished from the kingdom. I reckon he'll wish he'd let you run him through with your sword by the end of it."

"I agree, *mon ami*," Roget concurred. "And the assayer will not even have the consolation of a faithful wife to sustain him. I am sure this Iseult, by the sound of her, will have another man in her bed before her husband even comes to trial. What folly Partager committed on the day he took such a jade for a wife."

LATER THAT DAY, AFTER THE EVENING MEAL HAD BEEN served, Bascot watched from a place at the back of the hall as John Blund, with Lambert and Gianni, presented the abridged version of the book of gestures to Stephen of Turville. Bascot had moved away from his place at the table alongside the other household knights, fearful that his emotions would betray him. Gianni looked full of confidence as he walked up to the dais, both he and Lambert keeping pace a step behind the elderly secretary. It seemed to Bascot that on this day all the young boy's dreams had been fulfilled. He was now accepted in the scriptorium as an assistant and had even been the inspiration, and co-compiler, of a book. Soon, if he kept to his studies—and Bascot had no doubt Gianni would do so—the waif the Templar had found starving on a wharf in Palermo would become a clerk and be awarded a place in the retinue of Nicolaa de la Haye, the hereditary castellan of Lincoln castle. Bascot felt as though his heart would burst with pride. Only the knowledge that he would soon be leaving Lincoln marred his pleasure in the boy's achievements.

As Bascot watched Stephen of Turville receive the book from Blund's hand and heard Lady Nicolaa's voice ring out over the company as she explained its purpose, all of the company broke into a round of applause. On the dais, both of Stephen's parents stood up beside their son and made the gesture that meant "thank you" to Gianni and Lambert. Beside them, young Stephen did the same, but added the movement of placing his hand over his heart, meaning his thanks were heartfelt.

Through the moisture that blurred the Templar's eye, he saw Lady Nicolaa present Gianni and Lambert each with a silver gilt medallion on which was engraved the Haye emblem of a twelve-pointed star. It was given, she said, in appreciation of their services and would let all men know she held them in high favour. As applause rang out once more over the hall, Bascot turned away and went outside.

The bail was silent, except for the odd murmur of conversation floating down from the guards pacing along the walkway at the top of the parapet. The huge empty space of the ward was lit by flaring torches around the perimeter and alongside the steps on which Bascot was standing. How familiar these surroundings had become to him. When it came time to leave, he would sorely miss Lincoln and the people who lived here.

He thought back over the events of his life. So far, it seemed as though God's decree was that he travel from place to place. Some of the destinations had been within the confines of his homeland and others in such far-distant places as Outremer and Cyprus. But despite his roving, it was Lincoln he had lately come to regard as home. He knew that wherever he went, he would always feel a longing to return to the castle high upon the hill.

Gazing up into the clear night sky, he sent up a prayer asking for God's mercy and a plea to allow him to come back to Lincoln just one more time before his earthly life was finished. As he stood there, a stiff breeze swept across the bail and caused the flames of the torches on either side of him to flicker. For a moment, the brief darkness dimmed the sight in his eye and then, as the torches flared up again and his vision cleared, he heard a faint clatter near his feet. Looking down he saw it was a small piece of limestone that had become detached from the facade of the castle wall. He picked it up and ran his fingers over the surface of the shard. The fragment was not large, perhaps half the size of his palm. One side was jagged; the other had a rounded smoothness, as though it had been cut from a larger piece with a mason's hammer and chisel.

He put it in his scrip. He would keep it; it would be a little piece of Lincoln to carry with him wherever he went. Turning, he went back into the hall. Only the passage of time would reveal if God looked favourably on his plea to return. With that he must be content.

Author's Note

The setting of *Murder for Christ's Mass* is an authentic one. Nicolaa de la Haye was hereditary castellan of Lincoln castle during this period and her husband, Gerard Camville, was sheriff. In this book, I have introduced Gilbert and Egelina Bassett and their daughters, Eustachia and Lucia. They, along with Nicolaa, Gerard and Richard Camville, are characters from history. In 1203, the year following the conclusion of events in *Murder for Christ's Mass*, Richard Camville married Eustachia Bassett. Although the date of their betrothal is not recorded, it is likely their pledges would have been given in a public ceremony and so I have included the occasion in this story.

For details of medieval Lincoln and the Order of the Knights Templar, I am much indebted to the following: *Medieval Lincoln* by J.W.F. Hill (Cambridge University Press) and *Dungeon, Fire and Sword* by John J. Robinson (M. Evans and Company, Inc.) And for information on coinage to *English Coinage 600–1900 AD* by C.A.V. Sutherland.

Edgar® Award–Winning Author

MARGARET FRAZER

The Dame Frevisse
Medieval Mysteries

penguin.com

M191AS1107

From national bestselling author

VICTORIA THOMPSON

THE GASLIGHT MYSTERIES

*As a midwife in turn-of-the-century New York,
Sarah Brandt has seen pain and joy. Now she will work for
something more—a search for justice—in cases of murder
and mystery that only she can put to rest.*

MURDER ON ASTOR PLACE

MURDER ON ST. MARK'S PLACE

MURDER ON GRAMERCY PARK

MURDER ON WASHINGTON SQUARE

MURDER ON MULBERRY BEND

MURDER ON MARBLE ROW

MURDER ON LENOX HILL

MURDER IN LITTLE ITALY

MURDER IN CHINATOWN

MURDER ON BANK STREET

"Tantalizing."
—Catherine Coulter

penguin.com